Bartolomé de Las Casas

Chronicle of a Dream

A Novel

JOSÉ LUIS OLAIZOLA

Bartolomé de Las Casas

Chronicle of a Dream

A Novel

TRANSLATED BY RICHARD GOODYEAR

IGNATIUS PRESS   SAN FRANCISCO

Original Spanish edition:
Bartolomé de Las Casas,
crónica de un sueño
© 1997 by Editorial Planeta-De Agostini,
Barcelona, Spain

Cover art by Marek Rużyk

Cover design by Enrique J. Aguilar

CONTENTS

CHAPTER I

DON NICOLÁS DE OVANDO'S FLEET

In this year of grace 1565, here in the monastery of Our Lady of Atocha in Madrid, I am setting myself to writing that part of my life of which my superiors say I have given an insufficient account in my earlier writings. By my count, the reams of paper I have written in my own hand amount to at least four thousand pages; but with the frankness with which brothers should treat one another —and it is as brothers that we Dominicans regard each other, in our common father, Saint Dominic de Guzmán —they reproach me for how much I write and how hurriedly I write it, sometimes retelling the same things and at other times leaving fundamental things only half-told. They say that is the case regarding the years of my youth and my work in the Indies, before I took my vows as a Dominican. What is more, according to the Master of the Order, it is between the ages of eighteen and thirty that the soul is forged, and it is useful to know that period well when judging a person.

I trust that he to whom it will fall to judge me is God our Lord, and that he will do so quite soon, since I am eighty-one years old, because I place little trust in the judgment of men; but the Master of the Order insists that I am already being judged by men—by some as a saint, for all that I suffered on behalf of the Indians and for risking my life on that account, and by others as one who should land in hell for the damage I have done to Castile by bearing witness to how Spaniards destroyed the Indies.

I trust that God's mercy will spare me from having to go to hell, but also that I will not be canonized, either, when my wretched youth becomes known as I now write this memoir of it.

I must have been born with the Indies in my blood, because my first memories are about them. In March 1493, a year after Cristóbal Colón (Christopher Columbus) discovered them for Castile, the admiral himself disembarked in the Arenal of Seville, with his retinue of Indian slaves, green parrots, masks made of fishbone, precious stones, and fine gold in quantities never before seen in Spain. The villages emptied out, and the roads filled up with people eager to see these riches, all of whom dreamed that the riches would any day reach Spain in quantity. I was eight years old on that occasion, and I saw the admiral from half a palm's breadth away, standing next to the arch called Images of Saint Nicholas; we lived in the quarter of San Lorenzo, a stone's throw from the Arenal, and from that day on we lived only for the ships that came and went from and to the Indies.

My father, Pedro de Las Casas, was among those who did not wait for the riches to reach Spain, embarking with the admiral on his second voyage instead. I stayed in Seville, with my mother and my three sisters, Isabel, Catalina, and Marina, but my mother soon died of a fever, and it was my eldest sister, Isabel de Sosa, who had to take charge of the bakery that was our only source of income. The bakery did no more than bake bread for sale to the public, without a mill to grind the grain, without fields in which to grow it, and often without wood to fuel the fire. For that reason, my sister Isabel kept encouraging me to become a cleric, because some clerics were able, just by becoming a member of one of the four minor Orders, to earn an income that allowed them to support a family with modest pretensions.

I do not remember distinguishing myself for my piety during those years, although by nature I was not very lazy, either, and I would rise at dawn and go to the monastery near the bakery to help the chaplain, Noriega, with Mass, more for the alms that I was given than out of devotion. But the priest there, sensing that I could serve in a holy ministry, set me to studying Latin in the school that was founded in Seville at the time by Antonio Nebrija, who by then was already a famous grammarian. I did have a knack for Latin and did not find it distasteful, because I thought that it would at least serve me as a catechist in the Indies; that is what they called those who were sent out to those lands by the Council of the Indies to teach Christian doctrine to the infidels, and I was willing to do anything to get to the Indies.

As I say, we lived only for the ships that came and went from and to the Indies, and even the beggars wanted to get rich from all the hustle and bustle. It was around that time that we first heard the voice of Juan Ermitaño (Juan the Hermit), who had his hermitage in the marshes of the Guadalquivir and would come down to the Arenal during the Thursday markets to preach against all Sevillians. He accused the poor of wanting to escape their poverty by stealing from the rich, and the rich of stealing from each other without even fulfilling their obligation to pay the Crown its share. He was an uneducated man, of whom it was said that he had been a soldier in the regiments in Italy, and it occurred to people that what he said had been inspired by God, so they began to attribute miracles to him, until one day he was found drowned in the marshes, and it was rumored that he had been killed by thugs of the secretary of the Council of the Indies, who had the reputation of being the biggest thief in Seville.

The Dominican and Franciscan friars also preached from the pulpit against the widespread mania for riches, and the faithful listened contritely in church. But then they went back to their old ways, because no one in Seville thought about anything else.

In April 1499, when I was about to turn sixteen, we got the news that my father was returning in a brigantine that had sailed along the coast from Huelva to Sanlúcar de Barrameda and from there came up the river to the Arenal. He had been away for six years, and we had had so little news of him that there were times when we gave him up for lost, although it was agreed that those who had fathers or sons in the Indies had to honor them as being alive unless they received definitive news of their death; doing otherwise would have been to treat them as being dead. People were therefore not allowed to hold funeral Masses for them, nor were women who thought they had been widowed allowed to remarry.

My father was about forty years old when he returned, and I remember him as being of medium height and very erect carriage, with a graying beard. As was the custom among those who returned from the Indies, he wore around his neck a heavy gold chain with a medallion hanging from it, and he had two trunks so large that it took two mule drivers to unload each of them. It seemed to us that, when he arrived, wealth arrived with him. But, even though what emerged from the trunks was impressive, the true surprise was the Indian slave that my father brought me as a gift. Thus does God write the history of men; I who have suffered so much on account of the enslavement of Indians was among the first Spaniards to have one as a slave.

We were already accustomed to seeing them in Seville, because prominent Spaniards returning from the Indies were in the habit of bringing back natives and leading them through the streets, half-naked and wearing feathers, until the city council prohibited it. Even if they were dressed like Christians, we could distinguish them by the way they walked and their facial features; but as far as their dark skin being distinctive was concerned, some said it was no different from that of the Moors, or even of the mulattoes, who at the time were plentiful in Seville because it was common for gentlemen to have black slaves, and it was not unusual for servants, and sometimes the masters themselves, to breed with them.

The name of the Indian that my father brought me was Cristóbal, like that of the admiral. It was said that three hundred Indians had been baptized with that name, all at the same time, as a gift from the admiral to three hundred Spaniards who had served him faithfully, one of whom was my father. The Indian came dressed in the habit of

Saint Francis, a saint who was an object of great devotion on the part of the admiral, whom I saw dressed in dark brown when he returned from his second voyage in a caravel named the *India*. I called my Cristóbal "Cristobalillo" because he was a young boy, and I barely remember him because I had him for just a short time. Sometimes I played *chito* and other boys' games with him, but at other times I made him walk behind me so that people would know he was my servant. And there were times when I even put a rope around his neck, as I had seen the Portuguese do with the blacks they brought from Africa.

Cristobalillo was with me for just a short time because, within a year, the Catholic Queen decreed that everyone who had received Indians from the admiral was required, under penalty of death, to return them to their homeland. This ruling provoked a good deal of agitation because no one understood why some slaves had to be returned with such strictness and others not. Cristobalillo returned to his land, and I lost what I had gained from renting him out to do less difficult work than what awaited him in the mines of Hispaniola. Now that I look back on it, I remember how I gave him over to master Alonso Aguilar to harvest grapes in his vineyards in Jerez, in the month of September, and from that I garnered a fair number of gold pesos.

As I say, it seemed that my father came back from the Indies a rich man, but because he provided each of my three sisters with a dowry, and at the same time indulged in some ostentatious expenditures, we returned to our previous straitened circumstances. So he decided to go back across the sea, this time in the expedition led by Bartolomé Colón, the admiral's brother. No matter how much I pleaded, my father did not want to take me with him, saying that I had to finish my ecclesiastical studies, because as a clergyman I would have a great future in the New World. But I was so opposed to that, so afraid of having to go back to Master Nebrija's school and from there to the seminary, that at the same time that my father was going out one door, I went out another. And that other door was what led me to the Alpujarras, where there was an uprising by the Moriscos. The Christian troops were commanded by the Marquis of Comares, and I was under his orders for three months, at the end of which I was taken in hand by my great-uncle Juan de Peñalosa, who had served under the admiral as a recruiter of sailors in the port of Palos. He requested my release on the grounds of my age (I was about seventeen), but that was not the real reason for his request, because there were younger men who had very fine achievements under arms to their credit. The real reason was that my sister Isabel de Sosa said that she could not manage the bakery on her own and that I had to continue my studies at the same time that I worked in the family business.

I returned to Seville amid the commotion caused by the fleet that Don Nicolás de Ovando had organized, which was so well fitted out that anyone who was part of it was widely expected to become rich. To my sister's great regret, my uncle Juan de Peñalosa, seeing that I was not cut out to be a baker and did not want to be a cleric, either, and instead was bent on going to the Indies for better or for worse, arranged for me to become a part of that fleet, in which he had good reliable friends to whom he could recommend me.

The city of Seville, accustomed to living in a continuous state of shock since the discovery of the Indies, must have been amazed even more by that fleet, the like of which not even the most elderly members of the population could have seen before. It was made up of thirty-two ships, all of them fitted out to cross the ocean and carrying three months of provisions. Two thousand five hundred men embarked in it, many of them leading gentlemen, and one who stood out was Antonio Torres, the brother of Prince Don Juan's governess.

Don Nicolás de Ovando, the *comendador* of Lares, was of medium build but magnanimous in spirit; he wore a beard that was between red and blond, which he stroked whenever he had to give an order, as he often did because he was very jealous of his authority, which he exercised very fairly because he valued it so highly. He had the reputation of being an enemy of greed and covetousness, and it was that quality that led the king and queen to name him the governor of Hispaniola (which was tantamount to being the governor of all the Indies that were known at the time), so that he could put a stop to the outrages that the *conquistadores* were committing there. He brought credentials and orders, which were signed by the Catholic Queen and which everyone was obliged to obey, regarding the way in which the new lands should be governed. Her Catholic Majesty ordained that the Indians of the islands should live free and not be subject to any servitude, that they should not be harassed or harmed, that they should be governed and kept in justice in the same way as the vassals in the kingdom of Castile, and that therefore they should be instructed in the holy Catholic faith—not by force, but willingly. In pursuit of that goal, there embarked on the flagship twelve Franciscan friars, with Friar Alonso del Espinal, the most venerable of all of them, as their prelate, in imitation of the number and forms of our Lord Jesus Christ and his twelve apostles.

We weighed anchor from the port of Sanlúcar de Barrameda with the tide of February 13, 1502, on the eve of the first Sunday in Lent, and the people of Seville and other nearby towns came to bid us farewell with great emotion, because it was the widely held view that our fleet was on its way to establishing a new order in the recently discovered lands.

On the third day of our voyage, Don Nicolás de Ovando, having been alerted by a friend of my uncle that the fleet included a youth who knew Latin, ordered me to be brought to him, and it was the first time in my long life that I found myself in the presence of an authority who had no superiors other than God and the king.

In the Indies at the time, great store was set by the command of Latin because it was a language that lent great solemnity to whatever was being said, so the governors liked to use it in their reports to the kings. Clerics were obliged to know it because of their sacred ministry, but most of them only knew enough to sing the Mass, and that not very well, especially the ones who were headed for the Indies. Don Nicolás de Ovando was a highly educated man, capable of reading Virgil in Latin and a great admirer of the master Nebrija, and since he considered me to be a disciple of the latter, he treated me with a respect out of proportion to what my few years deserved. Who would have predicted that the suffering I experienced in Nebrija's school would earn me such a great honor!

He began to speak to me in Latin, very slowly, and

I answered him fluently, which was a gift that God had granted me without my having earned it and without any effort on my part. In fact, if it had been up to me, I would have put all my writings in Latin, but I wrote many of them in the vernacular so they could be read by all people, who would thereby know what was going on in the Indies and take action to remedy it.

His Honor asked me to take advantage of days of calm weather to chat with him in Latin, and I was more than surprised to find myself being received in the ship's sterncastle, when by my rank I should have been in the bilges. At the time, I did not see the hand of the Lord at work, and, God forgive me, I attributed everything to my own merits. Perhaps to punish me for my arrogance, I was unable to enjoy the privilege for long, because the following day, which was our eighth at sea and fell on the second Sunday of Lent, when we were not far from the Canary Islands, a southern crosswind that seamen call an *austral* came up, so strong that it scattered the fleet.

We had been traveling in convoy, which is the custom in such crossings so that the ships can act in support of one another if needed, and before the crosswind came up it was a beautiful sight to see the thirty-two ships sailing in pairs, each pair following in the wake of the pair ahead of it, with the ones that carried the most sail taking care not to go faster than the others so as to comply with the orders given by the *comendador* of Lares that no ship should fall behind and run the risk of being lost. The pilot of my ship, which was the *San Nicolás*, said two hours before the *austral* came up that we had the Madeira Islands, which are subject to storms, to starboard and that in two more days of sailing we would reach the Canaries. The sky was blue, the sea was a light green and foamy white under the keels of the ships, and the dolphins were playfully bounding about like small greyhounds with their master. As I gazed at the splendor of the spread sails, it seemed to me that we who were sailing in such a powerful fleet were called to be the owners of the world. When the *austral* began, it blew so pleasantly that it seemed like a zephyr, so gentle and smooth that we rejoiced in the thought that we would make an early arrival at the Canaries.

Luckily our pilot, Zamacoa, who was from the coast of Zumaia on the Bay of Biscay, saw the danger coming and ordered the halyards to be released, saving our lives; the ship with which ours was paired, the *Rábida*, kept her sails fully spread, and within the blink of an eye the crosswind dealt her a blow that sent her to the bottom of the ocean. None of her 120 men survived, because we could do nothing to help them. We stopped sailing in convoy, and each pilot did what he could to save his ship, but there was so much disorder that no two of the thirty-one ships reached the same port, each of them stopping wherever the winds took it, most of them on the Barbary Coast and at Cape Aguer, which is also in Moorish territory, near the Canaries. Ours fetched up in Tenerife, so we were the ones who came out the best, thanks to the decisions made by the Basque, Zamacoa. He ordered us to jettison all our supplies, including the wine we were carrying, despite the taste he had for it, but since the water continued to pour into our ship and we could not stem the flow, he ordered us to throw overboard our trunks and everything else except the clothes we were wearing. The gentlemen on board, and many were of very high rank, wanted to object because of the richness of the jackets and brocades they had brought, but to no avail because Zamacoa was a ferocious man, and he threatened to throw them, too, into the angry sea. In the end, they had to obey because Governor Ovando had decreed that, with respect to all matters of navigation, every pilot ruled in his ship the same way the king rules in his palace.

That is how Zamacoa saved our lives, and I have prayed a great deal for him, although I do not know whether my prayers have done him any good because no sooner had he arrived in Hispaniola than he partnered with another Basque shipwright, whose name was Chomin de Guetaria, to whom we will need to return later, and they were among those who fitted out the most ships to go and capture Indians on the coast of Cumaná and then sell them as slaves in Jamaica and Puerto Rico. If on that Sunday in Lent he had drowned fighting so bravely to save our lives, he would be in heaven now, but having dedicated himself to such a contemptible occupation, only the mercy of our Lord Jesus Christ could have saved him from the flames of hell. And he was on the verge of losing his life, because once he had lightened the load of our ship, he ordered that we be lashed to the masts so that we would not be dragged overboard by the waves, and he stationed himself at the helm of the ship, artfully managing to save us from that hell. So great was the fury of the wind that now and then the waves threw him to the deck, but Zamacoa, without a glance at the blood that was pouring from a gash in his head, threw himself back into his task. We could do nothing but pray for him not to be swept away by the sea, because our hopes would have been swept away with him.

I promised our Lord in those prayers that if I did not perish I would become a cleric and that I would fulfill my vocation in Seville and not in adventures in the Indies, to which I was going solely out of greed for riches, crazed as I was by what my father had told me. I also promised our Lord that I would never again cross the ocean sea and that when we reached the first port, I would return without fail to my homeland, never to leave it again. I was late in keeping the first of my promises and only kept it against my will, so it was the Lord himself who did so, in the same way that he pulled Saint Paul from his horse on the road to Damascus and thus forced him to see what he had not wanted to see. I did not keep my second promise at all, because by my count I have crossed the ocean ten times, and they say that only the admiral has done so more than I have. The theologians are right in saying that the promises men make in the face of death, like the loves of students, are but flowers that bloom for just a day.

And a day and a night was how long it took us to sight Tenerife and forget on that beautiful island all that we had been through. We were there for two weeks waiting for the other ships that had been scattered; thirty-one were reunited in the end because, by Divine Providence, the *Rábida* was the only one that was lost, although so spectacularly that two caravels that were making the crossing to Castile loaded with sugar came upon the remains of the ship—along with the provisions, crates, wood, and casks that we other ships had jettisoned to save ourselves, and they deduced that the entire fleet had gone to the bottom. That was the news they brought to Spain, where it reached the king and queen in Granada, and they were plunged into such pain that it was said they were in seclusion for a week and that no one could see or speak to them. They had had very high hopes for the mission of the powerful fleet, because they believed that upon the arrival of Ovando, invested with royal powers, all the Spaniards in the Indies would have to obey him and end their abuses. But Their Majesties did not take into account that, although those who were already in the islands were wicked, we in the fleet were no better, because I can say for myself with certainty that we were entirely motivated by the riches we thought we would find in those lands. And this was true of everyone except the twelve Franciscans, their prelate, and the governor, although the latter showed that, as just as he was, he did not know how to treat the Indians.

On the fifth day of March, all thirty-two ships having gathered together in La Gomera, we embarked for Hispaniola. I say thirty-two because *Comendador* Ovando wanted to be punctilious about the commission he had received from Their Majesties, so he bought and outfitted a ship so that the same number of ships would arrive in Hispaniola as had been commissioned in Sanlúcar de Barrameda. Would that he had been equally punctilious about the other expectations, relating to the treatment of the Indians, that the king and queen had commissioned him to fulfill!

CHAPTER II

THE MINES OF THE HAINA RIVER

We entered the port of Santo Domingo on April 15, 1502, after such a calm crossing from Tenerife, and with such propitious winds at our backs, that our earlier transit past the Madeira Islands seemed like a bad dream that would never be repeated. My arrival in these lands, aboard the flagship thanks to the value Governor Ovando placed on speaking Latin, could not have been better. Everyone saw me as his protégé, for good reason, because he had offered me a post as a notary to the council, and I knew, through my father, that that post was a highly coveted plum with many attendant benefits. But it was not to prove so for me, because no sooner had I arrived than I went mad for gold, as if I had caught the plague, and it took me twelve years to cure myself of that ill.

I can only say that, even now, old as I am and ensconced in this monastery of Atocha, I yearn for that island where I sinned so much and which I so loved. It was in every way just as my father had described it, and I think it must have been the site of the Earthly Paradise, as I have said at greater length elsewhere.[1] What awed us the most were

[1] This is a reference to the description that he gives of the beauty of those unspoiled lands in his *History of the Indies* (chaps. 128 and 129)

the green and delightful groves, because the soil was so fertile that flowers, bushes, and trees, of a beauty unknown in Castile, take root even in stony mountain terrain reminiscent of the Alpujarras; and the marshes along their rivers do not resemble those of our Guadalquivir at all, because their sands support more than just rushes and osiers, so that trees producing the sweetest fruits flourish in the most arid parts. To this can be added the subtlety of the breezes and the clemency of the hot spells, about which some complain because they say they are bad for rheumatism, though they are not at all like what we suffer through in Seville when summer is upon us. Besides, we usually went about more lightly clad, not to mention the Indians, who cover only what nature requires, and here, too, I see a resemblance to the Earthly Paradise, where our first parents were not ashamed to be seen naked.

But all this beauty had little effect on me because the colony was in a frenzy when we arrived, and all the Castilian Spaniards, who numbered no more than three hundred, never tired of marveling at the good luck of Francisco de Garay and Miguel Díaz, who had found a thirty-five-pound lump of gold the size of a loaf of Alcalá bread, for which the Crown paid them 3,600 gold pesos. They found it, or rather an Indian slave woman who worked for them in the Nuevas Mines of the Haina River found it, twenty-seven miles from Santo Domingo. They called the mines *nuevas*—new—because they had

---

and to the line of argument, with a great profusion of citations and comparisons with the River Nile, that that was the Earthly Paradise.

previously been mining gold from mines that were called *viejas*—old—which they said were played out.

That did not surprise me because one of the abuses of Governor Bobadilla, whose service there was to be the subject of an investigation conducted by Don Nicolás de Ovando, was to grant licenses to mine gold so liberally that the licensees, with work gangs of thirty or even forty Indians, men and women, set about sifting the sands of the river and building galleries and boring into the earth in search of the precious metal. There were encomenderos who held licenses for several work gangs that they set to work for the whole day, and if they hit upon a vein, they went on into the night working by the light of the moon, if it was full, or, if not, by torchlight, and they gave as a reason for such cruelty the fact that if they were to wait until the next day a freshet in the river might carry away the grains of gold. Though he was an honest man, *Comendador* Bobadilla made no objection to any of this because he wanted to curry favor with the encomenderos.

Francisco de Garay, who was later the governor of Pánuco, had become the partner of one Miguel Díaz, and they were the first to establish themselves with their work gangs in the Nuevas Mines of the River Haina, with so little to show for it at first that they considered going back to the old ones. But one morning, at the hour of the midday meal, when the Indians were resting for the little while that was allowed to them, an Indian woman named Tajima was eating with one hand and chipping at the earth with her mattock in the other, paying little attention and not looking at what she was doing. But she felt a flintiness in the soil and, looking down, saw something shiny. Digging farther, she discovered and unearthed the thirty-five-pound lump of gold that I mentioned earlier.

These people are so good by nature that Tajima was as happy as she would have been if the lump had belonged to her, and she called the foreman over and said, "Ocama quaxeri quariquen caona yari", which in her language means, "Look, Sir, come and see this gold stone." The news spread quickly, and as everyone began to celebrate this great event, Miguel Díaz ordered a suckling pig to be roasted and served up on the great gold loaf, preening himself on the fact that no king had ever eaten out of such a rich dish.

I saw the lump when it had been turned over to Bobadilla for storage, and I was so captivated by its size that it seemed to me its luster would be capable of lighting up the darkest night. And my soul did enter into a dark night, because right then and there I decided to follow in the footsteps of the Garays, forgetting what Governor Ovando was offering me and expecting of me. With the meager funds that I had, which amounted to barely a hundred pesos, I acquired what I thought would equip me to extract gold: a sack, cassava flour to make bread with, mattocks, and pans that are used to sift the river sands. Those funds, which in Seville would have gone a long way, were barely enough in Hispaniola to buy what I have listed, because those who arrived with me in Ovando's great fleet were seized by the same madness that had seized me, and we all thought that we were bound to grow rich overnight by simply rooting around in the river sands, so we paid whatever they asked for tools that in Castile would have cost a pittance. The only person who was interested in giving me good advice, despite the offenses he committed thereafter, was Zamacoa, the pilot, who warned me, "Look, nobody's made himself rich with a mattock, but many have with a pen, which if you know how to use it is more useful than a sword."

He said this to me so I would not turn my back on Governor Ovando and his offer to appoint me as a notary. Zamacoa was about thirty at the time, burly, with a bushy black beard, and he was given to alcohol and women. Seamen held him in high esteem, and so did I because I thought I owed him my life. When he saw that I would not be going back to the governor, he invited me to go with him to some mountains where an uprising of the Indians had broken out, which was another reason that things were in turmoil in Hispaniola. The law, which was applied very liberally, provided that rebellious Indians could be attacked and any captives could be enslaved and then sold to the encomenderos, to work either on their farms or in the mines.

"Take it from me", Zamacoa insisted, thinking only of what would be in my interest. "Gold doesn't grow on trees. You have to hunt a long time for it and won't always find it, but the Indians are there waiting for us, and when it comes to capturing them, they're not as fierce as the Moriscos, because when the Caribs hear gunpowder, they quickly lose their nerve and surrender."

He was right about that, because I remember that my Cristobalillo, the slave my father gave me, could not have been more docile. In any case, Caribs had a bad name, and enslaving them was permitted wherever they were because of their ugly practice of consuming human flesh; the friars were the first to correct them, talking to them very lovingly about what our Lord Jesus Christ did for all of us.

I cannot say that what Zamacoa proposed to me was anything new, because we did the same thing in Spain with the Moors, and the Moors with Christians, when they took each other prisoner: either they paid a ransom or they were enslaved. I saw it myself, with my own eyes, during the rebellion in the Alpujarras. The Marquis of Comares, in command of the troops, was authorized to enslave any Morisco who had rebelled, and he did so. The same fate befell the Guanches in the Canary Islands when they rose up against Alonso de Lugo; he enslaved them all and then became a major slave trader, in a business to which his son Alonso Fernández de Lugo succeeded. Not to mention the blacks that the Portuguese brought from Africa, for there was no nobleman in Seville who did not pride himself on having slaves of that color. These blacks' children met the same fate as their parents, and they were called *ladinos* because they had been born in Castile and spoke our language, unlike those who came from Africa. The latter were called *bozales* and fetched lower prices.

Suffice it to say that saints as great and learned as Saint Bonaventure and our Saint Thomas Aquinas, though admitting the odious character of slavery, understand that slavery is the right penalty for odious crimes, for if a judge can condemn a man to be deprived of life for his crimes, there is a still greater justification for depriving him of his liberty. And it is well established that all criminals would rather be taken as slaves than be hanged, because from the gallows they can go directly to hell for their sins, while as slaves they always have the hope that they will one day regain their freedom or earn the favor of their owners and end up ruling over them: there have been women who were captured as slaves and were ultimately enthroned as queens. In another context, I have been told that there is a black in Castile called Juan Latino, born in Baena the son of slaves and therefore a slave himself, who now holds the chair in grammar in Granada, where he gives classes at the Royal College by appointment of the archbishop himself. I am more amazed by that than I am by the enthronement of a slave as queen, because in such things there is always a part for the flesh to play in its great power to affect the emotions, whereas in the teaching of humanities all that counts is intelligence, and in that it is demonstrable that color is not an important asset and that all men are equal in that respect.

It took me many years to learn this last point, but ever since I did learn it, thanks to my Dominican brothers, I have made such a point of communicating it to others that I have spent my life doing so. But when Zamacoa made his proposal to me, I did not have these scruples because I was as ignorant as the rest, and I did not even stop to think whether the law the Basque invoked that permitted shackling the Caribs as slaves was among those that Saint Thomas and Saint Bonaventure thought legitimate, and all that concerned me was to get hold of the Indian Tajima, who was said to be a dowser, which meant that, just as others find water underground, she could find gold. How pathetic it was of me, with no more than small change in my pocket, to believe that I could obtain such a valuable woman! While I was eagerly trying to do so, a gentleman from Toledo named Esquivias had bought her for 150 gold pesos, which was more than double the price of a black, who has always been more expensive than an Indian. They say that Francisco de Garay and Miguel Díaz sold her with great amusement, for they knew that it was mere superstition to think that one could know where metals were to be found; they were not wrong, because Esquivias was among the first to die in that madness for gold that seized those of us who came in the fleet. We repaid our king and queen badly for the trust they had reposed in us.

I will add about Tajima that they sold her as a maiden, which at no more than fourteen years old she was young enough to be, although Spaniards have few scruples about such things; she was not bad-looking, for an Indian, and we will have occasion to return to her.

The human soul is a great mystery, as our Lord will take into account when he comes to judge us, for Zamacoa, despite my disdain for him—perhaps because he was moved by my being young, around eighteen—did give me some good tips regarding my work as a miner and loaned me eighty pesos when the purchases I made as described above left me penniless. I kissed his hands, the way I would those of a father, unaware that years later he would be my great enemy, for the pity he took on me turned into cruelty in his treatment of the Indians of Cubagua and the coast of Cumaná.

This was the Basque's third voyage to Hispaniola, and because he knew the wiles of the old miners well, the first thing he told me was to go upriver to the area where the mountains begin and the Haina is a crystalline stream. In this I did listen to him, and it may have been the second time he saved my life. Of the 2,500 of us who arrived in Hispaniola with Ovando, fully two thousand went—with all the turmoil and haste that greed fosters—to the mines. Ovando went along with this outrage, thinking that he was acting for the great benefit of the Crown, because the king and queen, after the battle for Granada and other wars in Europe had so completely emptied their coffers, were deeply in debt to the Jewish bankers, and this governor is one who cannot be said to look out for his own interest. That does not, however, lessen the mistakes he made. How can it have been thought that our Catholic Kings underwrote such a powerful fleet so that those of us who sailed in it, including the highest and most elite gentlemen, without taking time to think things through, should throw ourselves at the mountains equipped with nothing but a mattock and a little cassava bread? Well, Governor Ovando consented to it, requiring nothing more than the commitment to deliver half the gold we discovered to the royal treasurer.

The miseries I have endured have not been described, and I am one of the few who remain to tell of them. The Nuevas Mines of the River Haina were twenty-four miles from Santo Domingo, but those twenty-four miles, and 120 more, were taken over by the seasoned miners amply supplied with Indians, black foremen, and mastiffs, so that no one could get near them. This is where the mourning first began; those who were newly arrived from Castile, some of them with the arrogance of their status as gentlemen, did not recognize what the miners called their rights; and so the fighting got under way. The gentlemen had right on their side in that there were no mining concessions, and the whole river was free so that no one had the right to fence off a piece of it as being his. I will just say that in the first week, on Pentecost Sunday, more than a dozen Spaniards, not counting Indians, died in one encounter. No one was called to account for this crime because there was no authority in Hispaniola that could have done so, since Governor Ovando had sent the armed men he brought with him to suppress a rebellion by the Indians on the island of Saona, ninety miles from Santo Domingo, as I have related at greater length elsewhere.[2] That is to say, while the Christians were stabbing one another for a few grains of gold, Their Majesties' troops went about persecuting Indians who were just seeking to defend themselves against bad Spaniards. This was the expedition in which Zamacoa was marching, and he benefited a good deal from it.

I say bad Spaniards because there were also very good ones, and I had the good fortune to come across one of them, Pedro de Rentería, on the fourth day of my journey to the mountains. In the first two days, no fewer than a hundred Christians, all of them with the same eagerness that I understand to be not very Christian at all, were marching on the wide road that runs along the right bank of the Haina. Most of them, seeing a water-

---

[2] This is a reference to chapters 7 and 8 of volume 2 of his *History of the Indies*, in which he recounts how a mastiff of some callous Spaniards tore to pieces a cacique of that island and, in reprisal, the natives killed eight Spaniards.

fall or bend in the river that seemed as though it must have sands containing gold, stopped marching and in very unruly and disorganized fashion set about digging with their mattocks, though back in Spain they would deem it beneath them even to touch them. All it took to convince them of the presence of gold was the sight of others doing the same thing in the same pools, which prompted the fighting. Some of them had supplied themselves with Indians, using their own money to buy them, and they thought that, because those Indians were from the region, they would know where the gold was, so ignorant were we—was I, first and foremost, in view of what I have already said about my search for Tajima. It makes me so sad to recall how the poor Indians suffered when they did not find gold and their owners, thinking they were being cheated, punished them. On my fourth day on the road, I was walking alone, following a map that Zamacoa had drawn for me showing the way to a more rugged site, in which he warned me that I would not find gold nuggets but, rather, fine sand that would have to be sifted. Although I dreamed about coming across another lump like the one that fell into Francisco de Garay's hands, I followed Zamacoa's advice out of the respect and credit I owed him. In spite of my greed, I could not stop taking delight in the great beauty that surrounded me, and in contemplating it, I admired the greatness of God the Father, Creator of heaven and earth, and I praised him for that alone because, in other respects, I did not think of him at all except to ask that I would soon find gold. Here and there in my climb, I found lakes and pools of water that were as clear as the surface of the finest mirror

and so cool that just dipping my feet in them relieved
all my weariness. The flowers and bushes, which were
not known in Castile, were so profuse and so fragrant
that the most inconsequential of the lakes glowed more
beautifully than the gardens of Granada in spring, with
the added advantage that the year did not have seasons
and the flowers were always in bloom, as though original sin had never reached these lands, and for that reason I think it must have been the location of the Earthly
Paradise. In the presence of such beauty, I could not but
kneel down to give thanks to the Lord, on more than one
occasion, and I now think that being able to see the hand
of the Creator in the gifts of Mother Nature was what
made it possible for me, in those years of greed, not to
lose my soul altogether. It was on one of those occasions
that I came upon Pedro de Rentería, or, more accurately,
he came upon me, for he was in flight, a gentleman on
a mule.

He was fleeing because in those years nothing could
have been more coveted on Hispaniola than a horse, since
there were no more than a hundred of them on the whole
island and almost all of them belonged to those who were
in authority. As for mules, the first one to arrive was that
of Pedro de Rentería, who was a gentleman of great common sense and thought that mules would certainly be of
greater use than money, brocades, and pomp and circum-
stance, and he was not wrong about that. But some hard-
bitten persons wanted to buy his mule from him, and because he did not want to sell her and the rule of law did
not extend to the mines on the Haina River, they tried to
take her away from him by force, so he had to put some

distance between them and himself. Seeing that all the miners who were scattered along both sides of the river, of whom there were hundreds, looked at his mount with envy (and for good reason, because there is no animal more useful than a mule on which to get around on the steep terrain of mining works), he got onto an uphill path to get away from those people, and he then came upon me in an especially delightful place, which the Indians call the Flower of the Sun, because that king of stars, reflected in the waters of their lake, looks like a gigantic amber flower. Luckily for me, Providence arranged for Rentería to find me while I was kneeling, which reassured him because of the confidence that men at prayer inspired in him.

Pedro de Rentería was a man of proven virtue, prudence, charity, and devotion, and humanity and chastity shone in him, because he was very upright and humble. His father was a Basque from Guipúzcoa, and his mother a gentlewoman of the village of Montánchez, in Extremadura. He set so little store by the things of this world that I am not sure I understand why he was taken by a desire to come to these lands, and even less do I understand why he was wandering in the impenetrable ruggedness of the mountains in search of gold that he cared about so little. He explained it to me many times, but I never understood it.

The first thing Rentería said to me was, quoting the Gospels, "If it's not an imposition on your honor, allow me to pray with you, because the Lord has told us that where two or three gather together in his name, he is in their midst." He always carried the Gospels with him, together with commentaries on them by the saints. I acceded to his request, but not without suspicion, because we were suspicious of each other in those mountains, and we saw in every Christian an enemy who had come to fight over gold; I was not suspicious yet, but I kept Zamacoa's map in my bosom because, in my delirium, I dreamed it would lead me to a treasure that I did not want to share with anyone but the king, and even in his case I wondered whether I could cheat him of the part that was due to him. For that reason, when we finished our prayers, which Rentería prolonged by reading aloud some passages from Holy Scripture, I started to take my leave of him, and he reciprocated, although he warned me with his natural goodness, "If the only provisions you have are what you have in that sack, I'm afraid you won't be able to go very far."

In the sack I had cassava bread, which we made there with manioc, a very abundant plant that is excellent food even when dry; with that in their sacks, Spaniards conquered immense territories in Mexico and Peru, and in their frugality they did demonstrate great virtue. I was also carrying a little bit of cured pork, which was the only meat there was on the island. Rentería, though, was carrying well-stocked saddlebags on both sides of his beautiful mule, and although he offered to share them with me, I decided to forgo his company because I was unwilling to share with him the gold that I dreamed of, and I went on my way after inventing some clever excuses so as not to be followed by a person who, in the end, would actually become more than a brother to me.

On the sixth day of my travels, I found the place about

which Zamacoa had told me. It was in very rough terrain on the right bank of the Haina River, about six miles from the main stream at the foot of a tributary that fed a small waterfall, which fell from a rock in the shape of an eagle, and for that reason Zamacoa called it Eagle Cliff. In that remote place were singing some nightingales like the ones in Castile, but more melodious, not to mention parrots of the most varied colors. But I was in no mood for music, and as soon as I stopped, I pulled out my mattock and set about digging in the sand, right and left, sifting with my pan in search of gold dust with all my heart. When I saw it, as fine as flour, I wanted to cry because I thought that by finding gold I had ended all the travails of this world.

If there are any sins that I think are excusable, they have to do with gold, which in addition to being a sin is an illness that deprives a man of his senses, at least in my case, for I never tired of admiring the golden brilliance, which I imagined in the form of a large gold chain around my neck. I had an itch that would not let me rest, night or day, and I did nothing but dig in the sands of the riverbed to sift them. To save time, I ate some of the cured meat and cassava bread without looking for any of the wild fruits that might have been there in that paradise or even less for the beautiful fish in the river, the size of a barbel, although there would have been little point in it because, I am ashamed to say, I had not even brought any fishing gear with me. In a week my sack was empty, and I was almost happy about it because it could serve for carrying the gold I found, weighing (at a guess) a quarter of a pound. I lost track of the days, which is not very relevant, but it might have been on the eighth day that I had a dizzy spell and fell to the ground, and although I thought I was dying, I clutched my sack as if I could carry it with me to the other world.

But I am not good at dying, which I have had many opportunities to do in my long life. I have escaped from all of them, and even at my age now, when it would be only natural for me to die, the Lord is not yet ready to take me to his bosom. On that occasion, when I emerged from my dizzy spell, I had nothing to eat and began to jump around like a goat in search of wild berries, until I found some gnarled vines that are called *aje*, the roots of which are tubers resembling sweet potatoes, and I ate some of them raw and others that I roasted in a fire. I had enough strength to keep myself alive, but not enough to work with the mattock or the pan. I was in such misery that my devotion returned to me, and it seemed to me I was like the prodigal son of the Gospel, who remembered his father's house when he had only acorns to eat; I remembered the bakery in San Lorenzo and the scraps of bread we used to give to beggars, which in my affliction I would have liked to have for myself.

When Pedro de Rentería finally appeared, led by his guardian angel, I took him for a heavenly vision. At the time he was no more than thirty years old, although he seemed older because of the gravity with which he carried himself and his manner of speaking, which at times was sententious because of his taste for quoting Holy Scripture. He explained to me later that it was not his guardian angel who had brought him to me, but rather his mule, because she followed whatever track she found, and the only one there was in that dense vegetation was the one I had traced on my way to Eagle Cliff. When I restored my strength and saw that I was not going to die, thanks to Rentería's saddlebags, the first thing I wanted to do was to wipe out all tracks to our hiding place so that we could not be found by any other prospectors.

"What, do you think that you may have found El Dorado?" my good friend asked me. "Or how do you think this part of the river differs from the others that you've passed?"

Like someone confiding a secret, and in order to show him my appreciation for what he had given me to eat, I showed him the gold dust that I had in my sack, and, after looking at it and weighing it up, he did the same thing with what he had in a little leather bag, which was about the same as mine.

"Do not doubt, Your Honor," he said, "that in following this trail those who come behind us have to go to the same gates of hell, although many of them will not be unwilling to go through them as long as they can do so with bags full of gold."

What he meant was that there was gold in the sand of all these streams of Haina and that other explorers from Ovando's fleet were climbing that infernal trail. I thus came to know that my very beautiful waterfall at Eagle Rock was not very different from the other banks of the river, and the proof of that was that Rentería, six miles back, perhaps with less haste and effort, had sifted out as much gold as I had. He climbed the mountain, not for the pleasure of it, but to protect his mule from the envy of those who were coming up behind him. It was curious

that this saintly man, so generous with all earthly things
and so ready to take bread out of his own mouth in order
to give it to the needy, should have been so attached to
his mule that he would seemingly be so ready to sacrifice
so much in order to keep her.

From that day on we were partners, and until I renounced
wealth, twelve years later, we shared everything equally,
even though it seemed that everything was mine because,
while he was carrying on with his prayers and acts of charity, it was I who took care of managing our income.

The miners kept coming, although not all of them because many died on the way, some of them of hunger because of their lack of foresight, but the majority died of
the fevers that are endemic in those lands, not counting
those who were stabbed in disputes about food or the
placers in the river that they thought were the richest.
According to the account that was compiled by the town
hall, of the two thousand men who set out on the road to
the Nuevas Mines, a thousand died and another five hundred fell so ill that they had to take ship for Spain, and not
all of them arrived there. The clerics could not handle all
the work they had to do to give them a Christian burial,
so it was not strange that some of the bodies attracted the
attention of some vultures, the size of hens, called turkey
buzzards. None of the remaining five hundred struck it
rich, and it was a sight to see them selling their clothes so
they could eat. Everyone who gave himself over to the
mines was always in need, and quite a few ended up in
debtors' prison. Those who stayed in Santo Domingo, on
the other hand, devoting themselves to raising pigs and

cultivating the land for cassava and other edible roots, like *aje* and sweet potatoes, always were more productive and had more leisure time and abundance. I learned that lesson well and therefore applied myself, when God showed me the right path, to bringing workers from Castile, as I will describe in the proper place.

Rentería and I did not do so badly, which he said was thanks to his mule while I said it was thanks to the initiatives I undertook, and we joked about it. I say the initiatives I undertook because at the end of a month the banks at Eagle Cliff were crowded with miners, and, even without the rule of law, we respected each other's rights to our respective placers. But food was a different issue because the hunger was such that the slightest carelessness provoked robbery. One night they tried to take the mule, saddlebags and all, so I decided to buy an arquebus and went to Santo Domingo mounted on the mule, at a fast pace, taking less than three days to get there and less than three days to get back. On one of those days, I came upon the Indian Tajima, the one who had found Francisco de Garay's lump of gold. She had by then changed owners twice, and the only thing she gained from those changes, if "gained" is the right word, was the loss of her maidenhood; in all other respects, she had nothing but pain and suffering, because her owners were not satisfied with her sifting the sands and demanded instead that she find gold nuggets, as though they grew on trees. Perhaps out of pity for her, I bought her for only thirty gold pesos, and I could even have bought her for less because her owners were utterly ruined, more so than anyone else.

We stayed at Eagle Cliff for a full year because there was gold there, although it was very hard work to extract it, and what we did extract we spent in large part on buying food, which in that area could be described, most aptly, as being worth its weight in gold. After we got the arquebus, no one dared to bother us, and with Tajima we enjoyed a very restful period because, although she was a woman, she had a real knack for sifting, and she could do in one hour what took us two. I have already said that, for an Indian, she was very attractive, but we respected her; this was nothing new for Rentería because he was very honorable in his conduct and acted the same with all the Indian women, but the same cannot be said of me.

Every two weeks we had to go down to Santo Domingo or to a little store nine miles from the city to get supplies. I tried to get Rentería to go, for fear that *Comendador* Ovando would see me and require me to be his notary, although I think at the time he would have been dealing with too many problems to be concerned with me. It was at that time, if my memory does not betray me, that the island was lashed by a hurricane of such proportions that it destroyed the entire city, which was then called New Isabela in honor of our queen, and in its passage Ovando's entire fleet sank, so the governor who had arrived in Hispaniola with such pageantry was left without his gentlemen, who lost that status by prospecting for gold, and also without his ships.

But since misfortunes never come just one at a time, a plague of ants such as had never been seen before ravaged what was left of New Isabela and the surrounding fields. Luckily for us, they did not reach Eagle Cliff, but

I saw them, and it horrified me that such an insignificant animal could leave so much pain in its wake. Seen
from a distance, they resembled the shadow cast by the
sun at sunset; they passed in columns of hunters, and
the smallest ones, which were called soldiers, with tiny
saws in their forefeet, cut the leaves of whatever plant
they came to, and the ones that followed behind, which
were the workers, carried the leaves away. Thus were the
most beautiful cornfields left barren in their wake, and although the ants were not carnivorous, they would climb
up onto animals and kill them. The Indians call them
la marabunta (the horde) and are so terrorized by them
that, if they see them, they quickly break camp and flee.
That is what Governor Ovando ended up having to do,
transferring the location of the settlement to what is now
the site of Santo Domingo. And, fearing that *la marabunta*
would return, he ordered all of the buildings to be built
of whitewashed stone, and he was very right to do so.

La marabunta did not reach the mines, but the misery
it left behind did. Our gold barely served to buy bread,
and until some ships arrived from Jamaica, bringing pigs
and cassava, we had to turn to what we could find in
the forests and whatever fish we could catch in the lakes.
There were serpents in these. Some of them, called igua-
nas, are more than seven palms' width in length and like
little crocodiles, although they look more like lizards, but
with bonier mouths and noses; on their backs they have
a ridge of spikes that gives them a frightful appearance,
but they do no harm to anyone, and, because they lack
courage, they are very easy to catch. For the Indians, there
is no greater delicacy, and Tajima showed us how to eat
them, especially their tails, which those who have tried

them say are more delicious than chicken breast. I say
those who have tried them because I, despite the many
good things that were said about them, was incapable of
tasting them and preferred to eat the twisting roots that I
have mentioned, which are like sweet potatoes, and birds
that we could bring down with the arquebus.

This was when some of the thousand men I mentioned
above who died did so of starvation. But because every
cloud has a silver lining, so much misery prompted us
to undertake a mission to visit Governor Ovando and
convince him of how onerous it was for us to turn over
half the gold to the king. And the governor, who was
a fair-minded man, though he did not have a good understanding of how to treat Indians, agreed to reduce the
king's share to a third, which is what the cotton farmers
paid him. Six months later, because as time went by we
had to go deeper and deeper to find the very thin veins of
gold, it again seemed to us that a third of the gold was too
much in comparison with how much we had to sweat and
suffer. Because Ovando told us that he did not have the
authority to make any further adjustment, we agreed to
send the king and queen an emissary from Seville whose
name was Juan Esquivel, and he found them at Medina
del Campo. The king and queen, despite the great poverty
in Castile, agreed to our request, and Esquivel returned
with a royal decree that no more than a fifth of any metal
was to be their share from that time on. And that is how
it has remained down to the present.

Thanks to this last ruling, Rentería and I were able to
economize and did not end up in misery—or in prison,
like so many other prospectors.

CHAPTER III

THE CONQUEST OF XARAGUÁ

In the spring of 1503, when Governor Ovando saw how little gold we were mining with our own hands, he began a program in which the Indians from the villages were distributed among the Spaniards, so we could teach them how to work while at the same time we taught them our holy Catholic faith. We undertook the former promptly and skillfully, whereas in the case of the latter, what the friars did not do we laymen also failed to do, since we were thinking only of making up for the work we had done in the Haina River.

My partner and I were allotted two encomiendas in Concepción de La Vega, good mining country north of Santo Domingo. Each encomienda was of fifty Indians, as Ovando's usually were, but because my partner and I lumped the two encomiendas together, we ended up with a hundred Indians, which was a lot in those days. It was the first time that I was able to build a good substantial house in the Indies, which was what I had missed the most at Eagle Cliff.

The Indian Tajima came with us, and she was so faithful to us in every way that she recommended that we buy a black and make him the foreman of the mines in Cibao, because the natives were so terrified of blacks that they would work without stopping so as not to displease them. The blacks that were brought from Africa were very tall and strong and could handle the Caribs easily; knowing that this pleased their masters, they behaved very cruelly with the workers and developed a reputation as good foremen. Let me add that this was not their fault but that of their masters and their unscrupulous intentions. We did not pay attention to Tajima at first, but we ended up owning blacks because we reached a point where we felt the need for them.

It was a relief to go from digging with a mattock on the banks of the Haina to ordering others to do it in the fields of Cibao; we did not think about the injustice of it at all, and we did nothing but praise Governor Ovando for having the wit to think of it. We saw nothing wrong in it because we knew that the gentlemen of Castile did the same with their workers.

The natives granted to us were not our slaves: we had to take care of them, feed them, and pay them their daily wage, which *Comendador* Ovando set at a half peso of gold. But they got the benefit of this boon for just a short time, because the greediest masters protested loudly and sent lawyers to Castile, who got the Council of the Indies to reduce the amount to three *maravedís* for two days' work.[1] I do not want to think ill of the council, but they were deceived by the fact that a worker in Castile could buy himself a pair of trousers with three *maravedís*, whereas everything in Hispaniola was so scarce and high-priced that a gold peso was barely enough to pay for a

[1] At the time, a peso of gold was the equivalent of 450 *maravedís*.

bit of cloth. That is the kind of mistake that can happen when laws are made so far away from where they will be applied. But anyone willing to think ill of the council would see the malicious part of all this business in the fact that it spread to the members of the council themselves, because soon they also received encomiendas in the Indies, though they lived in Seville or Burgos and had never set foot in this part of the world, and it is human nature not to legislate against your own interest, especially when you do not see with your own eyes how these poor Indians suffered in the cruel labor of the cursed mines.

I have already confessed, and I repeat it here, that nothing distinguished me during those years from the other encomenderos; I thought of nothing but gold, and my greatest happiness was to see the storage sacks brimming over. When I say that nothing distinguished me, you should understand that I, too, sinned in the flesh, and even now, when I think back on it, my soul weeps, and I console myself by thinking that Saint Augustine suffered from the same evil and went on to be a great saint.

If we in any way distinguished ourselves by not being as cruel as the other encomenderos, it was because of Pedro de Rentería's goodness. The mines at Cibao were twenty-one miles away from Concepción, and many of the Indians had to do a round trip between them in the same day. Some of the Indians were from villages even farther away—up to sixty miles—and their strength would be completely exhausted just by traveling along the road. Rentería decided that we would buy a field near the mines and build huts on it for them, thatched-roof and made of wood like the ones they typically had, which they called *bohíos,* and I think they therefore worked more comfortably because they did not have the burden of having to cover so many miles on foot. Rentería also took care not to separate husbands from their wives, or children from their parents, but he was not always successful in that effort.

At the time, a law was promulgated that would have been of great benefit, but its potential was realized only where there were encomenderos who shared Rentería's concerns—and these encomenderos, to the discredit of our holy faith, were in the minority. The law provided that all of us who had Indians had to build a straw building to serve as a church, with an image of our Lady inside, and a tall bell tower to call the Indians to prayer at dusk. They had to be accompanied by a person who would pray the Ave Maria with them, and the Pater Noster, the Credo, and the Salve Regina. The churches were built, but they were of little use because there were no clergy to attend to them, not even catechists to preach the faith to the Indians, so it fell to the miners and ranchers themselves to rush through these prayers, either in Latin or in Spanish, as though they were parrots, so the poor Indians learned nothing from the exercise. And many ranchers, to be rid of this work, taught the prayers to some bright Indian lad and then left the task to him.

That is what Rentería did, but very sensibly, because he made Tajima responsible for teaching afternoon prayers. She had been baptized by that time—by Friar Alonso de Espinal, the same Franciscan prelate who had arrived with Ovando. She took the name Isabel, although we continued to call her Tajima, especially Rentería and I; she was dressed like a Castilian woman in every way, and she even looked like one, because she dressed so gracefully, and to make the resemblance complete, she even was able to wear shoes, which were what the Indians hated the most because they were used to going barefoot from their early childhood on. Tajima understood our language, thanks more to me than to my partner because my experience as a pupil of Nebrija, the grammarian, enabled me to teach what I had learned from him. But it was Rentería who taught her the truths of our faith, not by teaching her to parrot prayers, but rather by explaining the underlying principles to her—that there is a God, whose substance and divine being are beyond everything we see and hear. She then explained those principles to the other Indians in their own language.

Pedro de Rentería attended to the prayers, and I took care of the gold sacks at the same time that I was satisfying other appetites; but amid so much misery for my soul, I remember with nostalgia the pealing of the little church's bell tower, at dusk, as the only call to my heart. The fields of Cibao were then like a continuing spring, always in bloom, and they were especially beautiful and fragrant at that hour of the evening. I never missed the bells calling us to prayer so I could be present when Tajima was directing them, for I was enchanted by her, and she seemed more beautiful to me every day. The admiral says in his diary that all the women of the islands were very good-looking, and I think he said it so that the king and queen would value the lands he had discovered all the more, but those of us who went there were not of the admiral's opinion. What most surprised us about them was their tawny color, verging on yellow, and the way they dressed was not very modest even though they now wore more than just a little skirt to cover their private parts, which was all they were wearing when the admiral first reached these islands. By contrast, when the first women began to arrive from Castile, their brocade dresses and their pale complexion were all that was required to make them seem like goddesses to the Spaniards in the islands, and even the ones who came as prostitutes went on to get married and be ladies. This was a virtue of the conquest, and an important one.

But Tajima, after she stopped digging with the mattock and started dressing like the ladies of Castile, took on a different appearance, and it even seemed to me that her complexion had lightened. Her speech was very sweet and calm, and I found it delightful to teach her our language and also, as a diversion, a little Latin. Pedro de Rentería soon noticed it, and he said to me, "Watch what you're doing, because although we owe all of them respect, we owe it to her even more, having converted her to the truth of our faith, and she understands it so well that she could be of help to many souls."

He was referring to other souls who understood no language other than Taíno, which is what Tajima spoke. I was a twenty-year-old stripling at the time, and she was a couple of years younger. But she appeared in every way to be a grown woman, because women in the islands mature earlier than they do in Castile, which people attribute to the mildness of the climate. Rentería, regarding things that interested him, knew how to be very convincing, and when the prelate of the Franciscans paid us a visit, I do not know what Rentería told him, but Friar Alonso spoke very feelingly to me about the beauty of love between man and woman, so long as it led to legitimate marriage, for a difference in blood was not an obstacle because all were one and the same after Jesus Christ shed his own blood for all of us. The twelve Franciscans who came with Ovando, and those who were arriving after them, were bent on seeing to it that the Spaniards who lived with Indian women did so in order to procreate, in accordance with God's law, and they preached so eloquently and with such holiness that many marriages followed.

This, too, amid so many evils that we committed, was another virtue of our conquest, because those who married Indian women were not snubbed or frowned upon, as happens in other countries. Instead, they were honest and set an example. Friar Alonso's preaching was all that I needed to respect Tajima, although I did not stop taking delight in being near her to the point that I would have followed the holy prelate's preaching if the Lord had not had other paths for me to follow. I say that I remember the pealing of our little church's bells with nostalgia because of the pleasure it gave me to hear Tajima explain the truths of our faith in her Taíno language, which I now was beginning to understand, and also the Lucayan language, which is very similar. She explained great truths in just a few words, and a theologian would not have been able to choose better ones. That is what I think now, but at the time I was more attentive to every gesture that this beautiful woman made, to the vivid color of her lips, the whiteness of her teeth, and the grace of all her movements; so that I was respectful toward her in my behavior but not in my thoughts, because at the time my soul was wretched and not very inclined toward things of the spirit.

The proof of this is that when Governor Ovando organized an expedition to pacify the village and province of Xaraguá, I was one of the first to enlist, with an eye to taking advantage of the benefits the campaign would bring me. On one hand, I wanted to curry favor with the *comendador*, who granted more encomiendas as a reward to those who served him in that way. And, on the other, I saw an opportunity to acquire Indian slaves from among the prisoners we would take, because the war, being a just war, gave us the right to make them slaves. Well, that war had little of justice about it. There had been an uprising of sorts in the province of Xaraguá, yes, but only in self-defense against the evil Spaniards—who seemingly were the scruffiest, crudest, and most vicious men in all of Castile, many of them fugitives from justice who had banded together in that isolated region.

As the proverb says, birds of a feather flock together, and the flock in Xaraguá was largely made up of those who had served under Francisco Roldán, the local governor who rebelled against the admiral and who had the admirable habit of making slaves of any Indians in his path. This Roldán was the one who extorted tribute, either in the form of enough gold dust to fill a Flemish jingle bell or in the form of from twenty-four to thirty-five pounds of cotton—every three months—for every man in the village older than fourteen. Because the poor Indians could not satisfy such an outrageous demand, they fled to the mountains, where he hunted them down with the help of his workers, the most loutish men in Castile. His brazenness rose to such a point that in 1496 he had sent three ships to Castile, under the command of Alonso Niño, with three hundred Indians to be sold in the market at Valencia, one of them a seven-year-old girl, whom they sold for three thousand *maravedís* to a widow named Inés Rodríguez, who bought her, luckily, to bring her up as her daughter. But she would have paid Roldán as much as the girl would have fetched if she had been bought to be put to work in a brothel.

I recount this in great detail on the basis of the documents I had to collect in order to argue before the Council of the Indies, some time afterward, regarding the bad treatment meted out to the Indians and the measures that should be taken against it.

If Francisco Roldán was bad, members of his retinue were not far behind him, and Queen Anacaona rose up to defend her people against them in Xaraguá. This brave woman was the sister of King Bechechio, whose kingdom was at the end of the island on the southern coast, in the middle of ruggedly mountainous country, where fleeing Indians were seeking refuge more than 240 miles from Santo Domingo. This is the region that the admiral described in his diary as being populated by an infinite number of people, all of them very happy, whose women went stark naked, covering only their private parts with a white half-length skirt of densely woven cotton, which they called a petticoat and covered them from the waist to the middle of their legs, and the admiral said that they received him and his men with green branches in their hands, singing and dancing their dances, which they call *areytos*. There was no gold in this region, or at least the natives had not searched for it because they did not value it, so they paid their tribute in cotton and cassava bread. But the ones who had served as Roldán's thugs knew no tribute other than gold, for which I pardon them because we all worshipped it. In that regard, I confess that if I wanted more Indians, it was because I wanted them to mine gold for me and make necklaces out of it with which to awe my relatives in Seville. I even chose very specific persons, in my barrio of San Lorenzo, to whom I would show off my necklaces. I imagined the awe on their faces, and in pursuit of such a pathetically trifling distinction, I committed despicable acts, not the least of which was enlisting in the expedition against Queen Anacaona.

This woman was very striking, gracious, and regal, with an air of great authority. Contrary to the custom in those lands, she inherited the crown from her brother King Bechechio, upon his death, and, because she had also been the spouse of Caonabo, king of Maguana, she ruled over that whole province with such strong-mindedness that she did not accept what her brother and husband, two battle-hardened men, had accepted. They had agreed to pay tribute to the king and queen of Castile, after the admiral and his brother Don Bartolomé Colón, convinced them that all the peoples of the world had submitted to them and those of Xaraguá could be no exception. But when those evil Spaniards insisted that the tribute had to be paid in gold, Queen Anacaona decreed that no tribute would be paid in any form, and in the ensuing revolts, some Christians lost their lives, as was to be expected.

Those brutish Spaniards reported these developments in Santo Domingo in such a way as to make it seem that the Indians of Xaraguá were devastating those lands with blood and fire, which led Governor Ovando to decide he would teach them a lesson. He formed an army of three hundred foot soldiers and seventy cavalry, and I was one of the latter. At the time, one had to be very rich to have a horse on that island, and I had one thanks to the generosity of Rentería, who said that if he had a mule there was no reason why I should be in a lesser position, and we bought a mare out of our shared funds, as a great sacrifice, because the gold we were mining did not amount to much. I managed to become a decent horseman and was fairly skillful in mock battles on horseback, and I taught her to prance on her hind legs to the sound of a guitar. The Indians were in great awe and took us for gods on account of it; besides, in battle they fled when we attacked them, with our lances, on horseback, because of the terror the animals inspired in them.

Of the three hundred foot soldiers, seventy-five were armed with arquebuses and the rest had crossbows, so the Indians, armed as they were with swords made of fire-hardened wood, or arrows and stones, could do little against them. But we Spaniards entered into such encounters fearfully, because it was said that they dipped their arrowheads in curare, a poisonous liquid extracted from lianas that would kill you if it just grazed you. It is true that on the coast of Cumaná, in Venezuela, where the Indians are braver and more warlike, they often used this trick. I do not remember that they did so in the islands, but out of fear of what might happen, we just charged at them without thinking. And that was what, on that occasion, *Comendador* Ovando did, too.

When Queen Anacaona learned that an army was approaching, she sent out emissaries to meet it, and when they brought back word that the approaching army was coming to pacify the region, she summoned all the nobles of the kingdom and the villagers to the city of Xaraguá to honor the Christians' *guamiquina* (which means "great lord" in their language) and afterwards to present him with the grievances they had against the Spaniards, which were many.

As we were crossing the mountains, some of which have peaks higher than any in Spain, with very green meadows and good grasslands for grazing, the Indians came out to receive us, bowing to us and performing their *areytos*, which is a mark of great friendship. But one Robledo Cejudo, who was cut from the same cloth as Francisco Roldán, inseparably accompanied Governor Ovando, whom he ceaselessly urged to put no stock in these demonstrations. The governor, as a military man, wisely did not trust them, and we marched along every day in an orderly formation, arms at the ready, with a vanguard of forerunners and scouts on horseback. I was one of those forerunners, because of my equestrian skills, and I was very proud of them, trying to make a good impression in the saddle. When the others could see me, I made my horse rear up and walk on its hind legs, with its forelegs in the air, as if the guitar were playing. I remember that one evening at dusk, which in that area is exceptionally beautiful, cool, and fragrant, when it was time to set up camp, a wild boar that was very similar to the boars of Castile burst out of the edge of the forest. I chased after him, my lance at the ready, and despite his evasive maneuvers I managed to lance him in front of the *comendador*, who called out to me for all to hear: "I see that you are as skilled a horseman as you are a Latinist!"

Hearing that public praise gave me the feeling that I had touched the sky; all I can say in the way of forgiving myself is that I was young—not yet twenty, if I recall aright. For that and other reasons, the governor continued to single me out and sometimes gave me guidance as a father would; he was one of those who told me that, being so knowledgeable, I should pursue a career as a cleric, which was a role very much needed in those islands. It surprises me to think how he had hit the nail on the head, because I had so little inclination toward the holy priesthood at the time. What the *comendador* told me went in one ear and out the other, and if I took it seriously at all, it was to please him and receive more encomiendas from him. Would that the *comendador* had been as right in his treatment of the Indians!

I would be lying if I did not say that I remember this my first expedition of conquest as a festive lark, and the Indians who came out to greet us were a significant factor in making it so. As was customary, the pennants of Castile were at the head of our column, among them that of Governor Ovando, aglow with blazing fires and crimson maroon, along with the band of fifers led by the musician Ortiz. He went on to the conquest of Cuba and then of Mexico, where he garnered great fame. He was the one who said that he knew of no noteworthy battle that had not been won with the sound of drums and that a battle won without music might as well not have been won. He was gifted with such art in playing the guitar that he effortlessly adapted to the rhythms of the Indians' dances, and, when he accompanied them on his instrument, they went mad. They also went mad with the wine he gave them, which he loved, too, and one night there was such a ruckus in the camp (it was the night that some Indian women were brought in on the pretext that they would dance *areytos*) that the following morning the governor, who was very punctiliously devoted to good behavior, ordered him put in the stocks. The governor nevertheless held Ortiz in high esteem, because when he was sober he played all kinds of instruments, including those on which music was played in church, with great art and feeling.

The reception they gave us in the city of Xaraguá was beyond description, and it was every bit as fine as the welcome extended to the admiral's brother during the first arrival of Christians in their lands. Although over the years since then the Indians had suffered more than they had benefited at the hands of the Spaniards, they repeated their dances and honors once again, and though we were very numerous and hungry, they gave us all our fill of delicacies, in game from the forests and fish from the sea (which was several miles away from there), until we were sated and there was food left over. They provided the senior *comendador* with thatched-roof lodgings made of carved stone, with a number of rooms corresponding to his status as the *guamiquina*, or great lord. And they surrounded it with other, smaller, but well-built lodgings for the rest of our men.

Things got off to a bad start because we lacked a common language in which to understand each other, and we had to communicate through Robledo Cejudo, whose sole interest lay in coming to an understanding that provided for severe punishment of anyone who was unwilling to pay his taxes. Queen Anacaona, as was their custom, did not appear at first, holding back until the lesser caciques had paid their respects to the *guamiquina*. When she did appear, with all the grace and majesty of the great lady she was, it was late in the day, because Robledo Cejudo, and others of the same ilk as Roldán, had convinced the ranking *comendador* that it was all a trap to do away with him, which amounted to doing away with Castile. They made their calculations, which showed that no fewer than fifty thousand Indians, from all over the province, had gathered together in the city of Xaraguá and were encamped in the fields that lay at the foot of the town, which filled us with a great fear. And I have learned, in my long life, that fear is a bad counselor. Much of the damage that we Spaniards did in the Indies came from the fact that, wherever we went, we were few compared to them, and we had no choice but to fill their hearts with dread.

Under the pretext that we wanted to repay them for all their dances and festivities, the *comendador* invited the queen and her suite, which was made up of no fewer than eighty lesser caciques, to watch us joust on horseback, which for them was a great novelty, and they ac-

cepted with pleasure. This happened on a Sunday, after
the midday meal, and we first invited them to enter our
huts to enjoy a feast; at the same time, we ordered the
seventy cavalrymen to surround the huts on four sides,
thinking that the Indians would not dare to come near
the horses. The rest of the troops were distributed outside and inside, and at a signal made by the *comendador* by
touching a piece of gold that hung from his neck, three
of them were to throw themselves on each cacique and
tie him up. "Ipse dixit et facta sunt omnia." He gave the
signal when the noble Indians were most distracted, and
in the blink of an eye they were prisoners, bound hand
and foot.

Although *Comendador* Ovando was clumsy in the way
he handled the Indians, I never considered him to be
bloodthirsty, and yet, on that occasion, he was that in
plenty, because I was a witness to it, and my conscience
suffered for it. Taking Anacaona and her caciques prisoner so that they could be used as hostages was considered an act of good government in the Indies, and other
conquistadores did the same, among them Hernán Cortés
with Moctezuma, in the conquest of Mexico; but what
came after did not have the same justification. I think that
Robledo Cejudo and his ilk attacked the Indians because
they thought that the only way to teach them a lesson
was to impale their heads on the sharp end of a pike.
This Robledo Cejudo was the one who made himself
so rich that, in order to ship to Castile all the gold he
had stolen, he had a caravel built with heavily reinforced
decks made of okoume wood, which now must still be
at the bottom of the sea, and what remains of his bones

must be standing watch over his treasure, because off the Windward Islands his ship was seized by a crosswind that, given the burden the ship was bearing, sank it, leaving no survivors. I could tell a hundred such stories because, looking back from the vantage point of my old age, I can remember only a few men who enjoyed their ill-gotten riches and many who used theirs to hasten their descent into hell, unless they were saved by the mercy of Jesus Christ our Lord.

Either because the Indians wanted to rescue their masters or because they were defending themselves against Robledo Cejudo and others like him, we ended up in a fight to the death in which we had to engage in order to stay alive. So that the Indians' leaders could not be rescued, thereby fortifying the hearts of their subjects, we set fire to the huts in which they were held prisoner, which, being largely made of straw and very dry, burned like tinder. In order to allow Queen Anacaona to die a more honorable death, they kept her safe, but it would have been better for the good name of *Comendador* Ovando if she had suffered the fate of the members of her entourage.

The only good thing I did on that tragic day was to save a child no more than ten years old who was being chased by an enraged Spaniard. I lifted the child up to the hindquarters of my mare. The battle ended as it inevitably had to, because a body of some four hundred men well armed with arquebuses and crossbows, seventy of them mounted, were all that was necessary to devastate a hundred islands like this one. When most of the Indians fled, others were taken prisoner, and we were left owners of the field, we proceeded to execute the law that applies in

Castile in just wars against infidels, although, as I have said, our war was not one of them.

Given the fact that it was seen as a rebellion, and therefore slaughter of the rebels was justified, the person who was at its head could not be allowed to live, and Queen Anacaona was immediately condemned to death and hanged by the neck. She died like the great lady she was, and I believe she would not have wanted to remain alive, because it was through her trust in the Spaniards that so many of her subjects had died. Our practice of hanging criminals was very striking in those lands at first, but later they understood that it was a more merciful death than the one they inflicted on their own people, who were sometimes drawn and quartered.

Many of those who fled took refuge on a small island called Guanabo, twenty-four miles away, and all of them were condemned to slavery. I was given one of them.

I do not think Governor Ovando took a great deal of pride in his achievement, and I even believe that, when it reached the ears of our Catholic Queen, a judicial review of Ovando's residence in the Indies came very close to being ordered. But later it was forgotten, and now Ovando, who was made a commander of the Order of Calatrava, is regarded as the man who pacified Hispaniola.

CHAPTER IV

LOVE AND SORROWS

If God does not move the hearts of men, damaged as they are by original sin, they harden in such a way that we find justification for every evil. After what I have related took place, because we who participated in the event benefited from it, in the form either of Indians or of encomiendas, we pressed on doggedly, and for my part I participated in no fewer than three wars of pacification of the Indians, the most effective measure being to take their lives or enslave them.

One of the wars was that of Haniguayugua, ordered by one of Ovando's lieutenants, Diego Velázquez de Cuéllar, who later was the governor of the island of Cuba and with whom I had a great friendship, as will appear in its proper place. Another was the war of Higüey, around the year 1505, when I was no longer so young and therefore had more discernment and correspondingly greater blame; it was led by Juan de Esquivel, the same Sevillian gentleman who persuaded Their Catholic Majesties to reduce their share of the gold to one fifth. Because of the great prestige that this earned him, in addition to his behavior generally, he ended up being captain general of our fleet, and we fought in the province of Higüey for about a year.

This is a very interesting province on account of the

mountains of which it is formed: they are like plateaus, layered on top of each other, and all of them rising so steeply that even cats have to make a great effort to climb them. But they have the virtue of being covered with slabs of living rock, very rough, like the facets of a diamond, with holes among them filled with red soil that was so very fertile and excellent that simply sowing the cassava is enough for it to sink deep roots promptly, and the same can be said of melons that were grown with seeds brought from Castile and attained the size of a jug.

So the province became a breadbasket for the king, and, when a rebellion prompted him to do so, he ordered the governor to construct a wooden fort in the hinterland, but not too far from the sea, manned by a garrison of nine men led by a Spanish captain named Martín de Villamán. Although much was demanded of the natives to obtain the maximum value from the extraordinarily rich soil, because His Majesty's ships were always in need of cassava bread, life for the Indians was easier than in the mines, where the earth always had to be moved to extract the gold; and there would have been peace had it not been for the fact that the idleness of Martín de Villamán and his men—always a bad counselor—prompted them to steal from the Indians what would hurt them the most: their daughters and wives. Though they were not as zealously protective as Christians of the honor of their women, neither did the Indians allow what nature prohibited; of that I have proof. This violation prompted them to muster an army that set fire to the fort, which being built of wood burned very well, so although one man managed to flee, the other eight died. The one who escaped brought the news to Santo Domingo, and the governor declared a war of fire and blood against the inhabitants of Higüey.

This was a very cruel war because the rough terrain made it very difficult to track down the rebellious Indians, and when we took a prisoner, he was tortured so that he would reveal the whereabouts of his comrades. Also, the mountain Indians are always very ferocious, and that required us to fight with the utmost valor. Juan Esquivel told us that, by losing just one battle, we would inspire the Indians with greater courage, and, because they were so many and we so few, they would drive us out of Hispaniola in the end. It would have been difficult to achieve that (though not impossible if they had all joined in the effort) because the entire skill of the Indians consisted in hurling stones with great force, since they were not familiar with slings, but they had very good aim and any good shot caused great injury. But they were very brave, and they were not demoralized when they saw many of their men felled by our shots. Rather, it seemed that they took heart from it and defied us all the more.

One such act of defiance, which was very famous, took place when we were en route to the islet of Saona, where it was said that King Cotubanamá, the lord of Higüey, had taken refuge. Esquivel had assigned a caravel to sail to that island, and as we passed it, a detachment of troops came out toward us; among them was one who stood out by making gestures defying any Christian to come out and fight him. He was naked from top to bottom and very tall and burly; the breadth of his shoulders measured no less than a yard, whereas his waist was so narrow that it could be encircled by two hands; his arms and legs were very well proportioned; his gesticulations were those of a proud and serious man, and he carried a bow fit for a giant and an arrow with three points fashioned from fishbones in the shape of a trident.

There was a Spaniard named Alejos Gómez who was extremely experienced in killing Indians; it was said that he could cut them in half with a single stroke. He asked to be allowed to take the Indian on, and Esquivel agreed because of his great confidence in him and the desirability of teaching the Indians a lesson. Alejos carried his sword with a tight grip, his dagger in his belt, a short lance, and a shield made out of woven reeds. The Indian showed he was as agile as a hawk, and he did nothing but feint with his arrow and run circles around the Spaniard. The latter, at the outset, as if to avoid taking advantage of the superiority of his weapons, threw rocks at him that he picked up off the ground, very deftly, because as a child he had been a shepherd boy in Extremadura. And that is where the Indian displayed his agility, because he dodged them all with his hawk-like moves. In turn, he responded with rocks of his own, which Alejos warded off with his shield. It was a very fine fight, which ended in defeat for the Spaniard, who escaped death by curling up into a ball and covering himself with his shield when the Indian readied his bow. The fishbone trident broke against the Spanish shield, and the Indian ended the fight by retiring to the edge of the woods amid deafening shouts from his comrades. Esquivel did not try to stop him because he had fought so well, and even Alejos Gómez praised his strength and skill, recognizing that he had not been able to beat him. The fight lasted from two in the afternoon until shortly before sundown.

After ten months of suffering in those lands, enduring so much hunger that there were days when we ate only guáyagas (which are roots in the mountains out of which they also make a small amount of bread), we found King Cotubanamá on the islet of Saona and took him prisoner. The men wanted to crush him to death right there, but Esquivel spared him so cruel a death and took him in a caravel to Santo Domingo, where the governor more mercifully ordered him to be hanged.

From this pacification, which is what our wars were called in the Indies, we gained a great deal, not in gold or pearls, because the inhabitants of Higüey neither possessed nor wanted any, but in the great number of slaves that we gained. With the money we made in selling some of them, we bought some farmland in a plain in Cibao through which ran the river Xanique, and that was where I passed my happiest years in Hispaniola, before the Lord, in his infinite mercy, showed me the true way.

While I was off fighting, Rentería managed the farm, and the illusions under which all of us lived were such that, being an upright man who did not want to act contrary to Holy Scripture in any way, he accepted what I was doing because he understood that it was a way to open the path to preaching the gospel. That is how blinded we were and how we managed to justify our misdeeds, as I say at the beginning of this chapter.

This rugged land is composed of the tallest and stoniest

mountains, so the Indians aptly called them Cibao, because *ciba* means stone in their language. But, in delightful contrast, myriad rivers and gullies formed the loveliest valleys at their feet, with great, cool groves outside which there was nothing but sparse pine trees, widely scattered, which did not yield pine cones, and from a distance they resembled the olive trees of Aljarafe in Seville. There were tiny nuggets of gold to be found in all those rivers, but higher upstream there were some larger nuggets, and we found one that weighed sixteen pounds, for which we were paid eight hundred pesos of gold.

The land we bought was located high up on top of a delightful hill, surrounded by a river that emptied into the Xanique, in a stream so fine and sweet that the water in it seemed to have been distilled. We built a house there, made of wood and enclosed by a strong wall that was so well built that even in the midday sun we did not feel the heat at all. We moved our business there, leaving behind the mines of Concepción de La Vega, which were already exhausted; we began to work the land, which produced the first onions in the whole island of Hispaniola, grown from bulbs that Rentería had ordered from Castile. When this first harvest yielded its tender and fragrant bulbs, they seemed better than if we had found gold. From then on we never stopped reaping rich harvests of those liliaceous plants, and we also had, like the rest of the farmers, pigsties and land with which to produce cassava, for bread. And, for our own pleasure, we also had pens in which we raised brood mares, not for sale, but so we would always have fine horses to ride.

Although I liked working the land more than I had

the mines, I continued to occupy myself with the latter because if I had left them in Rentería's hands, we would have garnered little because he was so benevolent in his treatment of the Indians. Though I was not among the worst, I allowed the foremen to work them from sunrise to sunset, and it never entered my mind that it could be otherwise, because when a madness for gold enters a man's head, anything that fills the sacks is allowed. It enabled me to live the life of a great lord, and I would go ostentatiously to Santo Domingo with a train of horsemen to deliver the gold to the office of the royal House of Trade and, at the same time, give myself up to forbidden pleasures, among them playing card games, in which the stakes were small bags of tiny pebbles of gold and sometimes life itself, because it was not unusual for a game to end in a knife fight, to such an extreme that Governor Ovando had to forbid all games of chance; but, even then, the prohibition was not enough to stop us from continuing to play.

But I was always happy to return to our farm on the Xanique River, while Tajima was with us, because of the pleasure it gave me to be near her. Now my life unfolds in decades, one after another, as if each one were no more than a year, but at that time one year was worth ten, and at the end of 1506, I think, it seemed to me that I had known Tajima for many, many years. She resembled a Castilian woman in every respect, both in the way she dressed and in the way she expressed herself, and she was so coveted that, if she had been more aware of that, she would have had reason to become conceited. I say coveted not only in the sense that Spaniards coveted Indian women to take advantage of them, but rather also for her other virtues, one of them being her knowledge of all the languages of the island. Her reputation for being such an accomplished linguist reached as high as the governor, who at one point asked us for her so she could negotiate with a cacique from the northern part of the island whom no one was able to understand, and Tajima saved them from that difficulty. Things got to the point that the friar and prelate Alonso del Espinal, when he came up to Cibao, invariably visited us so that she could instruct not only him but the other Franciscans as well in the different languages of the Indians, in order to make it possible for them later on to be missionaries to the Indians who spoke those languages. And they sometimes brought her along so that she could preach in their company. She was in every way so sweet, so devout, and so obedient that Friar Alonso wanted to send her to Spain, where she could take vows at a convent of the Order of Saint Clare. The Franciscans were willing to pay not only the cost of her trip but also her dowry, saying that it would be such a benefit for the order (which was expected to send nuns to those lands soon, as they did shortly thereafter) to be able to count on her as one who would know so well the customs of those whom the Poor Clares were to evangelize. He was right, and Rentería was thrilled, eager to agree and even to supply her dowry, but I was against it, and not sorry to be so, because I did not see her as a nun but rather very much on the contrary, as captivated by me as I was by her, and taking in a nun who does not want Jesus Christ as her only husband would be a very unwise decision for a convent. Rentería got very worked up on the subject, to the point, I remember, that one day, at Vespers, he angrily reproached me—an anger that was very unusual in him. "How dare you fight with our Lord", he asked me, "over someone for whom you lack the proper respect?"

The Lord resolved the dispute soon thereafter, as he usually does when he has pointed out other paths for those he has chosen. Rentería beseeched me to marry her if I would not let her become a nun, and I was already inclined to do that, just when she came down with smallpox; it is impossible not to see in all this the hand of God. That is what I think now, but at the time it seemed to me a punishment administered by the Lord's avenging hand, because the smallpox had been brought by a black man whom we had purchased in Jamaica in order to increase the productivity of the gold mines and enable me to live more at ease. There were many blacks who brought this plague to the islands, and with it a greater mortality among the Indians than had been wrought by the Spaniards with their cannon. The blacks, because they were very hardy and had been more exposed to the disease, recovered from it with scabs and blemishes on their faces that their dark skin concealed. But for the Indians, because they did not know our illnesses, it was always fatal. Another link in the chain of death was their custom of bathing at all hours of the day, whether they were well or ill, given as they were to laughing and playing in the river and sea waters; and when they first began to feel the itching of the smallpox, they did so all the more.

Tajima was one of the first to show symptoms of the disease, in the form of a rosy complexion that, for a time,

enhanced her beauty by giving her a blushing color that
I thought was the result of my having mentioned to her
my proposals of marriage. She was laughing, very happy
about my intentions, and when the trembling caused by
her fever appeared, she laughed all the more because fever
was unknown among them. When she was wracked with
pain, we asked a Franciscan Father who lived in a hut in
Concepción, some twenty-one miles from our farm, to
come and see her, and it was he who explained to us the
disease from which she was suffering, which was already
beginning to be understood in the southern part of the
island, where the black slaves landed. She recovered consciousness and was able to receive all the aid and comfort that our Holy Mother the Church reserves for those
who die in her bosom. I believe that she went directly to
heaven, because ever since she had learned the truth of
Christ, she fully lived the gospel and even helped many
others do the same. She clung to my hand with hers,
which was burning hot, and it was one of the times that
I most held hers between mine, because she had thereto-
fore avoided close contact, despite the great love she had
for me. In the end, the horrible pustules appeared, and
I ordered her face to be veiled because I wanted to remember her as being as beautiful as she was when she led
evening prayer, in the little church on our farm. But that
did not stop me from thinking that human beauty was of
little value and that any beauty that is not related to the
soul quickly passes.

We buried her in a tomb that we built at the top of
the hill, in a place filled with the murmurs of a clean
and crystalline stream, and on the tomb, which was very

beautiful, we put her baptismal name, Doña Isabel, which is still there. A church was built on the same hill not long thereafter, along with a cemetery, but her tomb continues to be the most beautiful, and I am told that many ask who was this Doña Isabel, and no one knows how to answer them.

CHAPTER V

A CLERIC IN THE CONQUEST OF CUBA

Tajima's death left me in very low spirits and so unsettled by the life I saw ahead of me that Rentería urged me to go back to Castile; we always used to say that we had to make that journey to put our affairs in order, but we never made up our minds to do it. Together, we had about two thousand pesos in gold, and Rentería wanted to use his portion to buy himself a piece of land in his homeland of Guipúzcoa for his old age, and he advised me to do the same. We who were in the Indies during those years imagined that we were to some extent in exile, and we dreamed of making ourselves rich so that we could return to Spain. Only a few managed to do so because, although we did mine gold, a good deal of it ended up falling by the wayside, sometimes to the bottom of the sea, sometimes into the hands of pirates, and mostly into the hands of the officials of the council, who were the ones who dealt in it. For that reason, Rentería, who had more confidence in me than I did myself, insisted repeatedly that I pursue a career in the Church because I was so well qualified for it; he said it because of my studies in Latin and the ease with which I expressed myself both in speech and in writing and, above all, because it was a path to a secure income, since the clerics in the Indies earned their stipend as priests plus what they earned as catechists. That was true of the honest ones, though unfortunately there also were others, because being a cleric did not mean one could not be an encomendero, and I am ashamed to say that I was one of the latter.

Rentería also encouraged me because, after Tajima's death, I said that I was not going to marry, and, besides, I kept away from the company of women, I do not know whether out of virtue or because I had contracted a shameful disease of which I was cured, but it left me fearful of getting close to women. All this was written by the Lord, as he alone knows, and the scribe was Pedro de Rentería, who barely knew how to sign his name, but he dictated his homilies to me and insisted that, if I did become a cleric, I could even become a bishop. At the time I took what he said in jest, and later it turned out to be the case. So, I ask, who was it that was speaking through the mouth of my good friend?

My return to Castile was not so much in order to follow his advice as it was on account of my anxious nature and the fear that I would catch smallpox, which at the time was wreaking havoc in Hispaniola, to such an extent that I was not the only one who left for that reason.

I made the crossing, in a caravel called the *Guarama*, to Seville, where I spent a year; and then I spent another one in Italy, which was where I ended up being ordained as a priest. In Seville I studied humanities and received minor orders, which already qualified me to be a catechist in the Indies. At the time, I had dealings with the admiral's brother Don Bartolomé Colón, in whose command my father had served, as I have said above, which was how I came to know him. The Colón family was involved in major legal proceedings with the Crown, and I put myself at his disposal; Don Bartolomé took me as his notary and lawyer, although I was rather ignorant of the law, but I thought it was such an honor to participate in legal proceedings of such illustrious lineage that whatever I did not know I invented. Such is the arrogance of youth. I esteemed that friendship so much that I paid my own way to Italy, with Don Bartolomé, to make our case to King Ferdinand the Catholic, who was in Naples; it was the first time I had been in the presence of a monarch, and everything that happened there remains fresh in my mind, but because it has nothing to do with this account, I will move on.

It is relevant, however, to say that Don Bartolomé was a man of talent, very accustomed to court intrigues because, before the discovery, he had had dealings with the kings of England and France, when he offered them in the admiral's name what the latter ended up doing for Castile. Don Bartolomé was a fine cartographer, very well versed in foreign languages, of which he spoke no fewer than half a dozen, and, at that time, he bore the title of governor of Hispaniola, although that was challenged by the Crown. To me, being under the protection of such an illustrious man seemed the peak of distinction, and I lived only for what the governor said or thought. And the governor, seeing that behavior on my part and that I was reserved in my interactions with women, was among those who encouraged me to be ordained a priest, helping me to see the advantages I would gain from it. It was not insignificant that at the time Don Juan Rodríguez de Fonseca, the bishop of Palencia and later the bishop of Burgos, was the absolute owner of the future of the Indies, to whom the Crown delegated all responsibility for those lands, so that any cleric who enjoyed his favor had much to gain in the New World.

With all that in mind, I was ordained a priest in the Eternal City in February 1507, because Don Bartolomé Colón joked that Roman priests all ended up being bishops. With his backing, I was relieved of the necessity to complete some of the studies that I needed in my ecclesiastical education, and I do not regret that because I later did complete them, and others as well. Don Bartolomé was as cruel in his treatment of the Indians as the other governors, but it can be said in his defense that, because he was one of the first, he did not understand how much damage and injustice was caused by the encomiendas. I have always defended him, as I have Don Diego, the admiral's son, without receiving any favor from them other than their counsel along the path to the priesthood, but that always seemed sufficient for me to break lances in their favor. Besides, in my comings and goings from and to the Indies, I spent all the gold that I brought from Hispaniola because the Colón family was hard-pressed for money and there were occasions on which their hospitality was at my expense, and even so it seemed to me that they honored me with it. It is certainly true that in that year in Italy I learned a good deal about chancelleries that later served me well in my attempts to defend the Indians.

I bought Rentería the land he wanted in Guipúzcoa,

which was very productive and suitable for grazing cattle, although, because I was used to the expanses of Hispaniola, it seemed to me to be very small, but it was what he wanted and I did it, and I went back to Santo Domingo with my pockets empty.

There is not much to tell regarding my first years as a cleric, and I think I paid more attention to the income from my farms than I did to my holy ministry; that is shown by the fact that I did not sing my first Mass until three years had passed, around 1510, on the occasion of a visit from Admiral Diego Colón, who was the son of Don Cristóbal and by then the governor of Hispaniola, which is to say of all the Indies.

This period saw the arrival in Hispaniola of the first Fathers of the Order of Saint Dominic, and the youngest of them, Friar Pedro de Córdoba, being the holiest of them, became the vicar. He was twenty-eight years old at the time, and because he came from a very rich and noble family, he lived like the poorest of the poor, with four other religious who came with him. A neighbor, a good Christian named Pedro de Lumbreras, gave them a hut next to one of his corrals, which was just the same as the huts of the most wretched Indians. They ate cassava bread, which without lard is good for almost nothing, and some egg or small fish every now and then. They usually ate their cabbage cooked, without oil, with a bit of *ají* at most, which is what the Indians call pepper; they slept on *cadalechos*, which are beds made of woven branches, and sometimes, but not always, they put on them a straw mattress. The rules of the Order did not permit them to ask for contributions of bread, wine, or oil, unless they were ill, but if they received any they could eat them giving thanks to God for his mercy. They wore only a shift made of very coarse cloth and a cloak made of rough wool, but these humble garments took nothing away from the distinctive elegance of Friar Pedro, a native of Córdoba, who was so tall and handsome that wherever he went all eyes were drawn to him. They always carried out their missions on foot, never on horseback, and they were able to walk ninety miles, eating bread made from roots and drinking cold water out of the streams, which abound there, sleeping out in the open with nothing to cover them but their cloaks. They thus preached, by example, against the gluttony of which we encomenderos were guilty, because we did not even respect the fasting or abstinence called for by the Church, and even on a Friday in Lent the butchers' shops were stocked as though it were Easter Sunday.

When they arrived at a village, they ordered the church-bells to be rung, to call together all the inhabitants who had encomiendas, and they tried to hear their confessions and after celebrating the holy Mass admonished them to bring to the church all the Indians they had in their service. Friar Pedro de Córdoba would sit on a bench with a crucifix in his hand, and, through interpreters, he would begin to preach to them about the creation of the world, continuing to the point where Christ, the Son of God, died on the Cross for all men. The Indians understood him very well, and so did the Spaniards, but the former paid more attention, and the doctrine he preached seemed to them to be beautiful and in all respects superior to their own religions, which were very sad and full of evil spirits that mistreated them.

I saw Friar Pedro and his fellow friars as beings from another world, and if they had told me then that I would end up being one of them, I would have thought they were joking, because, despite my being a cleric, I continued to be as greedy as ever for the cursed gold, and I preached one thing to the Indians (the few times that I did preach to them) and did another when I required them to work in the mines. Friar Pedro did not take this point up with me, turning instead to the most important one, showing me that it was not right for me, as a priest, not to celebrate the holy Mass, depriving myself of its fruits and depriving those who could benefit from them. Despite the fact that he was telling me something so fundamental, I resisted, arguing sometimes that I did not consider myself worthy and at other times that there was no opportunity for it because we lacked the kind of wine and bread that could be consecrated; which, to our discredit, was true, because we took care to see to it that the encomenderos kept our tables well supplied with delicacies brought from Castile but often lacked wine for the Mass.

In the end, Friar Pedro got his way, thanks to the mediation of the admiral and governor, Don Diego Colón, who along with his wife, Doña María de Toledo, the niece of the Duke of Alba, came to Concepción de La Vega for the month of September 1510. And what the theology of this Dominican Father could not do, the favor of the governor could, and he showed me that,

because it was the first new Mass that was being sung
in the Indies, it should be invested with special solemnity, which it was. How could a poor cleric, not very
zealous about his ministry, imagine that his first Mass
should be presided over by such high-titled nobility? The
church was packed, with a great number of residents from
all parts of the island, not because of my merits, but because of those who were at the head of it. Theologians
say that the Christian faithful, by instinct, know that they
earn special favors from the priest who is celebrating his
first Mass because he emanates a mysterious virtue that
the Lord imparts to neophytes; for myself I will say that I
noticed something like that virtue, and it moved me to see
at my feet, kissing my hands, the son of Cristóbal Colón,
his wife, and all the dignitaries of the island, because they
were all there. But, unfortunately for me, because it was
September and therefore the season for smelting the gold,
all the inhabitants brought me presents of coins made of
that metal, in the form of ducats and *castellanos*, or very
graceful and well-made figurines, and it pains me to remember that on such a solemn occasion I could not help
calculating what all of that misery was worth. And it also
seems lamentable that, with so much splendor, we could
only consecrate the bread, because it had been days since
the last ship arrived from Castile and not a drop of wine
could be found on the whole island.

From that day on, I celebrated Mass on the days of obligation, and on other days, when Friar Pedro required it, I
preached to the Indians in the manner that he customarily

did—with more learning, because I knew their language, but with less piety. And that piety was of such value that when Friar Pedro preached with expression and the help of interpreters, the church filled up with Indians, all of them very attentive and elevated, and when I was the one who preached, they had to be forced to come to church and soon were nodding off. How could it have been otherwise if the same person who was preaching to them on Sunday was the one who made them work like animals on the other days of the week?

But it seemed to me that if I obeyed the sixth commandment and celebrated Mass with the grace of God, I was doing my duty as a cleric; and I compared myself to others who were worse, who did no more than I did, and who in addition cohabited with women in sin. It did not occur to me to compare myself with the friars of Saint Dominic, whom I thought of as going straight to heaven, and I contented myself with thinking that I would go there through the gate of purgatory. So badly did others behave that I was considered on the island to be a good person, and when Diego de Velázquez embarked on the conquest of the island of Cuba, he summoned me to be his chaplain. I accepted out of my anxious nature and because the elders of Hispaniola knew that the first ones to reach a new territory reaped great benefits; and they endlessly anticipated that result in Cuba. At the time it was still unknown whether it was an island or part of a continent, which Cristóbal Colón mentioned in his diary; it turned out to be an island, but so beautiful that from the beginning it was known as the "Pearl of the Caribbean".

It is nine hundred miles long and, at its widest, 180 miles wide; one can walk the entire island in the shade of trees, which makes it cooler and milder than Hispaniola. Many of those trees are cedars, like the ones in Castile, but as thick as an ox and so tall that the Indians make a canoe in a single piece from one of them, with the capacity to carry up to seventy men, and we navigated on the sea in them. There are other trees that they call *estoraques*, from which they extract a balsam of a fragrance unequalled anywhere else in the entire world; during the night, the Indians make fires with their wood, and, intoxicated by their fragrance, they sleep in their hammocks (they do not use beds, but rather hammocks suspended between trees). There are other trees called *xaguas* that give a fruit in the shape of a calf's kidney, the pulp of which is as delicious as that of pears in syrup. The whole island of Cuba, which is very mountainous, is filled with wild vines the grapes of which are slightly bitter but good for making wine; when they are planted in the sun, sheltered from the wind, they become domesticated and mild. Not to mention flowers; there are some islets off the southern coast that the admiral discovered on his second voyage and named the Queen's Garden, which says all there is to say about it.

A very powerful river that the Indians call Cauto flows into the sea on the southern coast, and the crocodiles that inhabit it are even more powerful, not less so, than those of the Nile. We jokingly called them lizards, and that joke cost a soldier named Sandíez his life. He was from Montalbán and very valiant, but not very bright. He was among those who disembarked in the second expedition to Cuba, and those who were in the first warned him to be careful about the lizards that teemed on the banks of that river. "Is my mother's son, who is not afraid even of the cacique Hatuey, going to be afraid of lizards?" The others laughed at this question, which offended the man from Montalbán, who was very touchy and thought they were making fun of him, and he rashly took a nap on the bank of the river. Soon several of those reptiles emerged and dragged him into the river and gobbled him up. These crocodiles are so voracious that when they get hold of a man there is nothing left of him, not even his belt buckle. And when they get hold of a cow they swallow even its horns.

In all other ways, Cuba is nothing but sweetness and leafy glades; the Indians had plenty of food before our arrival because there are some birds called *biayas* that fly very close to the ground, and the Indians catch them on the fly; they make a very flavorful, saffron-colored broth out of them, and after the birds are stewed, their flesh is as good as pheasant. But the hunt that yields the most is that of the *guaminiquinaje*, which are the size of a little lap-dog, and just one will satisfy three men. They seize them by their feet and kill them with a club. Not to mention tortoises; in the Queen's Garden, they were the size of a shield and weighed a hundred pounds or more. Because the sea is quite calm there, fishing for them is so easy that one needs merely to go out and pick them up. They are very good to eat, and as food they are healthy; their lard is like chicken fat, as yellow as gold and very good as a cure for leprosy and scabies. Just one of them will serve to feed as many as ten men.

The Spaniards under the command of Diego de Velázquez reached this paradise, and it was a good thing that we
did so, to separate the Indians there from the cult of the
devil that was very powerful and had been galvanized by
some witch doctors called *pythios*, who were capable of
fasting for four months, drinking only the juice of herbs,
to enable them to cast their evil spells. But it was not so
good for other things that happened there.

Diego de Velázquez, who had been born in Cuéllar, in
Segovia, was the one who had lived the longest in the Indies, because he came with the admiral on his second voyage; he was the lieutenant of the latter's son Don Diego
Colón, who as governor of Hispaniola ordered him to
colonize the island of Cuba. He went to Cuba as his lieutenant, but he went on to win the conquest, getting the
king to name him governor of the island. That is how
the *conquistadores* treated each other. Years later, Hernán
Cortés repaid him in kind, when Velázquez sent Cortés
to colonize Mexico and Cortés ended up doing so for his
own benefit.

Velázquez was about forty-five years old when he was
sent to Cuba, and Don Diego Colón chose him for his
great experience in dealing with Indians and for being the
richest man on the island, always willing to use his own
money in the business of conquest. He was a fine figure
of a man, although he was putting on a bit of weight; his
amiable and happy demeanor (except in his treatment of
Indians, of course, which was much the same as that of
others) won the affection of those who surrounded him.

I was among those who, after participating in that con-

quest, went on to be prominent in the affairs of the Indies, including Hernán Cortés, mentioned above, who
later on would be a famous captain, but who served during the conquest of Cuba as a notary and treasurer, and
including Pánfilo de Narváez, a very magnificent man,
red-haired, who came from Jamaica in command of four
ships and contributed to making very quick work of the
conquest. The fleet that left Hispaniola at Christmas in
1511 was made up of three hundred men, well-endowed
with riflemen, archers, and artillerymen who let the gunpowder fly in a way that quickly depopulated the coast
because in those latitudes the people were not yet certain
that the Spaniards were not immortal.

The indigenous people of Cuba, because they were
peaceful by nature, put up the least resistance to the
Spaniards, and, as they surrendered, Diego de Velázquez
distributed them among those who participated in the
conquest, not calling them slaves but, rather, long-term
servants, thus soothing his conscience. It was in Cuba,
as far as I remember, where Indians were first called
"pieces", and the encomenderos said to each other, "I
need this number of *pieces* for my hacienda", as if they
were talking about cattle.

But in the region called Baracoa, there was a king
named Hatuey, who, because he had so much experience plying the waters in his hollowed-out canoes, was
very familiar with the coastlines of Hispaniola, which he
reached by way of the Windward Passage. And because
he knew the fate of the Indians that the Spaniards set
to work, he decided to hide out with his people in the
mountains. He chose some that were very rugged and

that we could not reach on horseback because they were surrounded by very swampy land, and this angered the *conquistadores*. Hatuey's men took up their positions in the difficult passes and shot their arrows at the Spaniards, without much result because their arrowheads were made of fishbones and could not penetrate our shields; but the mountain range turned out to be so very rugged that it took us two months to find King Hatuey. This was the time when the word *ranchear* became famous, which the soldiers used when they were searching for the Indians, who had scattered widely or in small groups, in order to capture them, so they said: "Tomorrow we are going to *ranchear* this mountain or that one, where we're bound to find something." And they did find King Hatuey because in one of their *rancheos* an Indian whom they had tortured confessed where he was hiding. Because the king put up an armed resistance to the tragic fate that awaited him, it was decreed that he had committed the crime of *laesae maiestatis*, and he was sentenced to be burned at the stake.

Diego de Velázquez, with whom I enjoyed a friendship that lasted several years, told me that it was necessary to mete out such a death as a lesson. It pains me now to look back on it, but at the time I was so estranged from God that I thought it was the same death that traitors, and those who committed crimes of witchcraft, met in Castile. I was the chaplain of the fleet, but our company included a Franciscan friar who was called Friar Esteban, whose duty it was to preach to the Indians and who took the occasion of King Hatuey's being bound to the stake to preach to him of baptism. As best he could, with the help of an interpreter that we brought from Hispaniola, he told him to become a Christian and die baptized.

All people who are at death's door listen willingly to anyone who lavishes consoling words on them, and on that occasion, although the executioners put pressure on him, the Franciscan Father skillfully explained what heaven is and how all of us are sons of the same God, who is our Father. The friar's eyes were tender and clear, and with that clarity he was able to communicate what the interpreter was barely able to stammer out. King Hatuey, who was very fat, which is esteemed as a privilege among the Indians, remained pensive and seemed as though he were going to accede, when he asked: "And do Christians also go to heaven?" To which the Father replied that the good ones would. "So," replied the poor wretch, "because I do not know a single one who is good, I do not want to go to heaven because I do not want to end up in their company." The Franciscan Father insisted with tears in his eyes, but there was nothing he could do, and they ended up lighting the fire.

Such was the pacification of the island of Cuba, and Diego de Velázquez and his lieutenant, Pánfilo de Narváez, were very proud of it, because they said they had done it without shedding much blood; but for me that death of King Hatuey, refusing to become a Christian because he did not want to cross paths with us in heaven, gave me a good deal to think about. Not to mention the Franciscan Father; he was one who did not stay in the Indies and, at the first opportunity, went back to Castile.

CHAPTER VI

THE ADVENT SERMON

Our rejection by King Hatuey at the stake gave me much to think about, but that did not prevent me from taking my share when Velázquez distributed the island of Cuba. He put the first settlers in the village of Baracoa, but because it turned out to be land that was short of gold, we kept on sailing along the coast until we reached the port of Xagua, in the eastern part of the island. As far as I can remember, this was the first time that we descended from our ships in order to travel in the canoes that the Indians make, which are very well suited to navigating along the coast. Instead of oars, they use paddles with great skill, putting them into the water next to the sides of the canoes, and, if the sea is calm and there is no wind, they go faster than the caravels. When the water is calm, its smoothness is such that the corals and sands on the bottom appear to be within reach but turn out to be six fathoms deep. The canoes glide so softly through the water that their passage barely makes any waves, so all kinds of fish, which are very abundant there, are not frightened and are very easy to catch with some little nets that they make out of agave fiber.

Navigation is very safe because as soon as a small cloud appears, announcing a storm, they head toward land, and, because the canoes are very flat, with no keel, they can cross the reefs undamaged. If the cloudiness takes them by surprise, they abandon the canoe and swim to the shore, because they are all very good swimmers and are never too lazy to jump into the water, whether it be the sea, a river, or a lagoon. As time went by, we Castilians started learning to swim, because it was very much in our interest, but there were some who were very stubborn and said they would rather die than get in the water, and a few did just that. One cleric, who was not one of the best ones, said that modesty forbade him to take off his soutane and therefore he could not learn to swim; one day, when he crossed a river doing something he should not have done, because the canoe was carrying a lot of gold, the boat sank, and he lost his life. On the other hand, the friars, who served as examples for us in everything, were among the first to learn, because in their missionary work they had to cross rivers that sometimes ran with as much water as the sea. They put their bundles with the little they had on their heads, and plunged in to swim, wearing the long underwear they all wore, made of very rough serge, which reached to their knees. They were also among those who learned to use the paddles that functioned as oars, and they did not shy away from making crossings, which sometimes took a day and a night of rowing and left their hands bleeding.

The rest of us, on the other hand, traveled like lords in those canoes, with no fewer than ten Indian oarsmen on each side, and sometimes, just for fun, we raced our boats and bet money on them. Rentería, in spite of his great goodness, was one of the biggest enthusiasts for this game, because in his homeland of Guipúzcoa this type of betting was very popular. And the poor Indians were left breathless because if they won they received extra rations of cassava bread, which was their main food.

When I traveled through Hispaniola, I was certain that this had to be the Earthly Paradise, so beautiful did it seem to me, but once I reached Cuba, I became enraptured and changed my opinion, or rather understood that God, in his magnanimity, had reserved the beauty of the original creation for these islands. On this part of the coast, the beaches were endless, with sand as golden as the sun and palm groves and coconut palms that reached the shore. But because the gold was in the rivers, not in the sea, when we reached the port of Xagua (which was then a natural inlet, very well protected from the tides by coral reefs), we went inland until we came to the River Arimao, wide and spacious, which emptied into the sea a mile and a half from the port and which proved to be one of the most gold-bearing that I have known; its gold is very fine, like that of Cibao, but because it is softer, the goldsmiths hold it in higher esteem.

What I had been told was true, although bad for me, that the career of a cleric was a good way to prosper in the Indies, because without my having to endure the sufferings and dangers of the soldiers, Diego de Velázquez gave me a share of this province that was double that of anyone who had served in the conquest. Suffice it to say that it included a village, called Canaoreo in the language of the Indians, with three hundred souls as inhabitants—souls that, to my great shame, I ignored, concerning myself only with the work their bodies could do in my mines and fields. And I did not have the same excuse I had when I arrived in the Indies as just a youngster, because between one thing and another the years had gone by and I was about to turn thirty. In addition, just because he was my partner, without ever having set foot in these lands, they gave Pedro de Rentería another encomienda, next to mine, and, joining them together as we were accustomed to doing, we were among the richest people on the island.

Meanwhile, Rentería had married a Basque woman whom he had brought from his village, to whom he had been engaged since he was twelve years old; for that reason, he did not become a priest even though he was a worthier and more devoted person than I was, although he was not literate enough to be able to sing the Mass. I had known his wife, who was called María Ubenzu, from the time I went to Spain to buy the land for Rentería, and I have no complaint about her, because she adapted to life in Cuba and gave Rentería three children; this pleased him greatly, because when he married he was no longer a young man, near turning forty.

I was not one of the worst in my treatment of the Indians, nor would Rentería have allowed it; in our hacienda in Canaoreo we respected the ration that Diego de Velázquez had ordered to be distributed to the Indians in the encomienda, which consisted of half a pound of meat per day, in addition to cassava bread. The meat was pork, from which we made a good profit, so the Indians only took a part of what they themselves had raised. But other encomenderos said that the Indians were not made to eat so much meat, so they argued against even that.

We had cells for the punishment of those who did not want to work, but we made little use of them. In spite of everything, I acquired a reputation for being greedy, which still pains me; but it pains me more that I paid so little attention to what I did for their souls, all of which I had tucked into a corner, and I considered that I fulfilled my duty as a cleric if I heard confessions from the people on the island, without asking them to recount the outrages that they committed with the natives, caring only about what is called the decency of relations between men and women, a subject in which they were all quite wretched.

If I did not treat our encomenderos cruelly it was because of my compassionate nature, not because of my status as a priest, but during those years I never stopped to think if it was justifiable for me to have Indians in servitude, and on that point I was as corrupted as the rest, although with less excuse because many of them were ignorant people and had not been educated as I had.

At around that time, some of the Dominican Fathers who had come with Friar Pedro de Córdoba began to come to Cuba, and the one who became the most famous of all of them, and was to have the most influence on my life, was Friar Antón Montesino. Unlike his vicar and superior, Friar Pedro, who was beauty and sweetness made man, this Friar Antón was skinny and short, so consumed by his duty that all one could see in his face were his eyes, which were like garnets. His irascibility came out in his preaching, but as if his anger was stirred up by a divine fire; his sermons were very fruitful.

There was a woman in the city of Santo Domingo who was sentenced to death by hanging, and for good reason, because she had murdered her husband in his sleep in order to rob him and run away with a young soldier, who was one of a group that at the time was committing misdeeds along the Pearl Coast, in Cumaná. But the soldier only wanted the gold, and when the woman gave him the bulging bag of it, he fled, abandoning the woeful woman to her fate, which was simply to fall into the hands of justice. Condemned to the gallows, this wretched woman showed no remorse for her horrendous crime and simply cursed blasphemously the young soldier who had so vilely deceived her. Because she was the first woman from Castile who was to be executed in Hispaniola, this created a big stir, and the Franciscan Fathers, who acted as the chaplains of the prison, attended her day and night to persuade her to repent her sin and cleanse her soul in confession. But the more they tried, the more she persisted in her blaspheming and insisted on dying impenitent; so it occurred to her prelate, the reverend Friar Alonso del Espinal, to bring in Friar Montesino. Some members of his Order resisted and said, "What can a Dominican Father do that we cannot?" They said it because there were rivalries between the Dominican friars and the Franciscans; but the Father Superior said that if, to save the soul of a Christian, he would be willing to go down to the very gates of hell, then he would be all the more willing to seek help from anyone as skillful as the Dominicans in fighting against the Evil One.

The Franciscan Fathers, as befitted the members of an Order founded by the impoverished friar from Assisi, had been all sweetness with that unfortunate woman, reasoning with her at length about the evil she had done, so she would repent; and the response of the woman was to make fun of them and tell them that she wanted to go to hell so she could come face-to-face with the soldier who had deceived her. Her madness and rage were so great that when they came to take her to the gallows, she said she did not want to be accompanied by any friar or to have prayers said for her. Friar Montesino, footsore from the long walk he had made so that he would arrive in time, appeared while she was in this frenzy and, making his way through the Franciscan Fathers, substituted for sweetness the fervor with which he preached, and with his eyes like garnets, he rebuked the woman by saying, "You don't want to confess, lost woman that you are! Do you not know that you will within an hour be subjected to the strict justice of God, who will condemn you to suffer forever in hell?"

The woman was stunned and taken aback, and she changed her spirit without any more reasoning or words, and she was filled with a compunction that made her burst into bitter tears of remorse. She immediately confessed with sincere repentance and received Holy Communion. Friar Antón Montesino led her by the hand to the foot of the gallows, and all the people could see her because it stood in a small square near the palace of Don Diego Colón. From the top of the gallows she asked for forgiveness, said that she would die happy and that, if by God's grace she went to heaven, she would pray for the soul of the man who had led her to commit such a heinous crime.

Friar Montesino had become famous for a much-discussed sermon that he gave in the city of Santo Domingo on the fourth Sunday in Advent of 1511, denouncing the outrages that the Spaniards committed against the Indians. These outrages were known to anyone who had any sense, but it seemed that God had covered them with a veil so that no one would see them, until God made use of an outlaw to open the eyes of the Dominican friars. And, through them, the rest of us were seeing the light.

This outlaw was called Juan Garcés, and he had been one of the most evil men in the wars we waged in Xaraguá and Higüey because he was one of those who had no qualms about taking children as slaves, and he brazenly abused women in front of their husbands. Every thief believes that everyone is like him, and at the end of the second of these wars, when he returned to Santo Domingo, he got it into his head that his wife (for he was married to a woman who came from Concepción de La Vega) had committed adultery, and in a frenzy that is characteristic of those who engage in war, he stabbed the poor unfortunate woman to death. Because the motivation for his crime was baseless, he had to escape, and he fled to the mountains for more than three years, until some Dominican Fathers performing their missions found him. Who would have said that such a lost soul would turn out to be so beneficial to Christianity? Moved by the life of piety and sacrifice of the reverend Fathers, he not only repented for his past life, he never stopped importuning them until he was admitted as a lay brother of the Order. And if he did damage in the past, he more than paid for it in this life, because he lived in total commitment to his vocation and in the end died a martyr on the coast of Cumaná for preaching the gospel to some Indians who were in revolt on account of some bad Spaniards.

This Garcés was the one who opened the eyes of the Dominican Fathers by giving them an eyewitness account of the appalling cruelties that were committed in those wars against the Indians and how abused they were after they had been pacified.

The prelate, Friar Pedro de Córdoba, gathered together the most learned members of the Order and joined them in a retreat for three days, in a hut they had on the bank of the river Ozama, and after great acts of penitence, a good deal of prayer, and studying Holy Scripture, they decided that keeping quiet would be the equivalent of consenting to the iniquity, and they agreed to denounce it from the pulpit. As the fiercest of them was Friar Antón Montesino, because of his special ability to denounce vices, it fell to him, as an obligation, to preach the first sermon, which as I have said took place on the fourth Sunday in Advent.

Friar Pedro de Córdoba took care to see to it that the most important people on the island attended the sermon, and for that purpose he invited the second admiral, Don Diego Colón, who accepted out of respect owed to men who led such austere lives and because he knew that the Dominicans were highly esteemed in Spain, where the Master of the Order was at the time the confessor of the aged Catholic King. And all the dignitaries followed the governor into the church, which was full to the brim.

The time for the sermon arrived; Friar Montesino climbed into the pulpit and based his sermon on the Gospel by beginning with, "Ego vox clamantis in deserto."

The governor and the other dignitaries accompanying him thought he was going to preach on John the Baptist, whose voice cried in the desert; they were therefore surprised when the zealous Dominican, with his accustomed fervor, said:

> I am the voice of Christ in the desert of this island, and I have taken this pulpit in order to communicate that to you. And this voice is saying to you that all of you are in a state of mortal sin, and you will live and die in it, for the cruelty and tyranny that you inflict on these poor people. Tell me: With what right and what justice do you hold these Indians in such horrible servitude? With what justice have you made such detestable wars? You say it is to pacify them, when they were docile and at peace in their lands before your arrival. With what right do you work them until they are exhausted, hardly giving them anything to eat or curing their illnesses? What care do you take to indoctrinate them so that they may know their true God and Creator, be baptized, and keep the feast days and Sundays? Are they not men with rational souls? Are you not obligated to love them as you love yourselves?

Thus, with an increasingly fiery spirit, he held forth in his sermon for a long time, and there is a faithful record of it, because it was not improvised. It was written and signed, with their names, by all the Dominican Fathers to let it be known that the sermon was not just the thinking of the one who preached it; a copy of this precious document is preserved down to this day in our monastery at Santo Domingo for the glory of God and as a testament of service lent by the Order of Preachers to the cause of the gospel. I could not be there to hear it on that occasion because I was very busy with the affairs of my hacienda in Cibao, then went to Cuba, as I have recounted, and only after three years did I meet up again with Friar Antón Montesino, but those who were in attendance say that everyone there, starting with Governor Colón, was astonished and in a state of lasting shock because it was the first time that such things had been said in the Indies and that some women were left prostrate, as though out of their senses, and others cried because they now saw themselves in hell, so artfully did Friar Montesino condemn the evils.

The most hardened listeners wanted to kill him with their looks, but Friar Antón was not a man to be intimidated, and he did not care if he upset his listeners by telling them truths, so he came down from the pulpit and ended the Mass as though nothing untoward had happened, and he went to the straw hut in which they lived to have their cabbage soup, without oil, which was the appropriate meal for that day, as a Sunday in Advent.

Meanwhile, there was a great commotion as those in attendance left the Mass, and the governor had a hard time of it returning to his residence, the palace that he had built for himself, because the whole city of Santo Domingo gathered there, after the midday meal (which they could not have found very tasty). The king's officials (the treasurer, the accountant, the tax collector, and the inspector, who were those who had the most Indians) told Don Diego Colón that what the Father had said could not be allowed to stand, because it was an attack against the rule of the king in these lands, of which the king was the sovereign, and for that reason he had the right to distribute the Indians to the encomenderos. The second admiral agreed with what they said and, accompanied by the more important men, went to the monastery of the Dominicans, the straw house that differed very little from the Indian *bohíos*.

They asked to see the prelate, Friar Pedro de Córdoba, who received them with the refinement that was characteristic of him, and they argued to him that Montesino must be insane or possessed by the devil to be preaching the way he did, doing a disservice to the king and damage to the kingdom, because what riches would there be to send to Castile if the Indians were not to work in the mines? The prelate listened to them very patiently and at the end replied: "Well, if Friar Antón is insane, his insanity must be contagious, because it is the insanity of our Lord on the Cross, and it was for that reason that all of us joined in signing his sermon, which caused you so much pain."

And to remove all doubt about what he meant, he showed them the document to which I have already referred. Don Diego Colón, despite being a very good Catholic, insisted that the written words were one thing and the offensive way that Friar Montesino spoke them was another and that the following Sunday he had to take back, with the same solemnity and in the same place, what he had said. The blindness of the officials was such that the treasurer ventured to say to the prelate that either the words would be retracted the following Sunday or they could all begin now to pack their belongings for the return journey to Spain. Friar Córdoba replied to this insolence with an ironic quip: "In that, gentlemen, we will have very little work to do."

He said it because all his jewels were habits made of coarse floor cloth and blankets of the same texture, plus what was collected at Mass and some little books, all of which could fit in no more than two chests.

Other Dominican Fathers intervened as the discussion wore on, including Friar Antón Montesino himself, who had little fear of this world's authorities, and they all insisted that the sermon was in accordance with the gospel in every way and that in preaching it they were attending, first and foremost, to the salvation of their souls because in the end the Indians, innocent as they were, could go to heaven, or at least to the limbo of the just, but those who exploited them would go to hell.

Knowing Friar Pedro de Córdoba, Friar Antón Montesino, and the other holy friars who were there as well as I do, I can vouch for the many arguments they made, all of them in the name of love, but the king's officials and the rich encomenderos of the island, seeing that the acceptance of such reasoning would lead to the loss of their encomiendas, together with their wealth, preferred to lose their souls, and so they turned a deaf ear to those arguments. No wonder that the gospel teaches us that it is easier for a camel to pass through the eye of a needle than for a rich man to enter the kingdom of heaven; and the proof of that is that we have seen how diehard criminals such as Friar Garcés and the woman who murdered her husband felt their souls touched by the friars' preachings, whereas these other men, rich men, did not want to listen and did not give up their importunity, so much so that, to bring the discussion to an end, the prelate told them that on the following Sunday Friar Montesino would return to preach again, moderating what was offensive to the people, and the admiral and the king's officials understood what they wanted to understand and, as soon as they left the monastery, published throughout the city that on the following Sunday the friar would retract all that he had said.

It was unnecessary to invite anyone to hear this second sermon, because the news spread joyfully by word of mouth, and not one person in the city was absent from the church. Friar Montesino, with a humbler air than was usual with him, took the pulpit and began by reciting a sentence from the Book of Job, chapter 36, which says, "Repetam scientiam meam a principio et operatorem meum probabo iustum. Vere enim absque mendacio sermones mei et perfecta scientia probabitur tibi."[1] Then he went on to say: "I will turn now to citing here at the beginning the knowledge and truth of what I preached to you this past Sunday, and I beg the pardon of anyone who was offended by my words, but I'm going to show you that they were true."

[1] I will repeat my knowledge from the beginning, and I will prove my Maker just. For indeed my words are without a lie, and perfect knowledge shall be proved to thee (Douay-Rheims 1899 American Edition).

And point by point, he once again repeated the sermon of the fourth Sunday in Advent and changed it only in his use of verbs. Instead of saying, as he had the first time, "You will go to hell for mistreating the Indians", he said, "You could go to hell for mistreating the Indians." He said that he was singling out no one but that it was important for him to make it clear, with no desire to give offense, that no absolution would be given in confession to anyone who, after hearing what he said, continued to keep Indians in servitude.

After this last statement, many of the people gathered there left the church without even waiting for the end of the Mass, and they agreed among themselves to send advocates to Spain in order to secure the removal of those friars. Their leader was the treasurer, Miguel de Pasamonte, who because he was from Aragón had the benefit of being in high standing with the Catholic King. Thus began the war between the officials of the Council of the Indies and the Dominican Fathers, which is ongoing still today. On more than one occasion, the Fathers, and I was one of them, were near death at the hands of the encomenderos; others were persecuted and deprived of everything, but that did not make them give up, because the Fathers, like anyone who has nothing, carried on very calmly, very freely, because he who has very little cannot be deprived of very much.

CHAPTER VII

THE ROAD TO DAMASCUS

It must have been around 1513 when the Dominicans first went to the island of Cuba, and for a year I had been the only cleric there. This made me more diligent in the performance of my duties, and, without neglecting my work in mining or in raising pigs and producing cassava bread, I never failed to celebrate Mass on Sunday and every day of obligation or to preach and hear confession from the faithful whenever they requested it. I thought that doing so put my conscience at ease, and it seemed to me that God rewarded me by enabling us to prosper from our labors, for we were on the way to becoming rich, as perhaps we already were.

In Hispaniola, on the other hand, they were very short of all manner of provisions, for the Indian workers on their haciendas had been so much decreased in number, not only by having been mistreated by the Spaniards but also by having frequently been hit by a plague, either of smallpox or of measles, which promptly led to their death. This was the period when the Indian women, saddened by so much misfortune, did not want to give birth and took potions to do away with the children in their wombs; many men were so consumed by sadness that they let themselves die, and not even the youngest of them had the strength to procreate.

But the misfortune of the residents of Hispaniola became the good fortune of the residents of Cuba, because they bought our harvests of cassava, corn, and sugar cane before we had reaped them. As for the profit from our mares, they bought the foals while they were still unborn for ten times the price they would have fetched in Castile, so this business of breeding horses, which we had begun for our own pleasure and in order to have good mounts for ourselves, turned out to be a business as profitable as gold mining. It is fair to say that the first person to bring mares to Cuba was Hernán Cortés, who was a rich landowner at the time, and the rest of us learned from him; it is unfortunate that the lessons he taught us later, during the conquest of Mexico, were not worthy of being applied.

So those of us in Cuba lived a life of luxury, governed by Don Diego de Velázquez, and it seemed to us that the woes that devastated Hispaniola would not reach us. We heard about the sermons that, in imitation of the fourth Sunday of Advent, the Dominican Fathers went on preaching, and we understood that they preached them in order to persuade the encomenderos to treat the Indians better. Rentería and I, as I have already explained, were in agreement with them, and I, for my part, preached in similar fashion at Mass.

So when we got news that Friar Pedro de Córdoba and Friar Antón Montesino were arriving in the port of Baracoa, we went to meet them and give them the reception that men of such a reputation for holiness deserved. In their honor, we harnessed a carriage pulled by a team of six mules, humble animals for which Rentería continued to have so much esteem. As soon as he saw them, Friar Montesino said to me, "In faith, Sir, you have a fine team of mules, and I am sure that even the bishop of Palencia does not have better ones."

He said it slyly because at the time, if I remember correctly, the bishop of Palencia was Don Juan Rodríguez de Fonseca, who became the president of the Council of the Indies, where nothing was done without his approval. Friar Montesino mentioned Palencia to make it clear that, as a prelate from that part of Castile, he had no knowledge at all about the Indies, in which he had never set foot. Rodríguez de Fonseca would turn out to be very much opposed to what I attempted to do in the Indies, but at the time of Friar Montesino's visit I did not understand the irony of what he said, which I took as a compliment, for there was no better team of mules in all the islands, and I was very proud of them.

But when it came time to get into the carriage, Friar Pedro de Córdoba, with the sweetness that was his wont, excused himself from doing so, saying that for his mission it would be better to walk. We were left somewhat embarrassed, but the slight was partly smoothed over, because they agreed to sit at our table, where they ate without awkwardness, for the rules of their Order required them to accept whatever was served to them, were it a lot or a little. Governor Velázquez put them up in a palm-roofed cabin, with a cool and beautiful bedroom and good beds, but we learned afterward that they slept on the floor. They were there for about a month, carrying out their mission among the Indians, which included deciding where on the island they should build their monastery; when they returned, I asked to make my confession to Friar Montesino, because as the only cleric on the island, I had not received that great sacrament for several months.

Just as Friar Montesino was very impassioned in the pulpit, so was he very loving and understanding in the confessional, but not any less upright for that. While I was confessing my peccadillos and vanities, all of them were received with nods of understanding and spoken caresses, but he changed when we reached the subject of the Indians, and things became complicated. I accused myself of a small lack of charity toward them or indiscretion in the way I looked at the women, and Friar Montesino, without going into detail, told me that the main lack of charity lay in maintaining them in slavery against all right and reason and, as far as concerned the way I looked at the women, that I should pay attention to whether I saw them as sisters in Christ or as creatures who were good for nothing more than to serve me. I was left confused, but not to the point of not answering, because if God has given me any talent it is that of having a ready answer. On this occasion, I pointed to the good treatment that both my partner and I gave the Indians, to which he replied that the treatment they gave us was better, because with their sweat they had made us rich with good mule teams and had dressed us in fine linen clothes.

We became embroiled in one argument and then another, as I knelt on the prie-dieu and he sat in the same confessional in which I gave absolution to the encomenderos in the parish, without feeling any scruples about whether they had just a few or many Indians, because the confession took place in the church where I was the lord and master, and that made what Friar Montesino said to me doubly humiliating. In the end, quite ashamed, I invoked the Laws of Burgos (which had been made public in the Indies in 1513), which prohibited abusing the Indians but not distributing them, and the confession ended at that point, because Friar Montesino said to me:

"Look, Father, the truth always has many detractors and falsehoods many supporters. The Laws of Burgos do not at all allow cruel and unjust trade in Indians, as all of the Indians are subject to in these islands, and in the tribunal in which we find ourselves here, it is not for us to judge according to the laws of men, but according to God's law. And according to the latter, you cannot own Indians who serve you in perpetuity. Are you willing to free them?"

Burning inside, because I have always had a very strong temper, and sometimes an angry one, I answered I would do what the laws of our Catholic King provided for.

"Well, then, let him give you absolution, because I cannot."

And having said that, he left the confessional with great dignity, leaving me in a deep stupor.

At first I thought I would talk to Governor Velázquez and go over to the side that condemned such preaching as a disservice to the king and harm to the kingdom, but then I decided to keep quiet so that I would not be perceived as having been denied absolution for a more shameful reason.

But now I was not so much at ease as I had been, because despite the confrontation I had had with Friar Montesino, some of the things he had said to me were very well founded and therefore left their mark on me, although I rejected them to avoid having to let go of my Indians and lands. After so much work and suffering in those lands, after having exhausted myself in the mountains of Xaraguá, after having dug gold out of the Haina River with my own hands, for me to give up all of that would have been like tearing out my soul. Just as I was very attached to what I had, I was even more attracted by much more that I hoped to gain from a gamble on some ships; I say gamble because during that time I had sent Pedro de Rentería to Jamaica, where he had a brother who was very shrewd, with whom we agreed to fill a ship with brood pigs and seed corn and take them to Cuba to be sold, because in Jamaica they would cost a quarter of what we would have to pay for them in Cuba. We had so much cash that, to carry out our plan, we chartered a caravel that belonged to the king for two thousand gold *castellanos*, and after that we thought of sending some more to do the same business with Hispaniola and the island of Cubagua, on the Pearl Coast. All of these were ideas of mine, because Rentería just wanted to live in peace with his wife and the children she was giving him; nevertheless, he did what I told him out of affection for me and also because he was compliant by nature. From all this, I acquired a reputation of being greedy, because, despite having so much, it seemed that nothing was enough and that I wanted to have even more.

Actually, I do not know whether I wanted more, but I

certainly did not want less, accustomed as I was to living in
the lap of luxury. We now had four foremen, very black,
who were the most highly valued: two for the mines,
one for the cassava and corn plantation, and the fourth
for the breeding of pigs and mares. After Rentería married, the house that we had built, all out of fine stone,
became mine, one of the first that were built in Cuba
out of that material, so beautiful that some that in Seville
were called palaces were not even half as fine. I had no
fewer than twenty *naboríes*, or domestic servants, each of
them with his particular task so that I did not need to
lift a finger. Some worked in the kitchen, in which, to
compensate for the periods of hunger that we endured
on the Haina River, the fires were always burning and
the pots were filled with all kinds of food, either fowl or
meat or fish; others served me at table, and I am ashamed
to say that the tableware was all made of gold, although in
those lands, so close to the mines, it is less ostentatious
than in Castile; other servants attended to my clothes,
and there were days on which I changed my coat four
times, not to mention my shirts underneath, which had
always to be of the very finest material, either of linen or
even of silk that came in Italian ships. What is more, I had
naboríes who, with a contraption that was equipped with
pulleys, moved very big fans that hung from the ceiling,
with which they moved the air in the bedroom during
siestas.

Our hacienda, called Canaoreo, was by far the best in
all of Xagua, and many visitors to my house came and
went, because without any breach of the decorum with
which I was obligated to act in my ministry, we had very

good meals, which normally begin there at dusk, and which were sometimes attended by Governor Velázquez himself. Another frequent guest was the musician Ortiz, who played the organ in the church and strummed the guitar on those nights of hospitality in our house. Otherwise, we went no farther than playing cards, which did not fit so well with my being a cleric, but gambling always appealed to me, and I think now that I got into the business of loading ships in Jamaica and selling their cargo on the Pearl Coast because I liked gambling; if the ship sank, all was lost, but the arrival of just one in port made up for any earlier losses.

For that reason, the visit that Friar Pedro de Córdoba and Friar Antón Montesino made to us roiled the waters of the placid lake along which my life glided in those years because, after seeing with my own eyes their leanness, the coarse cloth they wore, and the fact that they slept on straw, my body itched when I stretched out on my bed's mattress stuffed with feathers of birds of paradise.

I say that their visit roiled the waters, but what it actually did was to clarify them because, curiously, the anger that I felt after my confession soon died out, and in my long rides around the hacienda, I thought of nothing but what Friar Montesino had told me about the injustice of the trade in Indians, and I would answer him with quibbles about whether the king or the queen or the governor said such a thing, or some other, favorable to the encomiendas. But I always replied, in my imagination, with great respect; and everything I did with the Indians we had in our charge I did with the thought that Friar Montesino was there beside me, and from then on I treated them with greater care, as though to earn his approval. I even thought of sailing to Hispaniola to tell him how I had been reasoning and ask him to grant me the absolution that he had denied me. To obtain it, I was ready to do anything except to dispose of the fields where the mares grazed, the fields where the swine rooted, the land where the corn grew, or the mines from which we extracted grains of gold.

I did not want to give up all that, but God did want me to, and very much against my will I began to look at the Indians with other eyes, and they all appeared to me to be more downcast than when we arrived in Cuba. In our hacienda, we employed women in what we said was less difficult work, but even so they had to be there from sunrise to sunset, up to twelve hours in a row, sifting the sands of the Animao River with pans. The sight of them put me in mind of Tajima, the only woman besides my mother whom I have loved in this world; I remembered her sweetness, her fine outlook on life, and I thought that all the women could be like her if we treated them differently, although in my blindness I deceived myself by saying that by feeding them and not mistreating them, like the other encomenderos, I did my duty.

Around that time I got word of an Indian woman who hanged herself rather than procreating with a black man. At the time, blacks were held in high esteem, and just one would fetch the same price as five Indians. It occurred to one of the greediest encomenderos, called Tavira, who was married to a Portuguese woman, to cross a very brazen black runaway slave that he owned with some young Indian girls in his encomienda to yield more vigorous *mestizos* whom he could sell at a higher price. I say he was brazen because members of his race found Indian women repellent and wanted nothing to do with them, but this one agreed because he was a perverse and slippery black, although later he became somewhat famous, because he was among those who were taught by the musician Ortiz to play the guitar and kettledrums, and he played African songs that became very popular with some ladies in Governor Velázquez's retinue. This caused a lot of murmuring, but because it is not relevant I will move on.

The Indian was a young girl whom I had Christianized in the baptismal font, and when I got the news, I rode at top speed to Tavira's hacienda, which was about eighteen miles from ours. Besides being greedy, this Tavira was very clumsy because as soon as he saw me, all he could think of doing was to spit out at me: "If you're here, Father, to give the Indian woman a sacred burial, there's no justification for it because she killed herself of her own free will and she doesn't deserve a Christian burial."

At that, may God forgive me, I dismounted and began to hit him with my riding crop, to the great satisfaction of some Indians who were there and who were among the most oppressed of all Canaoreo. I was close to turning thirty and very limber, and I had plenty of strength, so all Tavira could do was to cry out for help, but it did him little good because no one came to his aid; he was such a bad person that even his wife, the Portuguese woman, was happy to see him punished.

Governor Velázquez, to please me (and not because the death of an Indian woman meant anything to him), held him in prison for a time, at which point the business of crossing blacks with Indian women came to an end. Besides which the black, runaway that he was, fled and hid in the mountains; but the musician Ortiz held him in such esteem for the beauty of his music that he ended up finding him and later took him along to the conquest of Mexico; they say he died very honorably in the battle of the bridges of Tenochtitlán, which the Spaniards call the sad night, though in the end it was even sadder for the Aztecs. It is worth noting that this black ended up leaving descendants, but they were mulattoes and not mestizos, because a woman from Castile, who was in the governor's retinue, bore him a son, and if I mention it (despite my earlier reluctance to discuss gossip), it is because that mulatto was the first of his color to become a lay brother of our Dominican Order, and, although he died young, he had time enough to render great service in preaching the gospel. The Lord works in mysterious ways, and his paths are sometimes tortuous.

Tavira's hacienda could not have been in greater disarray; when he was imprisoned, in order not to leave his Portuguese wife defenseless, Rentería and I wanted to lend her a helping hand, and we were horrified by the conditions in which he had kept his Indians, worse than animals, so starved and helter-skelter that if one caught a cold and sneezed, all of them sneezed, and some of them died of their colds.

I say that these Indians were among the most abused, but it would be misleading to say that those living on other haciendas did so in greater comfort, because there were three classes of encomenderos: the cruelest ones, who took no pity and gave no mercy, thinking only about enriching themselves at the expense of the blood of their unfortunate Indians; the less cruel ones, who took no pleasure in mistreating their Indians but who did not want to forgo their profits; and those who felt the pain of their misery and anguish and tried to remedy them, which was the case with Pedro de Rentería. But because this last group was the smallest, the scourge of the encomiendas was on its way to wiping out the Indian population in the islands.

I was plunged in these anxious thoughts when Diego de Velázquez, who had just finished populating the province of Sancti Spíritus with Spaniards, ordered me to go there to preach the sermon for Pentecost, which I could not decline to do because I was still the only cleric on the whole island. I embarked from Xagua in a caravel to sail along the coast to the western part of the island, carrying with me a fair number of presents for the church that I knew was unfinished and lacked what was needed to celebrate the sacred rites. I brought along, as a gift, pure gold vessels for the Consecration, well wrought and highly polished, and I enjoyed seeing myself reflected in them at the same time as I took satisfaction in thinking that they would contain the Body and Blood of our Lord Jesus Christ. In addition, I carried a bag of gold pesos to contribute to the completion of the church, thinking it would be an offering welcome to God and the governor, of whose esteem and relations with us the encomenderos took solicitous care, because he took good care of them.

During the trip, which took two days and was very calm, coasting along the abundant greenery, which ended in beaches of sand that was finer and more golden than I had ever seen anywhere in the whole world, I began to prepare my sermon, and my attention was seized by chapter 34 of Ecclesiasticus, in the part that says: "Immolantis ex iniquo oblatio est maculata, et non sunt beneplacitae subsannationes injustorum. Dominus solus sustinentibus se in via veritatis et justitiae. Dona iniquorum non probat Altissimus, nec respicit in oblationes iniquorum, nec in multitudine sacrificiorum eorum propitiabitur peccatis. Qui offert sacrificium ex substantia pauperum, quasi qui victimat filium in conspectu patris sui. Panis egentium vita pauperum est: qui defraudat illum homo sanguinis est. Qui aufert in sudore panem, quasi qui occidit proximum suum. Qui effundit sanguinem, et qui fraudem facit mercenario, fratres sunt."[1]

Pedro de Rentería was a great devotee of the book of Ecclesiasticus because of the good advice that it contains, not only for the next life but also for this earthly life; but since he was a man of little learning, and all the more so for not knowing Latin, we would read it together, and we

[1] The offering of him that sacrificeth of a thing wrongfully gotten, is stained, and the mockeries of the unjust are not acceptable. The Lord is only for them that wait upon him in the way of truth and justice. The most High approveth not the gifts of the wicked: neither hath he respect to the oblations of the unjust, nor will he be pacified for sins by the multitude of their sacrifices. He that offereth sacrifice of the goods of the poor, is as one that sacrificeth the son in the presence of his father. The bread of the needy, is the life of the poor: he that defraudeth them thereof, is a man of blood. He that taketh away the bread gotten by sweat, is like him that killeth his neighbour. He that sheddeth blood, and he that defraudeth the labourer of his hire, are brothers (Douay-Rheims 1899 American Edition).

had read this passage many times without paying it any
more attention than we paid to others. But that evening,
at some point before sunset, I felt a sudden blaze in my
heart, and it seemed to me that it was the Lord himself
who was singing to me the sacred verses. How could I
dare to offer those gold cups to the Lord, those exorbi-
tant gifts, which I owed to the blood of the Indians, who
were my brothers as much as Pedro de Rentería himself
could be? Could I not have known that the Most High
is not pleased with gifts given him by an impious man
at the expense of the sweat of his neighbor? If one who
withholds the pay of a day laborer is in effect shedding
his blood, how much more serious is it for those of us
who do not even pay a day laborer of ours for the work
to which we set him, all his life long, at our whim and
for our satisfaction?

That evening was my road to Damascus, and just as the
Lord brought Saint Paul down from his horse to say to
him, "Saul, Saul, why do you persecute me?" he brought
me out of my mines and fields to say the same. Because I
and everyone else who, like me, had gone into the mountains to persecute Indians persecuted Christ himself, and
when we shut them up in a foul prison, we locked up
Christ himself.

If the apostle, with all his sanctity, was confused after
the Lord illuminated him with his light and caused him
to fall from his horse, one can only imagine how I felt,
poor me, nowhere near as intelligent as Saint Paul. When
I was in that trance, what I had understood the Dominican Fathers to be preaching helped me a great deal, and
as for the scolding that Friar Montesino had given me, in

the light of the holy words, it even seemed to me that he could have said so much more.

They say that the love of God is the only thing that moves saints, but sinners are also moved by the agonies of hell, and I could not understand how I could escape them if I continued to persecute Christ in the person of those Indians. *In persona Christi.*

Thinking back on the great exploits of the wars in which I had participated, and on how close I was to the Indians we executed to attain that cursed pacification, I wept bitter tears and made a firm resolution to make amends, treating them like my brothers, paying them a fair daily wage, seeing to their health, and instructing them in the verities of our faith. In this first exercise of my soul, I was prepared to do many good things (including preaching these truths to the other encomenderos), but despite the bitterness of my tears, I was not prepared to free them, because like the young man in the gospel who was very rich, I did not take to the idea of being poor, dispossessed of everything I had acquired at such a high cost.

But I just could not find relief from my pains in that train of thought, and I felt more and more compelled to preach to the four winds the injustice that we were committing; but because I was unwilling to sacrifice my own profits, I said to myself, "How are you going to preach to others that they should not have Indians, when you yourself have them? They will say, 'If it is so tyrannical to have them, he should let them go.'" This seemed to me to be so logical that, as soon as I saw Diego de Velázquez in Sancti Spíritus, my torment was over.

So that I would not have time to change my mind, I then and there communicated to him my decision to release my Indians, unconditionally and completely, so that he could dispose of them as he pleased, with the exception that I will describe.

The governor, upon hearing something as new as it was monstrous, clasped his head in his hands and said to me, from the bottom of his soul:

"What is this? Now that you've made yourself the richest man on the island, you want to leave it all behind?"

And he looked at me as though I had gone mad, because in the Indies nothing was more esteemed than getting very rich, but I answered him, "I don't want at the same time, Sir, to be the richest man in hell, too, because wealth is worth very little there."

The governor, who was a very jocular man, burst out laughing, as though I were joking, and he said that, if I was right, they would all end up in hell.

"You are not wrong about that, Sir, and for that reason I have resolved to preach it to the four winds and, if necessary, to the king of Spain himself, for the sake of the souls of all of us."

We went back and forth this way for a good while, and Diego de Velázquez, because he held me in high esteem, told me not to follow the example of the Dominican Fathers, that it was one thing to preach and another to give wheat; that the friars, who had nothing, were consistent when they preached the same voluntary dispossession, but I, who had so much and could have even more, ought to take care of my wealth because it was by God's will that I had it. I do not know where he would have found this will of God regarding me personally, but he firmly and repeatedly insisted on it and at the end said to me: "Be careful about what you do, Father, because in the end you will regret it; what God wants for you is to see you rich and prosperous, so I do not accept your release of the Indians, and, so that you can think better of it, I give you two weeks, after which we will talk again."

"Pretend, Sir, that those two weeks have already gone by," I pleaded, "and if I repent of what I propose, which God forbid, do not return the Indians to me even if I weep for them. If you do, may God rebuke you for that sin and not forgive you."

But the governor went on making fun of me and told me that if I went ahead with my resolution, he would take it as a miracle, and one of the greatest miracles, because in his already long life he had known of no one who, being rich, was unable to square his conscience with his wealth. I made it clear that I was firm in conscience, at the same time being agreeable, because I did not want to leave the Indians adrift or put them in the hands of some cruel soul, but rather to wait for the return of my partner Rentería to take charge of them (he was again sailing back and forth to Jamaica with his ships, buying and selling). The governor acquiesced, and we agreed to keep my resolution secret for as long as necessary.

CHAPTER VIII

THE ROAD TO THE COURT

The governor did as he said he would, but it was I who could not wait until the arrival of Pedro de Rentería returned from Jamaica; and my inability was due to the fact that I could not get used to the idea of living without my riches. One sleepless night, of which there were many in that period, the devil assailed me again and again with questions: How was I going to get along without the comfort of my feathered mattress, without my fine linen shirts, and also without my splendid carriage pulled by six mules? And on he went, counting all my wealth, producing in me an intense anxiety that brought back to me even the temptations of the flesh, which I had for quite a while subdued. And if I woke up with a start, in the middle of the night, I even doubted the existence of a God who was equally the father of everyone.

But during those nights of fitful sleep, I started reading by candlelight, and I did not find a holy book, either in Latin or in any Romance language, that did not say that what we were doing with the Indians was against all that was right, although our governors were saying otherwise.

I was consumed by these thoughts for some considerable time, until the Feast of the Assumption of our Lady, and, taking the occasion of the solemn Mass that I celebrated in the same town of Sancti Spíritus, I sought to commit myself in such a way that the devil would lose all hope of catching a hold of me where he most tormented me.

I began the sermon, as was the custom in the Indies, by thanking the presiding authority (who on that occasion was Diego de Velázquez himself, accompanied by his entire retinue) and praising him in a way that came from my heart, because I told him how grateful I was for the favor he had shown me throughout our years of friendship, especially in his having given me so many Indians; so many that they would almost put me, not at the gates of hell, but inside them. "Sir," I went on in a thundering voice, "I give you leave to talk to anyone about what we agreed, and I will take leave now myself to tell everyone present here that God has shown me the danger in which I was living while I had dominion over innocent and docile creatures, whom I hereby renounce for life, in the presence of Christ, whom we have with us in this tabernacle." Afterward, to the horror and admiration of those present, I preached to them about the injustice of the encomiendas, and if some of them were left with feelings of compunction, most of them thought they were dreaming, because they saw it as a bad dream that they could not at the same time have Indians and be free of sin; it was as though I were telling them that they could not make use of beasts of the field, and they could not believe it.

From that day on, I learned that, whatever I said or did about the exploitation of the Indians, some saw it as being good and others as being bad; and I endeavored to do what appeared to God, our Lord, to be good, because I do not put much trust in the judgment of men.

I did not return to my hacienda of Canaoreo and was left without a single *maravedí* and the means of producing one, other than the charity of those who thought what I preached was good, who were in the minority. The only thing I had was a sorrel mare who could be worth as much as a hundred pesos in gold, and I used her to go from one place to another to do my preaching, but I soon realized that at this rate the island of Cuba would meet the same destruction as Hispaniola and that the Catholic King had to be informed of the situation. So I decided to sell the mare to fund payment for the voyage. Because it pained me to leave without letting Pedro de Rentería know, I sent him a letter to Jamaica, where he was carrying on his business, and by return mail he sent me a message telling me to wait, that he was about to arrive in Cuba. I went to look for him at Baracoa, and when the arrival of his caravel was announced, I went out to meet it in a canoe, about four and a half miles from the port. Rentería, leaning over the rail of his caravel, began to shout to me.

"What is this you've written me about going to Castile? I'm the one who needs to go there anyway, for something that, when you know what it is, you'll be very happy about!"

He was shouting, which he had never done before, trembling with excitement, unable to wait until we had arrived at the port; I climbed a ladder into the caravel,

and after we had embraced like two friends who loved
each other very much, he told me what seemed to me
to be a miracle greater than all the ones that I had experienced since the last Pentecost. While he was waiting
for the ship's departure from Jamaica, that ship was waiting for the arrival of another from Castile, and he went
into a Franciscan monastery that was then on the island,
devoted himself to his prayers, and during one of them
sensed a call that told him he had to go to Spain to ask the
king for power and authority to establish some schools,
in which to gather all the children of the Indians and give
them instruction, so as to save them from the perdition
and death that the Indians had suffered in Hispaniola. He
thought only of the children because he had given up the
parents for lost.

I say this is a miracle because, being six hundred miles
apart, neither one of us knew what the other was thinking and both of us decided to go to Castile to talk with
the king, something that, in our right mind, we would
never have dreamed of doing—especially Rentería, who
was not given to dealing with the authorities.

I explained to him that I proposed to go to Castile in
order to seek a complete remedy for those poor people,
whether they were children or adults, men or women.
He listened to me in awe, and we began to debate which
one should go; each of us, as befits gentlemen, said that
it was the other who ought to go, until Rentería (who
had not known about it) learned about my renunciation
and that it would be up to him, until Diego de Velázquez
made some other provision, to take care of the Indians I
was releasing. He embraced me with tears in his eyes, al-

though he lamented with all his heart the heavy responsibility that was being placed on his shoulders. (It was not very heavy for long, because when it became known in Cuba that I was going around Spain agitating for the abolition of the encomiendas, Diego de Velázquez took the Indians that I had given up away from Rentería and allocated them to an encomendero named Juárez, whose sister was his lover. And he did him a great favor, because Rentería, before long, followed my example, renounced his encomiendas, sold everything he had, and returned to Guipúzcoa to live on the property I had bought for him during the trip I took to be ordained.)

But, let me say, he was filled with pleasure, happiness, and admiration for my renunciation and said with great feeling: "Father, it is clear now that you are the one who should go to Castile to present to the king all the evils and perdition of these people and, at the same time, ask for the necessary remedy, which you will know how to establish better than I will, educated as you are, and with greater authority because it is the first time in the history of the Indies that someone has renounced what belongs to him. And now what I must do is sell everything I have in this caravel so that you can be at court for all the time you need and obtain this solution."

The ship was very full of pigs and cassava bread, which fetched us a goodly sum; I only wanted to take part of it, believing that my trip would last a few months, but Rentería insisted that I take it all, about which he was correct because the months became years.

Once my journey had been decided upon, I sought from the mayor of Baracoa, who at the time was Hernán

Cortés, a testament *ad perpetuam rei memoriam*, for I was just a poor cleric, unknown in the court to which I was going, and I wanted the court to know all the travails I had been through in the Indies and how much I knew about wars, pacifications, and encomiendas, and also how I had renounced their fruits. Cortés gave me a full account of all that, but Diego de Velázquez and his retinue began to get suspicious and afraid about what I might be plotting to do in Spain, and, because among them there were some who were so malign that they would not hesitate to get rid of anyone who was going to act contrary to their interests, even if he was a man of the cloth, I devised a ruse that I was going to Paris to study and graduate in ecclesiastical sciences, and with that ploy I was able to embark for Hispaniola.

The news about my life had arrived there, and I was received with great joy by the Dominican Fathers. The Father Superior, Friar Pedro de Córdoba, the handsome and holy man, when he learned what I proposed to do on this trip, said to me: "Father, not a scrap of the work that is waiting for you at court will be useless, because God will take all of it into account; but you can be certain that, while the king lives, you will get nowhere."

The reason he said that was that the Catholic King was already very old and ill, and his involvement in affairs of the Indies was limited to whatever was decided by the bishop of Burgos, Juan Rodríguez de Fonseca, and his secretary, Lope de Conchillos, who, with no scruples at all, agreed to the distribution of Indians, from which they themselves benefited, being encomenderos without having set foot in or knowledge about those lands. Lope de Conchillos y Quintana had an encomienda of three hundred Indians in Hispaniola and five hundred in Cuba; furthermore, in his role as the ranking notary of the mines in Hispaniola, he received three reales for each gold-mining license, and, what is more, he collected two reales each for the right to brand Indians as slaves. How could they not see the trade in Indians as beneficial when they themselves were profiting from it?

Because at the time I did not know as much about such malfeasance as I learned later, I was not demoralized by Friar Pedro's words, and I told him that I would go down every path that was open to me; if I got nothing, at least I would have done my duty as a Christian. He was so pleased by my good spirits that, to reward me, he arranged for Friar Antón Montesino to accompany me on the journey, and he could not have given me a greater gift. He was the same priest who had denied me absolution, which was a great blessing because that denial resulted in many good things. The man who put so much fervor into his sermons now was amazed by the fervor I was putting into mine, because on the eve of our departure I preached in Santo Domingo, in his presence, and he could not get over his surprise at hearing such a welcome exposition from the mouth of one who months before had enjoyed talking about making a profit and nothing else.

We left Hispaniola in the month of September 1515 after the Ember Days, and we had such felicitous conditions that by the beginning of October we were already in Seville, Friar Antonio in his monastery and I with my family. Fortunately for us, the archbishop of Seville was Friar

Diego de Deza, another Dominican, whom the Catholic King loved very much, and as soon as Friar Antón told him about me, he gave me a letter of introduction to the king, vouching for me and my undertaking. With that in hand, I set out for Plasencia, because that was where the court was at the time, and this humble cleric was received by His Catholic Majesty on the eve of our Redeemer's birth, on December 23, 1515. Suddenly, without further ado, the road seemed so smooth that I even arrogantly thought that in the same way, without resistance, all doors would open to me, as they had to the prophets of old, sent by God, who were able to pull down the walls of a city with trumpets.

But I would soon understand how difficult it is to demolish walls that are raised by wealth and the interests that hold sway around them.

The Catholic King received me in a very large house in Plasencia, which from the outside did not look at all palatial, in a warm and spacious room; without his royal paraphernalia, he had an elderly and paternal air, and he encouraged me to speak as though I deserved such respect. I say elderly, and that is how he seemed to me at the time, even though he was not much older than sixty, but since he had been through wars and sorrows since the age of thirteen, it was as though he had lived more than one life. He listened to me kindly, all the while warming his hands over a brazier that he had in front of him, because it was a very cold day, which was appropriate in that region for the day of the Lord's birth, and he invited me to place my hands over the same brazier. I did so for the honor it was to warm my hands next to those of the most powerful king in Christendom, but I did not need more heat than what I had inside me, with which I explained all the harm that was being done in the Indies, the innumerable Indians who were dying without having received the faith, and how, if His Majesty did not come to the rescue soon, the islands would be left deserted and he would be deprived of income.

He understood very well that the message I brought him meant as much to his royal conscience as it did to his finances, and he began to ask me about those lands with great interest, so we talked for about an hour. As I see it, and may God forgive my presumption, until my arrival little was known in Spain about the Indies, and as far as our Catholic Majesty was concerned, he thought it was a matter of a few islands, somewhat larger than the Canaries, with some deposits of gold, which were quite good; and that was excusable because, at the time, little was known of the immensity of the mainland or of the empires of Mexico and Peru or of the marvelous lands that were accessible by the South Sea that Núñez de Balboa had just discovered.

Sadly, His Majesty was embroiled in litigation with the Kingdom of Navarre over the division of dominions that were not worth a farthing, at the risk of marginalizing the immense riches in souls, lands, and income streams of which he was the sovereign on the other side of the ocean. I insisted emphatically on the latter, showing him how much income he could earn from such immensities if he treated the Indians like subjects instead of slaves. I told him about the profitability of my hacienda of Canaoreo, where, not treating the Indians at all badly, more was earned than on other haciendas owned by harsh Castilians, whose sole effect was to cause the Indians to allow themselves to die because of their inability to endure their situation; he understood all this very well and was amazed by my renunciation of so much.

Since then, I have never spoken to any other monarch with the pleasure that I felt on this momentous occasion, and the Lord put so much eloquence in my mouth that His Majesty, speaking in his capacity as king, told me that I was right in what I said and that we should meet again, in Seville, where he intended to go before the end of the Christmas season. I kissed his hand with tears in my eyes, and His Majesty put his hand on my head, as a father might do with his son.

I was happier still when I had the opportunity to speak to the king's confessor, Friar Tomás de Matienzo, who was also of our Dominican Order and told me that His Majesty had been so pained by what I said that he was preparing to leave for Seville on the Feast of the Holy Innocents, the fourth day of Christmas, to continue the discussion and try to find a remedy for such evils. In my foolish vanity, I attributed to myself all the credit for that achievement and even thought that the Feast of the Holy Innocents had been chosen because that was the situation of the Indians, because they died blamelessly, like those whose throats Herod had ordered to be cut. It was not bad to see it that way, except for how emphatically I believed that everything I was doing had been divinely ordained, as though the Lord had taken me as a prophet, although I lacked the humility of those sainted men, as will soon be seen.

There was a lot of talk about my visit to the king, and Lope de Conchillos wanted to see me. He was the secretary of the all-powerful Bishop Fonseca, and it was said that he ruled in the Indies more than the bishop himself. I did not give much importance to talking with such a person, after I had been dealing with His Majesty, but I accepted the advice of Friar Tomás de Matienzo, who told me that little could be done in the Indies without the support of Lope de Conchillos.

Despite the solemnity of the holiday, he received me on Christmas Day itself, being in such a hurry to rid himself of me. He was a young man at the time, in his early thirties, but he looked older because he had lost his eyebrows, his beard, and all the hair on his head, which people said was because of the tortures that Philip the Fair had put him through over the intrigues related to the succession to the throne of Castile upon the death of the Catholic Queen. Since those intrigues benefited King Ferdinand, he rewarded Lope de Conchillos by naming him to be Fonseca's secretary for the government of the Indies. He lost his hair and with it his shame about profiting at the expense of his fellowman, because I have letters that prove he made a profit of four million *maravedís* a year with the encomiendas and other malfeasance even less legitimate. In our interview, which lasted a little longer than a quarter of an hour, he outdid himself in praising me, my merits and virtues, as though he had known me all his life, to be rid of me, offering all manner of marks of distinction in the Indies, including a bishop's miter. Despite his evil character, he managed to be affable and avoid saying anything that would offend me, but I let him know with equal affability that I had renounced all the glories and riches of this world. Which was true because God, since my renunciation of my haciendas and businesses, gave me the grace of no longer being covetous of material goods: not silks, brocades, or slaves to scratch my back, or daily baths as though my head could not support a louse.

Of a different nature, but not more profitable, was the interview with Don Juan Rodríguez de Fonseca that I had to have so as not to disobey the king's confessor. Bishop Rodríguez de Fonseca, being the minister for all the Indies in his role as president of the Council of the Indies, was a man with an uncommon talent for plotting intrigues that would benefit his natural lords, the Catholic Kings, but especially King Ferdinand, to whom he was most faithful. In his service, the bishop was capable of any exploit, such as organizing fleets to go to sea, a role more suitable for Basques than for bishops, as well as crossing France in disguise, to arrange the marriage of Doña Juana with Philip the Fair. He was so clear-headed that, by royal appointment, he was given the task of organizing Cristóbal Colón's second voyage, with a salary of two hundred thousand *maravedís*, and he acquired such a taste for that teat that he did not let go of it until he died. But it was surprising that, with so much experience in business in the Indies—though he never set foot there— he should know so little about them and his government of them should be so bad. Except in his faithfulness to the king, which is no small virtue in a courtier, all the rest of him was blindness, greed, and other vices. Despite his ecclesiastical position, he surrounded himself with some titled nieces, whose relationship to him no one knew anything about and who had to be courted by anyone who was interested in enriching himself in the Indies.

An ardent enemy of his enemies, he saw me as one such from the moment he knew of my existence. And I was not among those for whom it ended the worst, if one considers the fate that befell Cristóbal Colón, who was put in prison and also deprived of the prerogatives that he received in the Capitulations of Santa Fe. There were many reasons why he would be against me, but the clumsiness I showed in that first interview in Plasencia, on December 27, 1515, was perhaps not the least of them. Ignorant of his many powers and orders, I delivered myself of a description of the calamities in the Indies, and when I arrived at the subject of the children who were dying of hunger on the island of Cuba, no fewer than seven thousand in three months, I related it so gracelessly that it seemed he had been the one who had cut their throats; the bishop, with that anger which was so known and feared, leapt up with: "Look at this brainless wit! What concern of mine, or of the king, is what you are telling me?"

I listened in disbelief and answered, just as angrily, "How can it be that neither Your Honor nor the king would care that these souls are dying? Then who will care?"

His reply was to throw the dossier of papers about my complaints in my face and order his lackeys to eject me into the street, which they did with pleasure, laughing loudly.

Thus did my relationship with Rodríguez de Fonseca get off to an unpromising start.

CHAPTER IX

RETURN TO THE INDIES

I headed for Seville immediately, not in anger, and because I am not easily discouraged I thought that as soon as the Catholic King arrived there, as he had promised me, and I had been taken under the wing of the archbishop of Seville, Friar Diego de Deza, things would be very different. In one respect, I was justified in thinking so, because the Order of Saint Dominic was held in high esteem at court, being the source of confessors for the king and queen, which may have been the reason my bones did not end up in prison after the fit of anger I allowed myself with the all-powerful minister.

The news of what had happened reached Seville before I did (because I can confirm that palace gossip travels faster than gunpowder), and Friar Montesino and even the archbishop were both surprised by my having been so bold, but they did not disapprove of it. Instead, they made me repeat again and again what had I said to Fonseca and what he had said to me, and how he had thrown the papers in my face; friars later told the story to each other, with great delight.

King Ferdinand kept his promise and set out for Seville on schedule, but the Lord had other plans, for he took him to his bosom the next day, January 23; I say that he brought him to glory because the Catholic King died on the way to Guadalupe, where he was going to seek the counsel of our Lady, and anyone who sets out on that road necessarily crosses paths with the Mother of God, and there can be no better champion of gaining entry to heaven. I felt it in my soul because I was convinced that, once the truth was known about the Indies, a truth that many had hidden from him, this exceptionally wise monarch was bound to apply a remedy.

It is not relevant to describe the comings and goings that I went through during those months to impart my account of the wrongs that were being committed to the powers that be, and, in the end, I decided that that had to be the monarch himself, our glorious King Charles, who at the time was in Flanders, and I decided to go there, using the money with which Pedro de Rentería was good enough to provide me.

The Dominican Fathers commended my decision very highly and encouraged me to pursue it, as I in turn followed their prudent advice; they then told me that until the king arrived in Spain, the government of the kingdom of Castile had been entrusted to Cardinal Cisneros, a member of the Franciscan Order, and to Cardinal Adriano, of Utrecht, who was called the Ambassador, which he was, of King Charles, and they said that I would be negligent if I did not present my grievances to them. That is what I did, and I was very happy to have followed their advice.

I presented my grievous account to both of them, and Cardinal Cisneros showed less surprise, because he already suspected that outrages were being committed in the Indies, but Ambassador Adriano, more innocently, as was fitting in a man so benign and mild, which is characteristic of the Flemish, was plunged in amazement at such an account of inhumane treatment. From that moment on, Cardinal Adriano became my champion, and because he had less responsibility for governing the kingdom than Cardinal Cisneros, he gave me a great deal of attention, being a pious, honest man who had no desire to consent to such a great evil. I will say no more except that, to enter his residence, all I had to do was knock on the door.

In June of this same year, a meeting was held to discuss the Laws of Burgos (of 1512), which in my view were promulgated as a result of Friar Antón Montesino's resounding sermon and would have improved the conditions of the Indians to some degree if the governors of the Indies had bothered to enforce them. This meeting was held to discuss reforming them, and my champion, Ambassador Adriano, at my suggestion sought the abolition of the odious system of trading in Indians. Palacios Rubios, an erudite legal scholar, was of the same opinion, so it was not just madness on my part to propose to nullify something that went against all nature. The meeting was attended by the foremost jurists and theologians of the kingdom, and it took place in an estate that belonged to Cardinal Cisneros, in San Andrés Square, in Madrid, and it was the first time that I was invited to such a solemn event, so I was filled by a sense of the honor that it entailed. Cardinal Cisneros himself presided, and he was so strict and tireless in his work that the days went by one after the other, without a break, in a point-by-point discussion of every corner of the law.

One Juan de Samano, one of the most prominent fa-
vorites of Lope de Conchillos, acted as the rapporteur
of the meeting, and when we reached the fifteenth law,
which covers the duty of the encomenderos to feed the
Indians allotted to them, he read it out with great assur-
ance, following the instructions of his master, to the effect that they had to provide a pound of meat per day to
each Indian. Whether it was because of the exhaustion
resulting from such long days or because many at the
meeting wanted to be deceived, even about something as
important as that, everyone accepted his statement until I
interjected, with that testiness that has on occasion done
me so much damage: "The law says nothing of the sort!"

Cardinal Cisneros, thinking it had been an involuntary
error on the part of the rapporteur, asked him to reread
the paragraph being contested, and Samano, who feared
his patron more than he did the cardinal, although he
was trembling, repeated what he had said about the daily
pound of meat. I, because I knew the law by heart, re-
torted again:"That law says nothing of the sort!"

The cardinal, not being able to imagine that, in his presence, the rapporteur would dare to perpetrate such deceit, turned to me and with that temper of his, which was
sometimes quick and acrimonious, scolded me: "Keep
quiet! Or be very careful what you say!"

But because I was certain that the law said the pound of
meat had to be doled out once a week (and, shamefully,
the Indians did not even receive that meager ration), I did
not hesitate to rejoin with what I now see was insolence:
"Your Most Reverend Grace, order my beheading if it is
true that the law says what the rapporteur says it says."

The cardinal ordered the law to be brought to him, so angrily that I think he would have had me beheaded on the spot if I had proved to be mistaken. But when he saw with his own eyes what the law provided, he ordered Juan de Samano to be expelled from the meeting and, knowing who was talking through the mouth of the rapporteur, he ordered the dismissal of the secretary Lope de Conchillos in a few days, and that was what we gained from this confrontation.

As for me, what I gained was a great deal of work after that day; Cardinal Cisneros valued my decisiveness so much that he entrusted to me, along with Palacios Rubios, the task of putting in writing how the Indians should be governed. I asked permission for Friar Antón Montesino to join us in our assignment, and, when permission was granted, he came to Madrid, and here, in Palacios Rubios' lodgings, I drew up a provision under which the Indians would recover their freedom, putting an end to the encomiendas. I drafted it, Friar Montesino gave his agreement, and Palacios Rubios, being more versed in the law than I was, improved it and put it in the style of court language.

This made me so happy that I thought, poor me, that such a great result had been achieved that there was not much left for me to do in this world other than to die peacefully. That was fifty years ago and, instead of nearing death, I am still suffering for the Indians, although we have gained a great deal during those years.

As the saying goes, how short-lived happiness is in a poor man's house! The draft that we prepared was approved, but there was little enthusiasm for it among those whose duty it was to give it practical effect. It provided that the Indians had to live in freedom in their villages, governed by their caciques, and that they had to deliver to the king a fair portion of what they produced, the same as subjects in Castile; there were also many provisions that favored the Indians and limited the abuses of the Spaniards. Some of those provisions were written, in his own hand, by Cardinal Cisneros himself who, in matters of doctrine and love of one's neighbor, was excelled by no one. And despite his many governmental duties, he himself took up the pen and, being the man of letters that he was, what he wrote was very well said.

I proposed that, in order to bring the law to fruition, it would be well to seek trustworthy persons to undertake the task, and after a good deal of deliberation we resolved that they would be three Hieronymite friars, very learned and charitable, whose names are of no significance. As for me, by a decree signed by Cardinal Adriano, in the name of the queen and king, I was appointed universal protector of all the Indians of the Indies, a title that could not be excelled in its beauty, and the decree explained that I had been appointed for my knowledge of and love for the Indians. It provided me with a salary of a hundred pesos of gold, which was no small sum at the time, because the hell of Peru had not yet been discovered, which produced massive amounts of gold that only served to impoverish Spain, for anyone who gets used to easy money will not prosper. I accepted this salary because it did not seem fair that Rentería had to keep on subsidizing the expenses I was generating in my travels, mostly because the Hieronymite friars were so poor that often all the expense came out of my pocket.

In November 1516, we set out for Hispaniola, my departure being thirteen days after that of the Hieronymites. And that was the beginning of a problem, because the inhabitants of Hispaniola, having learned of the Hieronymites' mission and the support that I was going to lend it, received them with great deference and flattery, concealing their treatment of the Indians and presenting themselves in everything as good Christians. What they did was such that the naïve friars at first believed that the things I had told the court were exaggerations.

I realized too late that I had made a mistake in selecting the three Hieronymites, who were learned and charitable but as naïve as doves and lacking in the astuteness of snakes. The work they were there to do was very beautiful, because the first remedy they had to implement was to free the Indians from their encomenderos, and once that was done they would build for them villages of three hundred inhabitants each, wherever they wanted, with their houses, streets, and squares; there would be private properties in the villages and also some communal ones; among the latter there would be a hospital and also a church. The village was to be governed by a cacique elected by the inhabitants, and he, together with a cleric or friar, would choose the other officials of the governing council.

Each Indian would work the land assigned to him, and he was obligated to work in the mines for two months a year; of the gold that the Indians extracted, a third was for the Crown and the other two-thirds for the miners. The latter seemed to me to be a lot, but I went along with it because working in the mines for only two months per year was better for them than working every month of the year and every year of their lives.

As for the Spaniards who were left without Indians, good solutions were sought for them, whether it was working in the gold mines and paying just a tenth to the Crown, being given land that they could work, or working as administrators of the Indian villages; all of these positions were very well compensated and would have been welcome to many hidalgos in Castile. Also, they were encouraged to marry some female caciques or daughters of caciques, in which case the Spaniard would have the status of a cacique and his wife's lands, by right of marriage, would be his.

The Hieronymites, instead of doing the work that had been assigned to them, set themselves to asking around about the treatment that the natives had received, and it seemed as though they had come to judge whether what I had said in Castile was true or just the product of my imagination. To answer that question, all they needed to do was to go to the monastery of the Dominican Fathers in Santo Domingo, because they were well informed about everything that happened in the islands. But because of some grudges that the Hieronymites held against the Dominicans, they did not want to do that, and they even fled from them whenever they could, accepting only the counsel of the judges of the court that governed Hispan-

iola at the time, who were the most despicable people
there could be.

Suffice it to consider that one of the highest judges, Lucas Vázquez de Ayllón, a converted Jew born in Toledo,
despite being married, corrupted the wife of Nicolás
Pérez, a resident of Santo Domingo and master of a military order, and the go-between was no lesser man than
the accountant Gil González Dávila; Vázquez de Ayllón
later took as another mistress the wife of another resident, named García de Roales, establishing a house for
her and at first threatening to kill him, but he then set-
tled with him by paying him thirty *castellanos* of gold and
forgiving some of his debts to the Crown; and finally, he
made sexual advances to yet another woman, who was
married to a trombone player and by whom he had a
daughter. Vázquez de Ayllón thought he could conceal
his lechery by always maintaining a grave and formal air,
but the scandal rose to such a pitch that Friar Pedro de
San Martín, the Dominicans' administrator, denounced
him publicly from the pulpit. And Vázquez de Ayllón
was not the only one he had to accuse for violating the
sixth commandment so shamelessly, because he also pil-
loried one Matienzo, a judge who had as many mistresses
as the year has months.

These characters, with a good deal of sophistry, told the
Hieronymites that the Indians did not have the ability to
support themselves, and it was not worthwhile removing
them from their settlements or building villages for them,
because they would flee to the mountains. And Miguel
de Pasamonte, the treasurer and best ally that Rodríguez

de Fonseca and Lope de Conchillos had in the Indies, dared to tell the Hieronymites that it was not possible to set the Indians free because they would ally themselves with the black slaves and rise up against the Spaniards. And the Hieronymites believed such absurdities, when even the most brainless person in the Indies knew that it would be a miracle wrought by the devil for the Indians and blacks to join forces to do anything.

At first I was very insistent with the naïve friars, showing them that those who so advised them had been allotted thousands of Indians and would be the first ones whose interests would be compromised by reform; they agreed to my face, but they did nothing of any value, except for one of the Hieronymites who, because he was a great devotee of working the land, devised a way of planting the sugar cane that improved the crops of the sugar plantations.

To enlighten them, I gave them examples of the damage and outrages committed by the encomenderos, and I even had the opportunity to witness with them a very dramatic case, but without much effect. The man involved was one Juan Bono de Quejo, with whom I had a friendly relationship when I was behaving so badly, because he was from the same place as Pedro de Rentería, having been born in San Sebastián. Like almost all Basques, he was a very good pilot, and when he was in command of the *Santa María*, he had been back and forth to the Indies several times, being a ship's captain in the admiral's fourth voyage. He knew all the channels like the palm of his hand, but for the last two years he had used his professional skills in the most abominable activities, the slave trade, with special cruelty, because in order to transport one live slave, it did not bother him if he had to kill ten of them along the way.

We came across this Bono on the island of Puerto Rico, on an excursion we took there to introduce the Hieronymites to it, and as soon as we arrived, we ran into a crowd of 180 Indians on the beach, herded together like cattle, some of them badly wounded, in chains and guarded by the Basque and his murderous thugs. It sundered my soul because, if it is painful to see a criminal in such a desperate situation, it is much more so to contemplate an innocent person in the same plight. Their gaze becomes elusive, and they look down at the ground, for fear of what their eyes might find if they look up, and that is understandable because sometimes the slave drivers who guard them say, boastfully and angrily, "You! What are you looking at?" and with the whip make them bow their head. I would like those who dictate the laws in Castile to see them in such dreadful circumstances so that they would be more diligent in enforcing them.

At first I thought that they were Caribs, whose capture was permitted on the pretext that they are very fierce and eat human flesh; but, judging by their appearance, it seemed to me they were Indians from the coast of Cumaná, who also were very fierce but not cannibals. I asked Bono in the presence of the Hieronymites, and the Basque told me, with the simplicity and curtness that are characteristic of his countrymen, that he brought them from the island of Trinidad (which is in that part of Cumaná), where he had been well received, and that after some loss of life it was possible to capture them. He even explained to me, as though it were a feat, that they built for him a beautiful hut covered with palm leaves in which to lodge up to a hundred people, very well made of wood and walled with very fragrant and healthy straw, which is abundant on that island, and that every day the Indians fed them fish, bread, and fruit. My question was a calculated one, because I wanted the Hieronymites to realize how the Indians were being transported, but my slyness was unnecessary because Bono recounted it himself, unreservedly and openly, and was proud of his accomplishment. Unable to tolerate such an ignominious account any longer, I scolded him angrily, "But, lost soul that you are, if you benefited so much from those labors, why did you repay them with the black ingratitude of attacking them, killing some, and taking others prisoner?"

Now it was Bono de Quejo's turn to be surprised, and he answered me with the candor that the devil infuses into lost souls: "By my faith, Father, because that is the *destruction* given me by the court; take into account that they told me that if I could not capture them in peace, I was to capture them in war."

With this scrambling of words that Basques often fall into, the *destruction* was the *instruction* that the judges of the Audience[1] had given him to go and take by surprise the Indians on the islands off the coast of the mainland. They told them to do so because Hispaniola was being depleted of Indians, and it became common to say that it was because they were very sickly and not industrious,

[1] The Royal Audience (Real Audiencia), which was established in Santo Domingo, was the first court of justice and the principal political entity in the Americas during the colonial period.—TRANS.

for which the remedy was to bring Indians from the mainland, who were sturdier: the remedy, clearly, that would
enable them to continue mining gold from the cursed
mines day and night. And it was the very same judges of
the Audience who fitted out the ships to go after them,
and under the pretext that they ate human flesh and did
not want to hear the preaching of the gospel, they took
them as slaves and sold them at public auction, which
turned out to be not so public, because it was the judges,
their relatives, and their friends who ended up with them.
I ran out of tears when I saw that so few were able to do
so much damage to so many souls! And much more damage to the preaching of the gospel, because if those few
were responsible for enslaving the Indians, how can the
latter have wanted thereafter to receive the gospel from
the good friars who preached it with so much love?

I got into a heated argument with Bono then and there,
and his entire defense was that he had seen them eating
human flesh and that it was for that reason that he had
taken them prisoner.

The Hieronymites, who were very distressed but faint-
hearted and indecisive, said that there should be an inquiry to determine these facts, and that satisfied all of
them. They were satisfied because there was no better
way in the Indies to continue an injustice than to start an
inquiry that would never end. There were so many such
inquiries that a strong stone building was built next to the
Audience, the size of a barracks for halberdiers, and even
when the files were piled one on top of the other there
was not enough room to accommodate all of them. In
my opinion, though the slave traders were a dreadful dis-

grace for the islands, the paper pushers were in the end an even worse plague; they wrote so much and so badly that the price of a ream of paper exceeded that of ten pounds of pork. If they had put all those scribes to work laying out orchards and vegetable gardens, Hispaniola would by now be the equal of the orchards of Granada.

Oh, just imagine the fear and trembling that was struck in the heart of Bono de Quejo by the inquiry that was brought against him! He just continued doing as he wished, safely protected by Bishop Rodríguez de Fonseca, who eventually named him lieutenant governor of the city of Havana. I believe this happened around 1526, and he soon after died in that city, where he was buried with full honors.

Rebus sic stantibus made me feel ashamed to say that I was *protector of all the Indians of the Indies*, as my appointment stated, and yet do so little for them, but I was consoled by the encouragement that the Dominican Fathers gave me. The only thing I got from the Hieronymites who had been sent, and it almost cost me my life, was that they put into practice the commission they brought from Castile, under which they were ordered to take away from all the members of the Council of the Indies, or from any other persons living in Castile, the Indians they had in encomiendas, which was the worst of all the abuses.

They did that, without being able to excuse themselves from it, because their commission was very categorical in that respect, having been written by Cardinal Cisneros in his own hand. That gave me some hope, and I insisted to the Hieronymites that the next measure to be taken

would be to do the same for the Indians who were un-
justly held by the judges and officials of the Audience. I
convinced them that if we took away the Indians from the
Council of the Indies and from the Audience of Santo
Domingo, we would have accomplished three-quarters
of our mission, because the other encomenderos would
eventually see reason and turn to one of the remedies
that were available, mainly that of being ranchers or of
administering the new Indian villages. The Dominicans
agreed with me in all respects, but as soon as they said so,
the Hieronymites said they would have to give it further
thought.

What I have recounted almost cost me my life because
the officials of the Audience, when they saw that their encomiendas were in danger, decided to be rid of me, which
was not a difficult thing to do because the life of a poor
cleric differed very little from others that were lost in the
Indies for the most trifling reason, if any. I slept in the inn
next to the second admiral's palace, in the city of Santo
Domingo, and a maid who worked for an official of the
treasury (I do not mean Miguel de Pasamonte, but rather
an official of his chancery) came to warn me about what
they had contrived in the house of her master and that the
crime was assigned to a pearl trader, from Cubagua, who
was to kill me in the course of a pretended robbery. That
poor servant took a big risk in warning me, but word
had already gone out among the Indians that I had come
to protect them, although as this incident showed, they
were protecting me.

I was deeply upset to see that the rage of these heartless men should have brought them to such a point, and

I cried bitter tears. Very few times have I been so willing to die, if that was necessary to remedy the madness of giving a higher value to riches than to the life of a fellow man, even without giving consideration to the fact that he had taken holy orders. I knew the wiles and habits of the Indies well, and I thought there was little I could do to leave Hispaniola with my life if the members of the Audience had decided to deprive me of it. Because of what could have happened, although night had already fallen, I went to the Dominican monastery to make confession; it was received by Friar Bernardo de Santo Domingo, one of the holiest in the Order, one of the first three who arrived in Hispaniola, who scolded me severely for not wanting to defend my life in the face of iniquity. He included citations of the Holy Fathers and examples of how the early Christians prohibited yielding willingly to wild beasts, which was what those who were persecuting me so savagely were. He asked me to relieve him of the secrecy of the confessional, to which I acceded, and requesting the presence of the superior, who was Friar Pedro de Córdoba, it was decided then and there that I should not go back to the inn, so I would stay and sleep in the monastery, which I did. They gave me the best chamber they had, which was simple, austere, and plain, like the rest of the monastery, and I can remember only a very few times when I slept with such pleasure, comforted by the love of those friars, who, because of what might happen, took turns keeping watch before the best guard that any man can have in this world: our Lord Jesus Christ in the tabernacle.

From that day on, until I returned to Spain, I spent

the night in the monastery, and by day I was always accompanied by two friars, one of them a lay brother who
had previously been a slave trader, and was of such an
exceptional height that his mere presence was frightening. "Praying to God and wielding a hod", Friar Pedro
de Córdoba said to me, laughing, when he gave Friar
Garcés, the lay brother, his assignment.

I wrote letters to the cardinal describing what was happening, but by the time I received a reply, other events
had taken us down the road of bitterness, so that, following the advice of Friar Pedro de Córdoba, I decided to
return to Castile. Friar Pedro thought that, with other friars more spirited than the three Hieronymites, it would
be possible to find a remedy, because the decrees that
we brought from Spain were extremely wise, and if they
could only be put into practice, the wrongs being committed in the Indies would necessarily be righted. In passing, he gave me some documents that had been signed
by him and other Dominican Fathers that attested to the
malice and injustice of the judges of the Audience, calling
for their replacement by others who were more upright.
   This was less drastic than it might appear, because there
were only three evil men who did a great deal of damage when they distributed their Indians among the others of their ilk; but there were also honest encomenderos,
such as Pedro de Rentería, and they would have been prepared to become ranchers and administrators in the Indians' villages. And those who were not so honest would
have no other recourse, if authority had changed hands
for the better. The passage of time has proven that those

who thought as we did were right, because the gold of Hispaniola is not even a memory, and what was mined at the time has been converted into jewelry for European chanceries or is in the hands of the bankers of Genoa, but the royal treasury in Castile is empty, and our kings are always struggling to fill them so they can continue their border disputes. Not to mention the souls that were lost, and there are barely any Taínos or Lucayos in the islands. May God have mercy on them. On the other hand, if the villages had been built, they would now be very prosperous, the Indians would be very Christian, and our kings would be receiving a substantial income. Also, they would have served as an example for the forays they made later into the Mexicos and Perus, instead of having to take them with such loss of life as was caused by those who conquered them, always with a hunger for gold and trading Indians.

I left Hispaniola on June 3, 1517. The judges of the Audience were very relieved to see me do so, and I had a full supply of reasons with which to convince Cardinal Cisneros of what had to be done, but they were useless to me because shortly after I arrived the cardinal gave his soul to God, in a manner said to be very holy. I had an opportunity to see him once, but he was already very ill and distant from the functions of government, because our lord, King Charles, was about to arrive in Spain.

CHAPTER X

THE KNIGHTS OF
THE GOLDEN SPURS

The death of the cardinal left me immersed in great con-
fusion, because I was unable to understand the ways of
the Lord and how, at such an inopportune moment, he
had taken from us those who had shown themselves to
be disposed to help us remedy the evils of the Indies. The
first to go was the Catholic King, whom the Lord took
while he was on the road to Seville, where I was waiting
for him with a heart full of hope; and now the supremely
wise cardinal was taken from us while I was bringing him
a plenitude of reasons for bringing to a good conclusion
what we had agreed upon before my departure.

I was bringing those reasons, and I communicated them
to various people, but they all thought that the Indies
could wait, because it was always more urgent to discuss
a few plots of land with the French or the Kingdom of
Naples. Even Cisneros, in our only meeting, was more
concerned about what he should say, or not say, to the
new king when he arrived in Castile than he was about
the thousands of souls who were waiting for us there in
the Indies, with no protection other than what we were
able to give them. And while they were discussing those

trifles, the islands were being depopulated and their riches were being blown away by the winds.

I was so deeply discouraged that I withdrew to Seville to be with my family, which I did indeed have, though I had very much neglected them. But on the way to them, in Aranda de Duero, I came down with some fevers that I thought would be my undoing because I had to stay in bed, something that I do not recall having done more than once before in my life. Because God had not given me the intelligence I needed to know what I should do, but he had given me health in plenty; I have crossed the ocean sea ten times, lost count of the miles I have had to cover on foot, and never have known what pain is; and even if I do not sleep, the next day I am up on my feet at dawn and never get tired. But on that occasion, when I was prostrate in Aranda, a friar and herbalist who was caring for me said that I had brought great fevers with me from the Indies, of which many were dying in Spain. He said this to me with the best intentions, so I could prepare my soul for its journey, although to prevent it he gave me some concoctions that caused me to vomit very copiously, which he said was to purge my blood. He was a Benedictine friar who would have been a saint if he had not been so proud of himself for his medicinal art, which almost was the end of me, because had I continued along this path, he would have purged my blood in such a way that I would have had none left. Until one night, with the little understanding that so many infusions had left me, I said to myself: "Can it be that God our Lord has saved me from so many dangers in those lands, which are so plagued by mortal pests, that I should come to die in this modest inn, in this clean and noble Castilian city?" And at dawn, without waiting for the Benedictine to arrive, I ordered a mule to be saddled and immediately took the road to Seville, where I arrived half-dead, but not totally so, which is what would have happened to me if I had kept on with the herbalist's cure.

My eldest sister, Isabel de Sosa, lived in Seville and had made a good marriage with a shipwright named Cristóbal Fernández. They lived very comfortably in a house they had received from my father as a dowry when he returned from his first voyage. The house, with its corral, was next to the Guadalquivir River in the very quarter of San Lorenzo where I was born. There I finished recovering from my fevers, and also from some of the wounds to my soul, because my sister and her husband cared for me incessantly. With the great number of ships that came through the Arenal of Seville during those years, the shipwrights were very much in demand, and since my brother-in-law was one of the best, he had plenty of work, so he was better paid, I think, than those who hunted for gold in the mines of the River Haina.

They prepared a room for me so meticulously that not even the senior canon of the cathedral would have had anything better; and I allowed myself to be spoiled. It was my brother-in-law Cristóbal who lent me the funds I needed to live on during those two years, as recorded in the loan agreement into which we entered before the notary of Seville, Manuel Segura; that is how poor I was, an unemployed cleric without a penny to his name. And I say this because the fault finders muttered, "And where did this cleric get the money to go from one place to another? Doesn't he say that he renounced all the riches he had in Cuba? Is it that the Dominican Fathers, for whom he is the spokesman, are giving him money?" I was their spokesman, and it was a great honor, but only because it was the same as being the spokesman of Christ himself, to whom they were as devoted as I was. But the money for the trips I had to make came from Cristóbal Fernández, and he also loaned me the money to pay for the mule I have mentioned above, without anything at all in return, and I returned her to him in very bad condition from our travels along trails and roads.

To stop being an unpaid cleric, I went to see the archbishop of Seville, Friar Diego de Deza—the same man who had given me letters of introduction to the Catholic King—so that he would incorporate me into his diocese as a regular priest. This archbishop was a man of delicate health (it was the Catholic King himself who paved the way for him to be given the see of Seville so he could have the benefit of its benign climate), not very knowledgeable about the affairs of the Indies, but dedicated, like all the Dominicans, to defending the Indians. He heard me out patiently and with understanding and, at the same time, asked me to tell him about those lands, which I did with the fervor with which I always talk about that subject, and as I was winding up, he said to me: "Father, you can now go back to where you came from. You were not born to give sermons to Sevillian ladies, nor can I put my soul in danger taking you off the road that, quite clearly, God has traced for you."

He said it to me with a touch of sharpness and with

the authority of someone who is used to giving orders and being obeyed. Because I was not very good at taking orders given to me in that fashion, I answered him with a hint of asperity that I understood the Lord to have other plans for me, which was why he took away those who could help me, referring to the Catholic King and Cardinal Cisneros. He let me speak as long as I wanted, and it even seemed that my audacity pleased him, and when I stopped, he said: " 'The king is dead; long live the king.' If King Ferdinand was so good (and you are hearing this from one who loved him very much), King Charles will be just as good, with the grace of God. And if you don't obey your conscience and tell him what you have seen with your own eyes is happening in the Indies, you will have very little rest no matter how well you preach to Sevillians during Lent."

At that point, I stopped fancying myself as a canon of the cathedral with a red hat, in the city where I was born, which, in my opinion, continues to be the most beautiful in the world and the best place in which to live.

It is now appropriate to take a step back in my account. When I fled from the herbalist friar in Aranda de Duero, I could not follow the usual road to Seville because the mountain streams were high, so I took the advice of some mule drivers by taking a detour toward San Esteban de Gormaz. After one of my days on the road, as nightfall approached and I could not stop shivering, with pitch-black clouds looming over me, I felt I had to seek refuge in an isolated farmhouse, which was not an

inn, where the husband and wife who were farmworkers
and the owners gave me shelter. I say owners, which is
an exaggeration, because they were vassals of the lord of
Burgo de Osma, whose lands they were, and they worked
the land for him. They welcomed me like the Samaritan
in the gospel, and when they saw that I was poor and
ill, they made me stay until the fevers subsided. They
gave me the first milk of the only cow they had, burnt
with a stone, because the wife, whose name was Andrea, said that it was the best remedy for fevers. Each
person has his skills in such things, and since my body
did not have a negative reaction to the treatment, it did
no harm to follow it; they also set aside some eggs from
the chicken coop, and Andrea put so much love into the
seasoning that, in order not to treat her disrespectfully, I
forced my appetite, which was very low, and so, thanks
to the love of these good people, I began to recover my
strength.

   This happened when autumn was at its height, and in
these lands it is very severe, with rain and snow taking
turns, and since the periods of daylight were short and the
nights were long, we spent the evenings in the warmth of
the fireside. I told them things about the Indies, and they
thought I was delirious when I described the softness of
the earth, which yielded as many as three corn crops in
a year, the fruits that hung from the trees, just an arm's
reach away, and the farmlands that the islands' governors
were willing to grant to anyone who wanted to work
them. I also told them about the harm that the Indians
suffered at the hands of the bad Spaniards, and Andrea and
her husband, whose name was Blas Hernández, could not

comprehend so much evil, and their eyes even brimmed with tears.

Two sons lived with them, already young men, as well as a daughter of marriageable age, and they all exhausted themselves working their stony lands, always dependent on a merciless sky that sent them ice storms in the winter and droughts in the summer; and for each harvest that they managed to reap, two fell by the wayside. And the first part of the harvest went to pay the rent on the land to the lord of Burgo de Osma, who was not one of the worst, but neither was he a man of lenience.

Señor Blas sighed and said, "Here was I born, and here I want to die, but for my sons to have lands of their own, without a landlord to whom they owe rent, I would be willing to go to those lands that you say are at the end of the world."

Jokingly, to repay them for their hospitality, and because Andrea gave me a tasty drink of fruit brandy that, heated on the fire, left me a little drunk, I encouraged her by saying, "Your sons, working in those lands the way they do here, would be gentlemen mounted on steeds, and they would have gilded spurs on their boots. And your daughter, as soon as you gave her a dowry, would marry a captain and be styled *doña*." I said I was joking, and yet everything I said was true, because there have even been prostitutes who ended up being ladies after they changed their ways. As for the gilded spurs, there were soldiers who wore them. Who would have predicted that that joke would produce the Order of the Knights of the Golden Spurs, as will be seen in due time?

I could not have asked for better and more modest

Christians. They blessed the bread that they were about to eat with the same devotion as we priests consecrate the Body and Blood of our Lord Jesus Christ. That is how grateful they were for whatever gift the Lord gave them. They walked fifteen miles so as not to miss the Mass on a feast day, and another fifteen to make the return trip, carrying their shoes to keep them from wearing out. From the little bit they had, they paid every *ochavo* of their tithes to the Church, and in no way did they want to allow me to pay them for the care they gave me, although I took care to repay them in other ways.

Not to mention how hard they worked. To produce one pig per year, they broke their backs digging for acorns; their vines were so miserable that if they yielded any grapes it was because of the loving care they lavished on them, doing everything short of wrapping their bodies around them in order to protect them from the frosts; and, at harvest time, they did not know what it was to sleep under a roof, being always at work next to the furrow, sickle in hand, pressing on at full speed to prevent the hailstones from bringing a year of effort and suffering to naught.

I was amazed, and they were amazed by my amazement, for they said that in Soria everyone had to work with comparable diligence, and they thanked God for giving them the health that enabled them to do it. In the days I was under their roof, and by my count they were no fewer than two weeks, I was able to confirm it, because I met their neighbors, who also seemed to me to be hard-working and good Christians, not better than those of other lands but more accustomed to hardship. I think of my fellow Andalusians, who suffered more from hunger but were less willing to work among stones and, as Christians, more fun-loving than the Sorians, but less punctilious.

I met these good people because my hosts spread the word about my stories, and their neighbors also wanted to hear them at the warming fireside. Later they invited me to their houses, all of which were made of fine stone, in the building of which they helped each other, and despite being impoverished, they had a great knack for making it possible to withstand the rigors of winter, which are very severe there. All of them had one large room, with the fire in the middle of it. And the roof was tiled with black slate tiles that, when put carefully in place, made the roof impervious to both snow and water. All of the houses were very clean, and while I was among these good people, they cured me of most of my fevers. They vied with each other in spoiling me, and I returned the favor by celebrating the holy Mass in a small chapel they had, which I believe was dedicated to Saint Procopius, and there was no question that they would all be present; in the case of one grandfather who was more than a hundred years old and who could not manage or cope on his own, four men carried him in on a stretcher.

Accustomed as I was by then to dealing with prelates and cardinals, kings and governors, I found great relief in my conversations with these people, and preaching to them was a particular joy for me. Some of them asked me what they had to do to go to the Indies, but when they calculated the cost, they did not have the money necessary to get even as far as Seville. That is how poor they were. What I most liked about them was that they would not talk to me at all about gold, because their only desire was to work the lands that would be theirs and would later on belong to their children.

I gave them very loving advice, with no ulterior motive, for during that time, between the discouragement I suffered from the cardinal's death and the weakened condition in which the fevers left me, I did not think about business affairs in the Indies at all, and, as I said, the only business I cared about was to be appointed a canon of the cathedral in Seville. For that reason, it was painful to part from them, but winter was already threatening, and I had committed to returning the mule to my brother-in-law Cristóbal.

I am convinced that the mule acted as a secondary mover, according to the scholars of our Order. The Prime Mover for everything that happens is God, who normally works through secondary movers. So that mule, while I was going along, half-lost, leaving Aranda, my head distracted by the fevers, took me to Blas Hernández's farmstead, and I found there, without even realizing it, a possible remedy for the ills of the Indies.

I did not realize it because, weakened as I was by the dregs that the concoctions of the herbalist friar had left in my body, it was already considerable work, mounted on that secondary mover, to find my way to the city of Seville. But when the archbishop, Friar Diego de Deza, persuaded me that I was called not to be a canon or to preach sermons in Lent, but instead to persevere in the matter of the souls that were being lost in the Indies, it dawned on me that the solution was to send good farmworkers there to tame the lands with their work and the souls of the Indians with the example they set as good Christians.

It was like a clarion call that relieved my pain and discouragement, which is why I say that God made use of the mule, as a secondary mover, to take me to where the remedy was.

At the time, I had a very good relationship with Friar Reginaldo Montesino, the brother of the other friar, Antón, who had done my soul so much good, when I was a cleric and encomendero and he denied me absolution. This Friar Reginaldo was more terse in expressing himself than his brother, calmer in every way, but more scholarly in his knowledge of doctrine, because he was one of the good theologians of the Order of Saint Dominic. He was very agitated, because at the time four Franciscan friars had just arrived from Hispaniola, one of whom, Friar Francisco de San Román, said that he had seen with his own eyes how forty thousand Indians had been killed during a foray onto the mainland by some heartless men, ordered by the most heartless of them all, Pedrarias Dávila, using swords and raging dogs. These dogs were mastiffs or hounds that had been trained by their masters to attack Indians, and they even allowed them to eat their flesh. The Indians were so terrified of them that they did not know how to defend themselves, for they never could determine whether they were animals or devils.

Friar Reginaldo insisted that we go to show King Charles (who in that month of November had arrived in Spain from his dominions in Flanders), that we had to activate the plan we had devised with Cardinal Cisneros to stamp out the encomiendas and create Indian villages. But I was no longer in favor of that, for we knew nothing about the commission of Hieronymite friars, and it was even being said that they had written a report in which they argued that Indians were irrational beings, incapable of faith and of taking care of themselves. It is certainly true that the good theologians of Salamanca declared this proposition heretical, but I had seen proof that what the good theologians said had little impact if the bad Spaniards, of whom there were so many in the Indies, said yes with their mouths but with whips kept on treating the Indians as if they were incapable of reasoning. What is more, while the only people who went to the Indies were soldiers, scribes, and gold hunters, the remedy was difficult, because it is difficult for a soldier to be satisfied with his pay and the scribe with his salary, not to mention those who want gold, who regard everything as being too little, as I well know from having been one of the greediest ones.

Man's wealth is in heaven, but if there is any in this world, it is none other than the land that, when it is worked with love, produces fruits that relieve hunger and misery. Is gold edible? Are pearls, or seed pearls?

Thus did I begin to discuss with Friar Reginaldo, and I convinced him that the remedy lay in taking couples of Castilian farmworkers, from the province of Soria, to whom lands would be granted for them to cultivate and, when they were well cultivated, pass on to their children. Friar Reginaldo laughed heartily about the fact that the farmworkers necessarily had to be from Soria, and I gave him my reasons about how they were long-suffering workers, excellent in their manner, and fervent in their piety.

So, as we chatted on, we began to write a petition, in which we said that every Sorian couple would be joined with ten Indians, so that every village would have a Christian couple at its head, who would have to teach the Indians how to cultivate the land, help them become good farmworkers, and also cultivate their souls, to make them good Christians. Friar Reginaldo took what I said very much to heart, and he made it his own with the same enthusiasm I had, but with more learning in theology, for he had that in plenty, and he gave very substantial reasons why each village had to be as we proposed and how it would have its council and its church, well served by a trustworthy cleric or friar. We did not fail to pay attention to how the Indians would have to work, in shifts, in the gold mines, because we knew that whatever plan we made that did not include gold for the Crown would necessarily fail.

We proposed that, at the Crown's expense, the council of every town in Castile that sent a married couple of farmworkers would be required to make a loan to them of twenty thousand *maravedís* with which to buy their hacienda, their farming implements and tools, and the horses or mules that would take them, together with their families, to the city of Seville, where they would embark. The Crown would also guarantee their return after five years, although we were sure that all of them would be so happy and hard-working that none of them would want to return because, among other reasons, the grown sons they took with them would have to marry Indian women, whom they would find exotic at first, especially due to the shape of their faces, which are flatter, but our fathers had also been suspicious of the Moorish women from Africa, and yet they later took a great liking to them, for they were man and woman, and soon, as passion was awakened, the differences would disappear. And the Indian women, having become good Christians like my Tajima, had no reason to envy the women of Castile, whom they even outdid, for they are more docile and obedient.

We talked about this last point at length, because we knew that in the Council of the Indies we would necessarily run up against the rabid opposition of the lawyer Luis Zapata, a pious gentleman but very stubborn, being one of those who would most tenaciously and aggressively argue that the Indians were not rational beings; he invoked a law from the time of the Catholic Kings that provided for sending white slaves to the Indies so that Spaniards would not have to marry Indian women, being people who lacked all reason. It was true that such a law existed, but it had never been applied; my goodness, where did they think they were going to get white slaves? Surely not from among the Moorish women in whom the Portuguese trafficked, who were not very different in color from the Indian women. We pondered, but the one who pondered the most was Friar Reginaldo, who delved into the laws, and in one of the Laws of Burgos it said quite clearly that, having been instructed, the Indians could receive the sacrament of marriage. I cared less about these disquisitions, because as one who had been in the Indies for a very long time, I knew very well how the Spaniards paired up with the Indian women and promptly had children, and the best way to deal with it was to marry them, if they agreed.

This first petition contained much more reasoning and many more proposals, which need not be belabored here, their essence having been explained. We insisted very much to the king on the great benefit that could be gained from all this, first for his soul, because continuing on the road to the destruction of the Indies would have to cause God to call him to strict account; and second, for his treasury, because from the wealth that would be created by the Castilian farmworkers together with the Indians who would become farmworkers, the king would take his share. Furthermore, we argued, the riches of the earth last forever; the years pass, and the fields that have been cultivated well are enhanced and, grateful for the fine treatment they receive, yield more and larger harvests. And because frost and hail are unknown, those lands are very fertile, watered by mighty rivers such as are unknown in Europe and by opportune rains that fall at night, whereas the sun shines during the day, where the granaries would always be so full that the ships could be loaded and sent to Spain, and no corner of Castile would be lacking in bread.

In contrast, those who look for gold and pearls leave nothing but misery behind them. The miners arrive, dig holes in the earth, cut down the trees to build small dams, pollute the streams, and destroy everything that gets in the way of their profit, which always is a flower that blooms for just a day. When I was engaged in such brutish work,

we thought nothing of burning down the forest, if by
doing so we could smooth the way to the veins of gold.
The birds and fruits disappeared with the woods, and starvation came. Not to mention the pearl fisheries, which
they call placers there: such a foul, rotten stench emanated
from the island of Cubagua (to which we will have occasion to return) that only the blacks could bear it.

But on this point we took care to explain that our farmworkers, and the Indian couples who depended on them,
would also search for gold and pearls for the Crown and
to repay loans, but without having to be as destructive as
those who care about nothing else.

Friar Reginaldo developed the principles of the petition, and I put them into words, although in the end we
decided that it would be Friar Reginaldo who would read
it before the Council of the Indies, because clerical habits
were not, in those days, well-advised, for—as in my case
—they had been very much involved in worldly business
matters, more concerned with their own benefits than
the good of souls. The friars, on the other hand, and especially those of Santo Domingo, were highly esteemed
for being unselfish and for having abnegated everything
except saving souls. Our decision was also dictated by
the fact that in the Council of the Indies, as soon as the
most eminent Cardinal Cisneros died, Bishop Rodríguez
de Fonseca regained all his influence; and behind him,
as night follows day, reappeared the secretary, Lope de
Conchillos, both of them competing to be the more contrary to anything I might say, for they knew that I would
certainly be against the encomiendas, from which they
had benefited so much.

I do not know whether it was at, before, or after that time (which is not very relevant) that we received letters from Friar Pedro de Córdoba, who advised us that what we were going to do (for the news of our petition had reached him) we should consider doing for the mainland, which was more unspoiled, with more souls and better land, for all of Hispaniola was half-destroyed. As if things were not going badly enough there, they were made worse by a new smallpox epidemic, more devastating than those that had gone before. As soon as it infected the Indians, they turned red, and with their passion for bathing, they would dive into the rivers and the seas, thinking that the coolness of the water would relieve their itching, but since the cure was worse than the illness, they soon died. They said in those days that only about ten thousand Taínos were left in Hispaniola, and that the island of Cuba was going down the same road.

As far as the blacks are concerned, it is useful to know that there were two classes of them: the *ladinos*, who had been born in Castile as children of slaves, so accustomed to the comforts of being servants in the houses of nobility that nobody wanted them in the Indies, and the *bozales*, who were the ones brought by the Portuguese, roped together, from the coast of Guinea. Some of these were brought to Hispaniola, and because trading in them was authorized by special royal decree, the uneducated people thought that, since trading in them was lawful, it was also lawful to make them work in the mines. I was one of those uneducated people, and I proposed that black slaves should help the community of Castilian and Indian farmworkers in their most demanding work. Thus, in order to relieve those I loved from one evil, I condemned others, who were equally my brothers, to another evil. When I professed as a Dominican, I learned the valid doctrine, and I publicly begged forgiveness for my aberration, advocating for the blacks with the same fervor as I did for the Indians.

But, to continue my account, there is a saying in Seville according to which God always forgives, man sometimes forgives, but Mother Nature never forgives; and that was borne out in the case of the blacks, for because it was against nature to remove them from their lands and set them to work far from their homes and families, in order to relieve the Indians from certain work, what happened was that the Indians were relieved of their lives, because smallpox, which for blacks is a disease that scars their faces, in Indians turned out to be incurably fatal. I have written at length on this subject for the reflection of those who govern nations.

The mainland was named Tierra Firme, and the word *firme* was used because it was the first land that was known to be not an island but a continent. It was directly opposite the island of Trinidad, and the first people who arrived there were in search of pearls; the richest pearl fishing in the Indies was on the island of Cubagua, which was so close to the coast that the Indians reached the continent in their canoes in less than a day. Because they thought that where there were pearls there would be gold not far away, they called it Castile of Gold, but in this they were wrong, and they came upon little gold there. Richer farmlands, however, they could not be, but that did not matter much to those who went there with other intentions.

The Indians who live there are called Cumanagotos, and they are sturdier and fiercer than the islanders, but also good Christians when the gospel is explained to them with love. The first to establish themselves there, as I remember, were the Franciscans and then the Dominicans; they built their missions there, with some vegetable gardens and orchards that were as beautiful as those that came before the original sin in the Earthly Paradise. The prelate, Friar Pedro de Córdoba, therefore advised us to go there with our Castilian farmworkers.

All this beauty came with a misfortune named Pedrarias Dávila, whose lineage made him the lord of Puñoenrostro, in Segovia. It was said of him that he had performed many fine feats of war in Granada and Oran and that, because of them, the Catholic King named him governor and captain general of Tierra Firme. It was also said that he got off to a good start, because he brought with him his wife, Isabel de Bobadilla y Peñalosa, a high-born lady, like someone who is ready to settle in and determined to discharge his duty and accomplish his mission. But it turned out that the mission was to see to it that no one opposed whatever orders he gave, and one of those who paid with his life for that mission was Núñez de Balboa himself, whose great achievement in having discovered the South Sea got him nowhere. Because arrogance was accompanied by envy (both of them capital sins that usually go hand in hand), with Pedrarias unable to tolerate that Núñez de Balboa's glory should put his own in the shade, he set a trap for him and, capitalizing on a perfidious letter, made him come to Acla, where he accused him of treason for no reason other than his own insanity; and right there, in front of him and for no reason, he dictated a death sentence, signed it with his own hand, and ordered him to be executed in the central square of Acla, where the throat of the illustrious discoverer was cut in the presence of Pedrarias Dávila himself, who quite openly took pleasure in the death of the man who was able to overshadow him in the conquest of the lands north of Darién. If he showed so little mercy for one who had done more for the glory of Castile than he had, one can only imagine how much mercy he would show for the Indians, whom he had to pacify. In every foray he made against them, he began by beheading all the caciques and anyone who had war feathers on his head, and he made the rest of them slaves for his pearl fisheries or for trading them with the residents of Hispaniola. When he found Indians who had arrows the tips of which were coated with curare, which is the poison that they use in defending themselves, he ordered their hands to be cut off, saying that it was a very treacherous practice that deserved exceptional punishment. He later wrote letters to the king, who by then was also Holy Roman Emperor Charles V, saying that all his territories were very peaceful and had submitted to His Majesty. And the letters that the Franciscans and Dominicans sent complaining about his great lack of piety had little effect, because Pedrarias was very much under the protection of Bishop Fonseca and his mischief-maker secretary, Conchillos.

Given all that, we declared very clearly in our petition that there could be as many inspectors as His Majesty would find appropriate, to gather the recollections of the farmworkers who had come to the Indies and to confirm what we said we would do in our petition; but in the territories that were granted to us, there would be no higher authority than ours. We set that as a *conditio sine qua non*, because we had had regrettable experience with plans that were to be carried out by others, even if they were as pious as the Hieronymite friars. Even more if they depended on the insanity of Pedrarias Dávila or people of similar ilk.

In this first petition, which we titled "A Remedy for the Continental New World", we asked for three thousand miles of the northern coastline, along which a fortress would be built every three hundred miles, along with other fortresses inland, in a triangle, and each fortress would have room for a Christian village of our Castilian and Indian farmworkers; our request was excessive, which was the custom because the Council of the Indies always granted less than what was requested.

We wanted the fortresses in order to protect ourselves more from the Spaniards than from the Indians. I say the Spaniards, but worse still were the English, French, and Dutch pirates, who as soon as they smelled riches in a colony attacked it. The Indians, however, according to the news that reached us from the Franciscans and the Dominicans, if one approached them in peace, replied in kind; Friar Pedro de Córdoba recounted at great length the excellent qualities of the mission they had in Chichiribichi, a valley watered by the Cumaná River, as productive of fruits as it was of souls.

We had a very apt idea along these lines, which was that, for the first hundred farmworkers who established themselves in the manner specified, cultivated the land with the love it deserved, and converted Indians to Christianity in peace with the example of their industriousness and the uprightness of their conduct and without forcing them, and if they paid the fifth due to the king, generously and when it was due, these farmworkers would be ennobled by being made Knights of the Golden Spurs. The idea came to me when I recalled the jokes I used to make with Blas Hernández about how his sons would be gentlemen mounted on steeds and would wear boots with golden spurs. This time it was not a joke but a very well-founded concept, because those gentlemen would wear a habit, like those of the military orders, but with a mission of peace and not war, so the habit would resemble those of the friars whom the Indians respected so much, in order to enhance their reception. It would be white on the outside, with red crosses in the same form and color as those of Calatrava, except that each cross would be adorned with some graceful, jagged little branches. They would not carry a sword at their waist but, rather, a leather strap with a cross suspended from it. We included all this detail in the petition, with an engraving that depicted it, and Friar Reginaldo described it very well, reasoning that kings bestow titles of nobility with less justification, and although the farmworkers were plebeians, they stopped being so when they rendered such full service to the Crown. And if those who conquered territory by force were made counts and marquises, there was greater reason to do the same with those who conquered for God and the king with love and decorum.

Later on, some who wrote about the Indies, such as López de Gómara, who had never even set foot there, like the ignoramuses they were, made fun of the Knights of the Golden Spurs and their white habits with crosses and little jagged branches, without realizing how important it was that the Indians not confuse them with the Spaniards of Pedrarias Dávila and others of that ilk who were wreaking devastation wherever they went.

The way I tell this story, it seems that day after day we had nothing to do but write the petition, but the fact is that we spent over a year on it, almost two years, because it is one thing to draw up documents and quite another to get results. And the whole purpose of the petition was to convey it to King Charles, without forgetting that first it would have to pass through the Council of the Indies, and Bishop Fonseca and his cronies, who were lying in wait for us.

When it came to the comings and goings of the court, the work fell to me, being more familiar with its duplicities than Friar Reginaldo. It is true that I had letters from the superiors of the Order of Saint Dominic that opened all doors for me, and the first one I knocked on was that of the great chancellor of the king, Jean le Sauvage, who was Flemish and the minister of Indian affairs. When I recounted to him what was happening there, and the forays that Pedrarias Dávila made on the coast of Cumaná, he clutched his head with his hands and agreed with me completely.

The great chancellor was a man of urbane manners, who spoke with a touch of fatigue and who sometimes said yes to avoid the need to speak at length. As a recent arrival from Flanders, he expressed himself with difficulty in Castilian, but luckily for me he was a good Latinist, and we understood each other in that language. Fat as the people of that country are, he suffered a good deal from the heat of the Castilian plateau, and he was amazed that it should be even hotter in the Indies and that we had the energy to mount expeditions of conquest in such hot places. Like the other Flemish courtiers that King Charles brought with him, he was resentful of the nobles of Castile, and he began to listen with pleasure to what I was telling him about the bad treatment of the Indians; because he told me that it should be ended, I encouraged him in that view, encouragement that he accepted because it suited him, and it seemed that we Spaniards were the only ones who committed evil deeds.

I emphasized to him that evil is part of the human condition, damaged as we are by original sin, and that all men, left to their own devices, tended to seek what most benefited them, without considering the damage they did. And that those in authority were placed there by God to remedy such abuses. I took care not to offend him, for we very much needed his help, but in order to tell the whole truth, I explained to him that the Germans who sailed up and down the coast of Cumaná were, by far, worse than the Spaniards. The Germans did not hesitate at all to seize Indian women, and later, if they left them pregnant, they would kill them so as not to have children by them, for they considered it a dishonor. Think about this outrageous manner of reasoning. I saw Spaniards kill pregnant Indian women, but not if they were the ones who had impregnated them, because it is against nature that a father should kill the fruit of his seed. I have already said that the Spaniards did not hesitate to marry Indian women when they had reasons that made it advisable; but in all the many years that I spent in the Indies (which now add up to more than sixty) I never saw a German, Englishman, or Frenchman who married an Indian woman; nor did I find anyone among them like Pedro de Rentería, Friar Montesino, or Friar Pedro de Córdoba, who sought to do nothing but establish the kingdom of God in those lands.

I explained this to him, but he understood it in a way that suited him, and I did not protest, for never before had a cleric who lacked money and erudition, as I did at the time, been treated with such deference by someone who was subject to the orders of no one other than the king. That is what I thought, although later it turned out that we also had to deal with Bishop Rodríguez de Fonseca, because he was the president of the council. I made it clear to the chancellor that the bishop necessarily opposed anything that originated with me, but the former emphatically insisted that I pay the latter a visit, for it was customary for the president to know beforehand what issues were to be presented to the council.

We were in Valladolid at the time, where I was received by Rodríguez de Fonseca, whom, despite his being the bishop of Burgos, I had never seen in his diocese; he resided where the monarch did, on account of his intrigues, and because at that time he was in the city of Pisuerga, he received me there, with very good manners, not because he cared at all about me personally, but because he knew that good theologians and Cardinal Adriano himself (who would soon become the pope) stood behind me, all of them sharing the feeling that the Indians should be acknowledged as having the power of reason and be treated as such.

He maintained his good manners until we reached the proposal that the royal officials would have an obligation to support the farmworkers until the first harvest, which would take a year, because to do otherwise would be to send them to the Indies to perish. Upon hearing a statement so founded in reason, the bishop leapt up with this outburst: "What, support farmworkers at the expense of the Crown? When has such a piece of foolishness ever been seen before? That would require the king to spend more money on your farmworkers than it would cost to mount an armada of twenty thousand men."

He said it with great conviction because the lord bishop was much more experienced in mounting armadas than he was in celebrating pontifical Masses.

And that is where peace came to an end because I, who have a suddenly volatile and inopportune temper, immediately replied: "Then what is it that your lordship wants? That I act as a bullock and lead the Christians to the bullring, unprotected, to perish there? Is it not enough that the Indians should be dying there, and now in addition we want to do the same with the Christians?"

We said some very angry things to each other, but because I had little to lose, I did not yield; Lope de Conchillos, the biggest troublemaker of them all but very unctuous in the way he spoke, appeared when he heard us raise our voices and attempted to arrange a peace. Oh, what a pity that such great matters should be in such small hands! What purpose could a twenty-thousand-man armada serve other than to depopulate the islands even more? If they sent the farmworkers that I requested, however, Hispaniola would be populated by no fewer than two hundred thousand inhabitants, with the Castilians well spread among the Indians, and the king of France would not dare show himself within six hundred miles of it. In contrast, he is constantly sending his pirates to commit their depredations, and, to defend against them, it costs the Crown in one year ten times what I was asking it to pay just once.

Friar Reginaldo reprimanded me for these attacks, but he helped me persevere and insisted that I had to visit the other members of the council to get their support when the matter was brought before them. That is what I did, and I learned a great deal in those years that served me well.

One person I visited, the lawyer Francisco de Aguirre, was one of the most illustrious Basques at the court. He was a member of the Royal Council and the Inquisition, and he had been the executor of the Catholic Queen, for which he was highly esteemed. A man who was very much in God's service, he listened to me patiently but with a sullen demeanor, and when I finished, he reproached me: "Does it seem right to you,

Father, that in order to defend the Indians you should promise an income to the king and want secular honors for your farmworkers? I myself do not believe that the preaching of the gospel can be mixed with human interests. In faith, Father, I do not find what you've told me very edifying."

He was so right in what he said that he would have left me speechless if it were not for the fact that I do not know what it is to be speechless. About my being speechless, Friar Pedro de Córdoba said that if they let me talk, they would never hang me. As others have the gift of prophecy, I have that of not keeping quiet, and sometimes people agree with me just to stop having to listen; but Thomas à Kempis correctly says that talking a lot is, in itself, more a tiresome virtue than a useful one.

"Sir," I replied, "if you were to see our Lord Jesus Christ being abused, would you not beg urgently for him to be given to you so that you could serve him and comfort him as the good Christian you are?"

"Yes, certainly," he answered, still frowning.

"And if they did not want to give him to you graciously," I went on, "but rather wanted to sell him, would you not buy him?"

"Without a doubt, yes, I would buy him."

"Well, that very same thing is what I'm doing", I concluded; "I have left Jesus Christ, our God, in the Indies, being slapped and crucified not once but thousands of times, because that is what they are doing there when they deprive the Indians of their lives without any chance of faith or sacraments. I have begged and pleaded with the Council of the King many times to put a stop to this tormenting of Jesus Christ in the person of those poor, ill-fated people, and although they say yes, they will, afterward they don't do it. Now, the religious, the servants of God, have begun to preach the gospel on the continent of the New World, but upon the arrival there of the bad Spaniards, who think only in terms of invading and looting, the ill-fated ones, seeing their bad example, blaspheme the name of Christ. But since the friars cannot occupy lands and deprive the king of income from them, others have to cultivate them, with the help of the Indians, as equals and not as slaves."

The lawyer Aguirre, like the very noble man he was, took me in his arms, and from then on, he was my most faithful ally and among those who helped me the most to move the petition forward.

I say the petition, but I no longer remember which one made progress or the number of meetings the Council of the Indies had to hold to accomplish what we were proposing. A session would begin and then always have to be interrupted when news of some trivial matter in France would arrive. I was wasting away watching how such very wise people turned their backs on thousands of souls and great wealth in the New World and, at the same time, never tired of arguing for hours over the most negligible frontier town with respect to which we cared very little about what side of the border it was on. And on one occasion, when I got carried away by my bad temper, I protested, "What do we care about France?"; people who were very fond of me warned me that, for my saying such a thing, my bones could end up in prison;

but no one went to prison for killing or enslaving Indians.

I have suffered a great deal on those seas, which are
sometimes so treacherous, for the bluer and calmer they
are, the more hidden danger there is that a ship and its
crew will be swallowed up by a powerful gust of wind.
And there are accounts of cases in which, when the air
is still and the sea is calm, a ship disappears and is never
seen or heard from again. Not to mention that inland, in
the jungles in which you can walk for a week without
seeing the sun, I once tried to ford a reedbed (this was in
Cuba) and found myself bogged down in a marsh where,
before I knew it, I was up to my chest in quicksand.
The dark sands were sucking me down, very gently, as
in a game, which I knew was one of inexorable death,
and I started to pray what our Mother the Church pre-
scribes for such situations. At the same time, I begged for
a miracle, and the Virgin Mary offered me a branch of a
nearby silk-cotton tree; it seemed so fragile that I feared
it would snap as soon as I clutched at it. But when the
sands reached my chin, I did clutch at it, thereby saving
my life. We who preached the gospel were surrounded
by so many miracles that we barely talked about them.

And the hunger we endured, the days without eating
and hardly drinking; the sleepless nights for fear of wild
animals, tending the fire; I do not want to talk about them
because other chroniclers have described them better than
I can. Besides, all these sufferings are nothing compared
with what I went through in the years that I pursued the
Council of the Indies, the Council of the King, and all
their chancellors and officials who had to have their say

and turned out to be, like the demoniacs of Gerasa, innumerable. I will just say that we began to read the first petition in 1517, a few days before the Lord's Nativity, and the final authorization was given in the spring of 1520, when King Charles sailed, again, for Germany. And what we had begun in Valladolid came to a conclusion in La Coruña, from which our lord and king embarked. During that time, I had to go from one place to another, always on the back of the borrowed mule, from Valladolid to Zaragoza, then to Barcelona, and finally to La Coruña. While he could, Friar Reginaldo Montesino accompanied me, but his superiors eventually got tired of the to-ing and fro-ing and called him back to perform other tasks for the Order, so I was left alone. That relieved the pains of our long-suffering pocketbooks, because Friar Reginaldo's was empty, and both of us had to make do with the loan that my sister's husband made to me.

We began the reading in Valladolid, and, as we had agreed, Friar Reginaldo did it, in his unhurried voice and with that wealth of doctrine with which he was able to reply to those who contradicted him. The sessions were held in a large hall with fine seats for the members of the council and the comfortable warmth provided by braziers that burned day and night, for it was a year of heavy snow. It was perhaps on the third day that I saw, very painfully, that some of the Flemish that we thought were very much on our side did not pay as much attention as such an important debate deserved, and they entered and left the hall on the smallest pretext. Or their secretaries came in to give them messages that had nothing to do with what was being discussed. We soon understood that they were not doing so out of malice but, rather, on account of their great fussiness about what they ate and drank; therefore, not far from the hall, they had a refectory that was very well-stocked.

One afternoon, after the midday meal (which the Flemish usually took at the hour of the Angelus), a debate began over whether the idea of sending farmworkers to the Indies was a new one or an old one, and Fonseca boasted that he had already tested it and no one had wanted to go. For that reason, they now sent fine gentlemen to teach the Indians how to work. It goes without saying that my blood was boiling when I heard such talk. Friar Reginaldo answered him with his usual gentleness, in such a cadence that the Flemish, between the torpor induced by the midday meal and the warmth and comfort of their seats, began to nod, as though in agreement, to disguise the fact that they were dozing. Except for the chancellor, Gattinara, who was the most prominent of all of them, who openly and frankly set himself to sleeping and snoring, from which no one, out of care for his dignity, dared to wake him.

Bishop Fonseca and his disciple Conchillos could barely conceal the delight with which they saw the sleepiness that our disquisitions produced in men whom we esteemed and considered our supporters. And the bishop insistently questioned the sending of farmworkers when there were noble and accomplished gentlemen in the Indies who could look after the king's affairs.

Friar Reginaldo answered him politely and prudently, but having reached this point, believing that the council members should hear a few other things, I exclaimed in a thundering voice: "I send you as sheep among wolves to tame them and bring them to Christ!"

Because they were all pious men, hearing the holy gospel shook them out of their slumber and even Chancellor Gattinara stopped snoring. They looked at me dumbfounded, thinking I was insane, and I went on: "I send you as sheep among wolves, says the Lord." And I added angrily, speaking to the president and the council members on his side: "Why do you, instead of sending sheep who could convert the wolves, send ravenous wolves, cruel tyrants, who waste, destroy, and scandalize the sheep and throw them to the winds?"

That was the end of siestas that afternoon, because we fell into a heated quarrel, and I was the one who shouted the most, although very much in conformity with what the gospel said, about how we had to treat our brothers the Indians. Many on the council came over to my side of the argument, and from that day on Bishop Fonseca took care not to be confrontational in the sessions, and he carried on all his intrigues behind my back.

I think that the intrigue that did me the most damage was the one that the bishop carried on using Luis Berrio, who began as my aide and ended as a traitor.

CHAPTER XI

THE TREASON OF LUIS BERRIO

Luis Berrio was from the province of Antequera, a man of little education but with a certain knack for navigating troubled situations. I met him in Zaragoza, in the summer of 1518, when I spent six months waiting to be called by the council, which at the time was in that city, but they only called me to delay things further, and I was on the brink of despair, even though my friends on the council told me that my project would certainly prosper.

This Luis Berrio knew how to present himself as a humble and well-mannered man, although because he was a little cross-eyed it was impossible to follow his gaze, so he could say one thing with his mouth and another with his eyes. He told me that he came from a region of good farmers (around Antequera) and that he very much agreed with my view of the good that those men could do in the lands that were as rich as they were neglected. He explained to me that he was responsible for the support of his widowed mother and that a cousin of hers was a notary of the council and could use his influence to bring to life the dossier that had been dozing there. All he would want to gain was a salary as my aide, for the support of his mother, and he was prepared to set sail for the Indies.

What he said about his cousin the notary turned out to be true, and his ability to dust off the dossier seemed likely to be true as well, because it has been proved that, on occasion, what the king cannot do a household servant can. As for his widowed mother, how that turned out will soon be clear.

Whether it was thanks to the cousin or because its time had come, the fact is that on October 12 of that year, when the twenty-sixth anniversary of the glorious discovery of the Indies was being commemorated, the petition that Montesino and the cleric writing this account had presented the previous year was approved. It emerged somewhat amended, as will be seen, but in substance it seemed that it would serve; the miles along the coast in which we would be establishing the communities of farmers were reduced to eighteen hundred, and in that respect we emerged with a good result. The most fortunate fact was that no limit was placed on the number of farmers that we could send, and I calculated that they amounted to three thousand. I could not contain my joy, certain as I was that three thousand of those good men would do more for the Crown and all of Christianity than three thousand of the fleets that Bishop Fonseca admired so much. I already imagined the whole northern region transformed into an orchard or garden, the Castilians working the land, and the Indians learning from them, with their respective children marrying each other, for the greater glory of God and the good of their souls. At the same time, I saw myself as being freed from the need to plead with those functionaries and sailing again through the blue southern waters to reach the riverbanks that were so very green and I loved so much. My dream was that that was how to demonstrate that the best way to pacify the Indies and maintain their wealth of men and women was to put them to work instead of plundering them for the benefit of a few; and this example would put an end to governors who thought only in terms of forays aimed at plundering and pillaging.

The Dominican Fathers shared my joy, and they celebrated a solemn thanksgiving Te Deum in their monastery in Zaragoza. They insisted that I exercise great care in the selection of those who were to go to the mainland, because much depended on getting it right. I was working on it and quickly prepared the mule to take the road to Soria. Meanwhile, Berrio strutted about as though the achievement had been his (after what Friar Reginaldo and that cleric had done), and I said nothing because it turned out that he had negotiated the salaries very shrewdly, and at the point we had reached, because I was living on the charity of a few others, that was not a trivial matter.

The result of this negotiation was that, by royal dictate, each of us was given a daily salary of 150 *maravedís*, and although it was notable that a subordinate would be paid the same as his superior, I thought it was a good thing because he was in great need of it. Afterward, by royal decree of November 1518, they granted me fifty ducats of gold for the work I had already done, without having been paid an *ochavo*, and with that I was able to pay the debt that I owed my brother-in-law, which was weighing heavily on my conscience.

On October 13, 1518, I received nine royal decrees that, because they were issued by His Majesty, required complete obedience, and they ordered all the authorities of Castile to help me recruit farmers to populate the Indies. I did not have time to set the work described there in motion, after the anxiety of my long wait and the trip to Soria, so I would arrive in a place, gather together its people in the church, and announce the king's intentions, which were: first, to populate those lands; second, to form such a population for the happiness, fertility, health, and resources of the natives; and third, I described to them the mercies that the king had granted them for doing so, both their designation as Knights of the Golden Spurs and the material benefits from the lands they would receive; for which, for less work than they were doing in Spain, they would be blessed in this world.

So much did this lift up their hearts that, in Berlanga, of the two hundred residents of the town, seventy enlisted. But it was not enough that they wanted to do so; they had to be examined, a task in which Luis Berrio helped me, and that was when I began to notice that the task did not interest him much, as though he took it amiss that he should be taking orders from me. I also summoned Blas Hernández and his children, the Sorians who cured me of the fevers I contracted in Aranda de Duero, and they, because they knew their countrymen well, were of great help to me in determining the intentions of those who wanted to go to populate the lands.

I remember one elderly man, seventy years old and the father of seventeen children, who was among the first to enlist, and when I saw him, I could not but ask him: "Father, why do you want to go to the Indies, being so old and so tired?" "By my faith, Sir," he answered, "because when I die I want to leave my children blessed in a free land."

Tears came to my eyes, and thinking that, if he was capable of dying far from his home for the good of his children, he would have to be a good Christian, I ordered that he be enlisted despite his very advanced age.

But this good old man was right to want a free and blessed land for his children, for Berlanga was not that, as I was able to verify on my third day there.

I was already suspicious about the fact that those who enlisted asked me not to let it be known, and they held secret meetings among themselves in preparation for the voyage, not in their councils, but behind haystacks and in other places where their words could not be overheard. I soon learned the reason for so much secrecy; at noon on the third day, a squire of the constable of Berlanga, who owned those lands, presented himself to me and in the name of his master ordered me to leave them. Seeing that I was a cleric with a well-worn cassock, because I had no other, he spoke to me with a haughtiness that plebeians use because they think it shows they have some power. I listened to him with ostensible meekness but with internal fury, because I quite feared the rogue's intentions.

The constable of Berlanga, like other such men in Castile, wanted to go on being a feudal lord, and he also wanted his farmworkers to continue to be his serfs; these feudal lords fought tooth and nail to defend their position, for it was with the work of those unfortunate farmworkers that they maintained their luxurious living, their wars, and their numerous bastard children.

I waited until the fool finished talking and then showed him the royal decrees that authorized me to recruit as I was doing, warning him that if he opposed anything that His Majesty ordered, I would have to order that he be hanged for treason. The man's face went ashen and, transforming his haughtiness into humility, he told me that he was just speaking for his lord and master, who at that moment was celebrating Easter with the bishop of Osma, in Berlanga itself, which was twenty-one miles from where we were, and I set out in that direction.

The bishop of Osma knew about me, and he explained to the constable who I was, and I think that saved me from being beaten and run out of his lands, because the constable, like the courtier that he was, was very used to being unafraid of royal decrees and to finding a way of not fulfilling them. On that occasion, he told me that His Majesty's wishes seemed to him to be very praiseworthy, but that I should go to other lands to look for farmers, because they were very scarce in his, and the few who were there were very happy in his service. (That was why they enlisted to go to the Indies, of course.)

By then I had been toughened up by holding my ground against people of higher birth than the constable, and I did not give an inch regarding my right to recruit; the bishop of Osma hemmed and hawed, wanting to please us both, because although he saw that I was a cleric, and one of the poorest, he knew how many good theologians supported what I was saying.

We had this argument in the atrium of the church in Berlanga, and the constable was full of eagerness to take me to his palace for our midday meal, as though by pleasing my palate he would surely convince me there of what was contrary to nature and the royal orders that it had cost me so much to obtain. When he saw that no solution was possible, with no respect for the presence of the bishop of Osma, he told me to go to hell and threatened me that I would leave empty-handed, no matter how many royal decrees I had.

And he succeeded. He ordered it to be proclaimed everywhere that anyone who bought belongings from those who had enlisted to go to the Indies would lose them. He could do such a tyrannical thing because of a proclamation that dated from the times of the Visigothic kings, and for one reason or another many of those who had enlisted withdrew, because their belongings were worth up to a hundred thousand *maravedís* (which at the time and in that area was a great deal of money), and they and their parents, grandparents and even great-grandparents had had to work to acquire those belongings.

A lust for money is worse than a lust for flesh, for I have known very lecherous men who have turned chaste from one day to the next or who, under the burden of the years, have lost their capacity for sin. But as far as wealth is concerned, the older they get, the more they cling to it, and they do not mind risking their soul to keep it. News of the success of the constable's threat spread throughout those lands, and all the lords of similar places conspired to threaten the workers who wanted to go to the Indies. One of them, from Almazán, who was very mean and stingy, threatened a farmer who was enlisting to take away from his elderly father his job as a shepherd, the only job he could still do.

I was wrestling with these difficulties, seeing that the greed of the lords put the Tierra Firme project in danger, when Luis Berrio came and stabbed me where it would hurt me the most.

He began by saying that Soria was a bad region from which to recruit farmworkers and that in his region, Andalusia, we would not have to deal with so many problems, because the lords there were of a different character. I told him he was right about that, at the same time that I explained that the workers, too, were of a different character; I knew the Indies well and understood that those who worked those lands had to be like the ones in Soria, very skilled at wielding the pick, while the Andalusians were accustomed to knocking olives from the trees; we therefore had to be patient and use the royal decrees to overcome the resistance of the tyrannical lords.

In pursuit of some help, we returned to Zaragoza, and Berrio promptly found it in the person of Bishop Fonseca: unfortunately for me, Berrio ran into him and told him about how I would not let him go to Andalusia to recruit workers. "Why is that?"—he who loved me so much asked with surprise—"Do you need his company to do your duty?" "Sir," Berrio answered, "I can do nothing without the cleric, because the decree that I have says that I must go with him and do as he says." Thinking about the fact that I should be able to wield such power clouded Fonseca's judgment, and right then and there, without respecting what the king had signed, ordered the decree to be amended, crossing it out and in its place giving Berrio the power to recruit on his own. And as if to encourage him to stop obeying me, he provided a healthy number of ducats for him to carry out his duties. I learned about all this when it was too late to repair the harm that had been done, because Berrio took his decree and money and without saying anything to me showed up in Antequera.

Thus a man who had left there a few years before as a squire without anyone to serve returned as a great lord, with a purse full of doubloons. I am not saying that there were no good farmworkers in Antequera, but the ones Berrio recruited were not among them, because he began with those who were close to him, all of them ne'er-do-wells, barflies, patrons of prostitutes, and ruffians. His widowed mother ended up being a bawd who was very well-known throughout Andalusia.

If this Berrio had been as impelled to do good as he was to do harm, we would have done better. In the blink of an eye, he had recruited two hundred people from Antequera, who were on their way to Seville to take ship, and what a rabble they were, for in their recruitment he got help from a concubine he picked up in passing (according to what I was told, she was a beautiful woman who picked his pockets almost clean) and his own mother, the bawd. He made the real farmworkers, who numbered no more than thirty, pay him five thousand *maravedís* each, which he pocketed for himself or his concubine.

I first got word from a relative in Seville, an official of the council, who told me that, invoking a royal decree that included my name, two hundred farmworkers from Antequera had set sail for Hispaniola. I never heard from Berrio again, but I did hear about the shady deal that

he struck with Bishop Fonseca, and I protested against
that with all my strength, but it did me little good because those who could have backed me up, the king and
his chancellors, were in France with their usual quarrels,
and meanwhile, the men from Antequera were dying of
hunger in the Indies. I was afraid of this, for when they
arrived in Hispaniola, it had been sucked dry, and they
were so lacking in provisions and in tools and equipment
with which to earn a living that they were doomed to
perish.

I soon received letters from the Dominican Fathers
in Santo Domingo describing how, of the two hundred
farmworkers, some had died, others were in hospital, but
most of them had taken up stealing Indians in the company of the usual miscreants. But the letters also said that,
if I sent resources without delay, it would be possible to
salvage something; I protested so much in every court
that I got some ninety thousand arrobas of flour and over
twenty thousand arrobas of wine for these unfortunate
people. When two hundred men were being sent to their
doom, a ship was readily available; but when we wanted
to send them something to eat, it took two months, and
by the time the provisions arrived at the island, the officials of Hispaniola said that there was no trace of them.

Thus ended Berrio's feat, and the only ones who got
rich from what it cost were the officials who sold the provisions that were meant for the people from Antequera.

Bishop Fonseca and Lope de Conchillos, despite being
most to blame for the disaster, especially the first one,
said left and right that it had been proved that it would
not be feasible to send farmworkers to the Indies. What

was clear to me was that I could not send anyone not chosen by me and that I could not do so unless the king ordered them to be supplied, for at least a year, with lodgings and food, because as thin as they were when they arrived, having been through the travails of the voyage, and some of them being ill, they would surely die.

Because neither Chancellor Gattinara nor anyone who was a confidant of the king gave me any guarantees in that respect, with a lot of heartache (but to the great joy of those in Fonseca's retinue), I publicly renounced the project. Blas Hernández and the other farmworkers from Soria, who were still ready to go there, could do nothing but cry, but I showed them that I could not repay their friendship by sending lambs to the slaughter.

We were already approaching the end of 1519, and I do not remember that I did anything productive during that year because everything I had in me was consumed in lamenting what had happened. I thought what had happened was God's punishment for my bad past life, because I was one of the first to abuse the Indians, and now, in wanting to atone for it, I was unable to make any amends at all, and on top of that I hurt other Christians who were in no way to blame. Or, as in the case of the ones from Antequera, who had been on the path of sin in their homeland, I was sending them to a place where that path was even wider.

Luckily, I had a Dominican confessor at the time, named Friar Abundio de Betanzos, who was very severe, of sound doctrine, not very familiar with the Indies, but very well versed in souls. He made me see that it was

foolish of me to think that way, because that was not
the manner in which God punished sinners. Since Friar
Abundio usually assigned very heavy penances, I tried to
free myself from such thoughts, and that way I calmed
my spirits.

At Christmas of that year, I was blessed with a great
peace because I believed I understood that God was asking me to leave behind the court intrigues, in which I
was doing so badly, and to return to the Indies to preach
the gospel and make up with love for the damage that I
had done to the Indians before.

But my good Dominican brothers did not let me take
that path, either; when I wrote to propose it to their
prelate in Hispaniola, my beloved Friar Pedro de Córdoba,
he answered me by return mail with a very severe letter,
in which he told me that the peace I said I had came,
not from God, but from the devil. How could it be that
God would ask that so many years of suffering should
have been spent in the chancelleries and that such good
friendships as the ones I had made in them should serve
for nothing? How could I waste the esteem in which I
was held by the chancellors of the king, and by Cardinal
Adriano himself, who was always ready to lend an ear to
my grievances? At the same time, the friar recounted how
the abuses continued, with the treasurer, Miguel de Pasamonte, the leader of the chorus for Bishop Fonseca in Hispaniola, at the head of all who were more and more committed to the flourishing of the abominable encomiendas?
Since they did not have Indians to sustain them, for there
were now hardly any Taínos and Lucayans left, no better
solution occurred to them than to make forays into the

islands near to the mainland, and under the pretext that the Indians there were Caribs and ate human flesh, they captured them as slaves. But they did not do it just every now and then, as they had done when I was there, but rather with fleets dedicated to nothing but that, in which the leading actors were one Gonzalo de Ocampo, whose tastes I knew well, and another man named Antonio Flores, the chief administrator of the island of Cubagua.

Friar Pedro de Córdoba insisted emphatically that I not think any more about going to the islands, because they were so bereft of Indians and so full of corrupt bureaucrats and other malfeasants, that anyone who went there would be infected with that evil; that I should just look at the Tierra Firme, which had turned out to be a continent like no other in the whole known world. Being fond of adages, he reminded me that Rome was not built in a day, and that one should not bite off more than he can chew, cautioning me not to bring thousands of farmworkers at a time but, rather, to be patient and begin with a few, because achieving a small but good result was better than making a haphazard attempt to achieve a large one, as had happened to me when I placed my confidence in Luis Berrio. As far as the lands were concerned, he advised me to content myself with a small but good part of the coastline, without aspiring to take on a hemisphere, for no matter how small the territory that was given us, there was so much work to do there with souls and other riches that, with God's help, we would surely be the marvel of the world.

We have a custom in Andalusia by which, in a bullfight, if the bulls turn out to be docile, their necks are pierced with little darts dipped in burning powder, and that way they are provoked to fight with spirit. This is the effect that the letter from the prelate of Santo Domingo had on me; I lost my tranquility and could not sleep, about which I cared not a bit because it gave me immense joy to return to the arena. Going back to the example of fire: if a man is branded with a red-hot iron, he will be a slave for life to the man who branded him. In my case, I had been branded by Christ himself, who is the only one who has the right to do so, and I was his slave forever. And when I wanted to shake off the branding iron, our Lord had good servants who came to subject me to it more firmly.

The king was in Barcelona at that time, and I went there, this time with some money lent me by the Sorian Blas Hernández, who would have given his life for the success of my project. God eventually paid him for his generosity, as we will see; I say God because I do not remember having paid him back the two thousand *maravedís* I owed him, which represented for him many years of work without spending a penny.

Things could not have gotten off to a worse start in that supremely beautiful Mediterranean city. Friar Juan de Quevedo, a Franciscan and a good preacher, with so many merits that he ended up being consecrated bishop of the Indies, had just arrived in Barcelona from Hispaniola. A man of upright intentions, he succeeded in reconciling Pedrarias Dávila and Núñez de Balboa, who had been enemies, and toward that end he celebrated the betrothal of one of Pedrarias' daughters to the discoverer of the South

Sea. But, as I have described, it did Balboa little good, because his fierce father-in-law ultimately cut off his head without a care for the fact that the latter was the father of his grandchildren. From then on, Bishop Quevedo was also against Pedrarias Dávila and among those who denounced his excesses.

But because he was one of the prelates who understood that it was helpful to the dioceses to have funds with which to build churches and schools, he was one of those who got his share of the spoils from the forays by Pedrarias' gang in search of Indians, pearls, and gold in the mines. What a way to generate tithes for the Church founded by Jesus Christ!

Unfortunately for me, on his way to Spain, he came through Cuba, on a pastoral visit, and there Diego de Velázquez, governor of the island at the time, spoke very ill of me, telling him how I wanted to free the Indians so that they could continue to be pagans as well as to end the encomiendas, which was tantamount to putting an end to the king's dominion over those islands. The bishop, a man of advanced age, perhaps with his mental faculties darkened by the years, believed Diego de Velázquez and promised him that, as soon as he arrived in Spain, he would do everything in his power to eject this bad cleric from the court.

And he came across me as soon as he arrived in Barcelona, for God arranges such things in that way. It was like this: Friar Juan de Quevedo was invited to the midday meal in the castle that was occupied by the bishop of Badajóz in Molins, near Barcelona, where we clerics were all very well received and tried to cultivate the bishop's friendship because of the high esteem in which he was held by the king. When I presented myself there, after the meal, the two bishops, along with the second admiral of the Indies (Diego Colón) and another person whom I don't remember, were playing a game at the table while waiting for a visit that the bishop of Badajóz had to make to the king. I kept myself slightly apart, along with other courtiers, so as not to distract them from their respectable recreation; but when I learned who the prelate was that was participating in the game, it seemed to me that I was obliged to approach him. I asked the host for permission to approach Friar Quevedo, and when I received it, I did so, kissing his hands and saying very respectfully, "Sir, on account of the role that it has fallen to me to play in the Indies, I consider myself obliged and honored to kiss the hands of Your Eminence."

I believe that he knew very well who I was, but as if he would not trust my reply, he asked Juan Samano, an official of the Indies who was present there, "Who is this Father?" His interlocutor replied, "Señor Las Casas, Your Reverence."

He looked me up and down, as though he was surprised at who I was, and he said to me with more than just a touch of arrogance, "I have brought a good sermon with me, Señor Las Casas, to preach to you."

I was seized by the anger that works against me so much, and with no less arrogance I replied, "I will be honored, Sir, to hear you preach, but I assure you that I, too, have prepared a couple of sermons on the treatment of the Indians, which may be worth more to you than the money you are making at their expense."

There was a deep silence, which did not last very long because everyone who dealt with court matters was accustomed to saying very harsh things to each other.

I looked at the bishop of Badajóz out of the corner of my eye, because I did not at all want to offend him in his own house, given the high standing he had with the king; I saw that he was washing his hands of the matter, as though he were absorbed in his card game, but my reply did not appear to me to have displeased him, because it was good doctrine with regard to the Indians. The bishop of the Indies said to me, very solemnly, "You have lost your way, Father, you have lost your way."

And he made as though to go back to his game, as if he were going to leave the sermon he had announced for another occasion. But Samano, to complicate matters, tempted the prelate: "Excuse me, Your Reverence, but many members of the council are very pleased with Father de Las Casas' intention."

To which the bishop replied, unable to suppress his indignation: "There are some who are so dim that, with every good intention, they do improper things that are a mortal sin." And he continued, turning to me with blazing eyes, "What learning and science do you have that would lead you to dare to negotiate against the interests of Castile?"

I answered him, still taking care not to anger the bishop of Badajóz: "Perhaps, Lord Bishop, I am even less learned than you think I am, and that allows me, as uneducated as I am, to say three things to you. First, that you have sinned a thousand times for not having devoted your soul to your sheep in order to free them from the grip of the tyrants that destroy them. Second, every ducat you carry in your purse has been bought with the blood of your sheep. And, third, if you do not make restitution for all that you have taken from them, down to the last *ochavo*, you will meet with a fate as bad as that of Judas, the traitor."

Some of those present laughed at my words, as though I were joking, and Friar Quevedo, although he was livid, also began to make fun of me, so I, who do not understand jokes in such a serious matter, said to him, "Are you laughing, Sir? You would do better to cry for your misfortune and that of your sheep."

"Yes," he answered as though I were insane, "I have the tears right here in my purse."

But that is as far as it went, because the bishop of Badajóz said, "Do not continue, Sirs, and let us go back to our game. There will be a better place than this to settle the matter."

I understood that he said it as a good host who wanted to avoid altercations among his guests; but what I could never have imagined was that that "better place" would be the presence of our lord, King Charles.

As I say, the bishop of Badajóz was waiting to be received by His Majesty, which is what happened shortly after what I have described, and when the monarch was informed of what had happened, following the advice of the bishop, he called for Friar Juan de Quevedo and me to appear before him. He also wanted others to be present who were familiar with the affairs of the Indies, among them the second Admiral Colón and a Franciscan friar who had just arrived from there, very scandalized by the bad treatment meted out to the Indians.

We were ushered into the presence of our king and lord on December 12, 1519, the Tuesday of the third week of Advent, and I felt very highly honored, because although the king had shown consideration for me before, I had never been invited to a Royal Council. Ever since the first time that Cardinal Adriano had taken me into His Majesty's presence, he had addressed me by name, calling me *Micer* Bartolomé, which is the form of address that the Flemish use with clerics.

His Majesty had not yet turned twenty, but he had already left behind him that air of indecision which he had had when he arrived in Spain; his chin was very prominent, and his mouth remained half-open, as though he were going to stammer, but later, although he was not talkative, what he said was said well and with great authority. He listened patiently, as he showed in that long session, and he was not distracted during the debates.

Knowing that he valued the salvation of his soul very highly, as is evidenced by his death, after he had withdrawn to the monastery of Yuste as a monk, I shaped my arguments to him accordingly whenever possible.

He was seated in his royal chair, wearing the Golden Fleece around his neck, as though to lend more importance to the meeting, and on his head he wore a lavishly embroidered maroon velvet cap. The grand chancellor, the bishop of Badajóz, the lawyer Aguirre (whom I have mentioned before), and another person of high birth whom I do not remember were all seated on lower benches. When one of them wanted to address His Majesty, he rose from his seat, stepped up to the foot of the king's chair, and there, kneeling on one knee, consulted with him regarding the subject under discussion. When he received a response, he bowed and returned to his seat. So much ceremony lengthened the debates, which, on the other hand, proceeded with such respect that no one dared to raise his voice or to say anything that was out of place.

The bishop of the Indies, as was appropriate to his high dignity, was placed in his seat of preference, although not as prominently as those already mentioned. And this cleric and the Franciscan friar were seated against the wall, because we did not even bear the title of doctor. I wanted the Franciscan to be at my side, because I had heard him preach in the church at Molins, and I found that he hit the mark in everything he said about the Indies.

The bishop of Quevedo began to speak, delivering a very graceful and eloquent sermon, as was appropriate to his position as the royal preacher, which he was in the days of the Catholic King. But as a person who came from the Indies, unaware of what the theologians of Salamanca had determined, he allowed himself to say that, as it seemed to him, the Indians were slaves by nature, and that is where we caught him out.

When the great chancellor gave me the floor, I told His Majesty that servants by nature were an invention of the philosopher Aristotle, to justify the idea that some people had been born to be slaves. But the philosopher was a pagan, and for that reason he was burning in hell. How can we be required to use his doctrine against ours, which is holy and revealed to us by God himself? I reasoned by extension that our Christian religion is the same and fitting for all the races of the world and does not place anyone in servitude on the pretext that he is a slave by nature.

I went on to explain what would have happened to the gospel if, instead of being preached by some poor fishermen of Galilee, it had been spread by Roman centurions with blazing swords. Who now remembers what so many Roman generals said and did as they roamed in triumph through the world, from one end to the other? In contrast, the words of some men who, like their Master, lacked a place to lay their heads will endure until the end of time. We would have to do the same in the Indies, preaching by example and keeping our swords in their sheaths, as Christ ordered Saint Peter to do when he cut off the ear of the servant Malchus.

The emperor listened inscrutably, as befit such a great monarch, without expressing approval or disapproval of what I was saying, but the bishop of Badajóz later told me that I had hit home with what I said about our holy religion and the way in which it should be preached.

I spoke for some three-quarters of an hour, and the Franciscan friar spoke after me, for a shorter time and focusing on the atrocities that he had seen with his own eyes in the Indies, which greatly impressed the monarch. King Charles understood that day, for the first time, what was going on in his dominions overseas.

Lastly, the bishop of the Indies asked to be heard again,

and after the usual whispered consultations between the
great chancellor and His Majesty, permission was granted
for a brief statement, and the lord bishop, as though he
had been touched by the grace of God, admitted that what
had been said about the damage that had been done in
the Indies was correct, but that he had not been able to
remedy it, because he did not have the authority to do so.

He thus did us a great favor, because one who had begun by presenting himself as our accuser became a de-
fender of what we were saying; and God paid him for the
great service he thus performed, because a few days later,
on December 24, 1519, he died devoutly while he was
writing a memorandum in defense of the Indians. How
beautiful it must be to die on the same day on which the
Lord was born.

CHAPTER XII

THE REMEDY FOR
THE NEW WORLD MAINLAND

Thus does God dispose the affairs of men. The bishop of the Indies, with all the authority of his high ministry, had come to Spain charged by the encomenderos with the mission of ejecting me from the court, and thanks to him I was established in it better than I had been before.

From Barcelona we went to La Coruña, following the king, who was on his way there to embark for Germany, to be crowned king of that country as ruler of the Holy Roman Empire, an office to which the kings of France and England also aspired. They say that to attain that office he had to pay eight hundred thousand florins, which some Jewish bankers loaned him, a loan for which all the gold that came from the Indies was not enough to discharge. If he had spent those florins in the islands and the mainland of the New World, he would soon have been the most powerful monarch on the globe, whereas being Holy Roman emperor was short-lived and only served to embroil him in more wars and require him to spend more money.

In La Coruña, he convened the Cortes for the purpose of raising the funds needed to cover the cost of the journey, which were substantial because of how important it was to him to maintain his hold on the empire. My champion, Cardinal Adriano, told me that it was now or never for advancing our plan to bring Castilian farmworkers to colonize the mainland of the New World peacefully, for His Majesty was very much in favor of it after what he had heard in the Council of Barcelona, but that I should not even dream of securing a single *maravedí* of support because the royal coffers were empty. It made me want to cry to see how there was money available for vain purposes, but there was not even a copper *cuadrante* for an empire of souls and riches beyond anything that all of Europe could offer. But because I am not one to lament and did not want to waste the opportunity that His Eminence was offering to me, I reflected that, if there was no money in Spain, there was money, in abundance, in the Indies. And how awful it would be if we could not find even fifty people in the islands who were in their right mind, among the friends the Dominicans and I had, who would want to concern themselves with such a good project and, in the process, gain more riches by legitimate means.

I said fifty, because in my analysis of the prospects of the business, I came to the conclusion that ten thousand ducats would suffice, which could be raised if each of the fifty were to contribute two hundred ducats. That sum would cover the cost of a year's worth of supplies and two caravels to carry the farmworkers from Hispaniola to the mainland, and then beyond that some items such as glass trinkets and mirrors, which we could freely give the Indians as gifts, fostering their interest in our friendship. Keep in mind that in those days one could do more with a thousand ducats than can be done today with six thousand.

When I finished thinking about it, a great peace came over me, and I realized that the project would go forward; I did not at this point want money from the Crown, even if they gave it to me, because working with just one *maravedí* of public funds involved meeting requirements of the officials of the treasury and justifying expenditures and giving up the freedom we needed so much for what we were doing.

The Cortes' session in La Coruña lasted a week, almost all of it dedicated to raising the money for the emperor's journey; but on one day of that week, Cardinal Adriano, with his great authority (which he would not have when he soon thereafter became pope), gave an extremely solemn speech saying that the Indians had to be brought to the knowledge of God by peace, not by war or slavery, all by proofs rooted in natural reason and citations from Sacred Scripture and saintly Fathers of the Church. No member of the council dared to oppose this doctrine, but when he added that I ought to be named to administer and evangelize the mainland of the New World, Bishop Fonseca said that was impossible, giving as his reason the scandalous life I had led in Cuba. He was not wrong, but if we were to inspect the sins of everyone's past, who would be worthy of preaching the gospel? I do not believe Saint Peter himself would be. Others defended me in this matter, and the appointment moved forward.

The king signed the Capitulation for the colonization and peaceful evangelization of the mainland of the New

World on May 19, 1520. The land grant ran along 780 miles of coastline, from the province of Paria to Santa Marta, but because it included inland territory down to the South Sea, it covered an area of 7,500 square miles, as much as an empire.

Added to this Capitulation were many provisions and decrees that I requested in order to fulfill what had been agreed, which were completed after the king had left. Bishop Fonseca himself had to sign them, and he did so with pleasure, I think in order to be rid of me and to satisfy Cardinal Adriano, who, in His Majesty's absence, became the highest chancellor of the kingdom.

By royal decree, I was named administrator of the Indians of the Pearl Coast, which seemed to me to be the noblest title, because it gave me, and no one else, authority to exercise power over them, and I already saw, in my dreams, that no governor, trafficker, or encomendero would dare to roam about my dominions, which were those of Christ himself, or to touch a single hair of those whom the monarch himself entrusted to me.

In addition, it was provided that, during the first two years, we would not make any payments to His Majesty, that fifty thousand ducats would be paid annually from the third year on, until the sixth year, when the number would rise to a hundred thousand ducats per year. Because it was income that was not earned by blood and injury, it was very good income, and His Majesty did not take it out of the mines of Cuba, where it was all smoke and no fire.

Since we were not given any money for such a noble endeavor, I sought generosity by another route, for there was one royal decree that ordained admission of the fifty good persons who subsidized the endeavor, and also the farmworkers who deserved it, as Knights of the Golden Spurs, with a coat of arms and the robe described above, so that the Indians would not confuse them with the bad Spaniards who were exploiting them, but rather take them for friars whom the Indians loved so well. The title carried with it the right to use silver in the cutlery used at their tables, but to avoid greed there was a proviso that the cutlery could not be sold or traded.

Those who took a hostile view of the undertaking mocked these provisions and even attributed delusions of grandeur to me, ignoring the fact that I needed no more than my clerical soutane and wooden spoon for my meals; I sought these privileges to lend dignity to the enterprise and encouragement for those who were embarking on it. But no paper ordered that I be named a Knight of the Golden Spurs or that I be given the right to use a silver spoon.

So, finally, we embarked from Sanlúcar de Barrameda, weighing anchor on November 11 of that year, 1520, the feast day of Saint Martin, the bishop of the poor. We had to obtain financing for this voyage, too, which was easy to obtain on account of the fact that we had generous guarantees from Cardinal Adriano, who was the highest authority in Castile at the time.

There were seventy farmworkers on board, counting men only, although some of them came accompanied by their wives and, in most cases, by their children. I named Blas Hernández to be at their head because of the

confidence I had in him and his wife, Andrea, who gave
as many orders as he did. They brought their two sons,
Ignacio and Isidoro, but their daughter could not come
because she was recently married and pregnant. I do not
recall ever having had a more pleasant voyage, and it hurts
my soul to remember it; we had nothing but fair weather
on both the sea and the ship, the winds were propitious,
and we were in high spirits. I believe all seventy farmworkers were from Soria and among the most battle-
hardened, because they were not afraid of the threats of
the constable of Berlanga, or of others of his stripe, and
they preferred to lose their haciendas in Castile (which
certainly were diminished) as long as they could be masters of their destiny in the Indies.

They knew a good deal about the lands to which they
were going, for after they enlisted, when Luis Berrio was
recruiting people, they had talked about nothing else and
spread news among each other about what was happening
there. For my part, after evening prayers, I gathered them
together on one of the lower decks, and I told them in
great detail what they were going to find in the Indies.
Their eyes widened, and the air was thick with questions
that I did not tire of answering, for I could not believe
my good fortune and could not even imagine the great
cross the Lord was preparing for me.

I say that I could not believe the joy of breathing the
sea air again, far from the great halls and intrigues of the
court; I could not believe my good fortune in being free
of pretense and of wasting time and hot air in discussion,
but instead making no bones about anything, teaching
them how they should work and how they should treat

the Indians, who were their equals, and telling them that they would be followed by other farmworkers, who by following in their footsteps would transform those lands into a crown jewel. Some people objected to that, which made me laugh; they must have thought that the mainland was like Soria, except a bit bigger, and that they would be able to cultivate the land without the help of anyone else.

They were so enthusiastic, so well-mannered, and so devout in prayer at the appointed time that the sailors on the ship, who were sinful people, used to transporting soldiers and scoundrels, felt edified by their conduct, and one of the sailors, whose name was Miguel Carriazo, and who was over forty years old, asked me to take him with me when we arrived. I took care to explain to him that what we were going to be doing was not to rob but to work the land, to which he replied that that was what he wanted, because he had worked on a farm when he was young, and since he last used a plow he had taken the shortest route to hell. He said it because he had participated in the trafficking of slaves.

It lifted my spirits very much that such a vitiated person should want to do what we were trying to do and to join us in doing it. I accepted it and did not regret having done so because this Miguel Carriazo was among those who persevered to the end.

It was a good crossing, not more than twenty-five days, with propitious winds, and our ship, the *San Juan*, arrived at the island of that same name (San Juan de Puerto Rico) on December 6, the feast day of Saint Nicholas of Bari, and from that moment on I was fated to drink nothing but bitter draughts, the deepest I have ever swallowed in my life.

The first swallow, as soon as I jumped onto dry land, was the news that the mission of the Dominican Fathers, on the Pearl Coast, had been destroyed by the Indians, and the friars who had lived there had been killed. They almost did not have to tell me, because when we entered the mouth of the harbor, the roadstead, I could see a fleet of no fewer than six ships well armed with cannon, and I knew from sad experience that, in the Indies, when one sees such a display of artillery, it is clear at whom it is pointed. Indeed, that fleet, under the command of Gonzalo de Ocampo, was going to punish the Indians who had killed the friars.

I could not have been wounded more painfully if someone had driven a knife into my rib cage; I was arriving as the administrator of the Indians on the Pearl Coast, and I found that a captain general, authorized by the Audience of Santo Domingo, was preparing to pacify them, which is to say, to destroy them, on account of a wrongdoing that they were said to have committed. I knew very well that if the Indians had done some wrong, it would have been because of some greater wrong that had been done to them: I set about looking into it, and before I continue my account, I should explain what had happened on the Pearl Coast.

They call this part of the mainland the Pearl Coast because it is directly across from the island of Cubagua, the richest pearl fishery in all the Indies. By that time, a greater volume of pearls had been harvested than all the wheat in Xaraguá. I do not know how many of them reached Spain, because the greatest thieves in the kingdom had gathered there, under the leadership of their mayor, Antonio Flores, the greatest thief of all.

When I first went to the Pearl Coast, around 1504, it was a paradise; a few years later, it was a hell. The work of the Indians in the mines was inhuman, but I hardly need say how it was in these fisheries, because the gold is near the surface of the water in the rivers, but pearls, which are a mysterious affliction of oysters, are at the bottom of the sea, which is where the Indians have to go. As though it were a game, and because of their love for swimming and skill in moving through the water, they had always fished for pearls in relatively shallow water, without being underwater for long; but when the Spaniards arrived on Cubagua, the pearls to be found in the shallows were soon all gone. So the Indians were put into canoes, with a well-armed enforcer in the bow, until they reached an area where the sea was some twenty or thirty feet deep, and there the Indians were required to dive, either willingly or under threat of being beaten, each with a basket of nets hung around his neck, which they had to fill with oysters. And that is what they did from sunrise to sunset; as food, they were given oysters and a little cassava bread. But so many oysters were gathered that many of them rotted and produced a stench that could be smelled many miles away. When a fishery was exhausted, it left nothing but misery behind, and it was a great pity that the governors in Castile did not understand that.

Sometimes the divers do not come back up, either because they drown out of exhaustion or because sharks, which are plentiful there, come upon them. There were very cruel foremen who, to enable the divers to dive deeper and for a longer time, hung a stone around their neck, and then they would tug on a rope to be pulled up, but I hardly need say how they came out if they did not do it in time. How is it possible for men to live the greater part of their lives under water, without breathing? The black hair of these Indians lost its natural color, and it turned straw-colored; their backs shed scales of saltpeter that made them look monstrous. The cold temperature of the water so rotted their lungs that it was common for them to die expelling blood from their mouths.

Of all the bad things I have seen in the Indies, this was the worst. Because the Dominicans were of the same opinion, they would leave their mission at Santa Fe de Chichiribichi from time to time to console the Indians and preach to the Spaniards about the great evil they were committing. And it was one of those missions that triggered the catastrophe with which we are concerned here.

The Dominican Fathers had built a monastery in Chichiribichi around 1510, I would say, and it became so prosperous within a few years that it was the apple of Friar Pedro de Córdoba's eye, and he told me about it in every one of his letters to me. It was set in the middle of very rich land, with such glorious orchards that Friar Pedro would say it could feed a whole fleet all by itself. He was among those who thought that, when the Castilian farmworkers arrived on the Pearl Coast, they would convert it into a garden, and instead of leaving misery behind them, as they did in the fisheries and mines, they would leave an oasis.

I was counting on that monastery to begin our work and thought I would build our first village there, to which Friar Pedro had agreed. It is therefore easy to imagine how upset I was when I arrived in San Juan de Puerto Rico and they told me that that monastery had been destroyed.

The friars got along very well with the Indians, as they customarily did. They call the people from this region Cumanagotos (because the region is called Cumaná), and they had already baptized several of them who helped them in their labors. As always happens in missions, it was not the Indians who caused problems but the Spaniards, largely because they were so close to the focus of evil, Cubagua. Because even all the Indians were too few for the fisheries, it became popular to organize expeditions to enslave them; three or four neighbors from Hispaniola, or other islands, set themselves to doing so, each of them putting up five or six thousand gold pesos, buying two or three ships that they loaded with fifty or sixty of the most heartless Spaniards, who would get a commission for each of the prisoners they took, and they were sent out to commit piracy.

The greatest infamy of all is that the Audience of Santo Domingo appointed an official to head these forays whom they called an examiner, and he examined nothing because he was the worst of all of them. This "examiner", when he arrived on a part of the coast that was densely pop-ulated, tried to convince its inhabitants by saying there was a God in heaven and a pope on earth, who was God's vicar, and kings of Castile, of whom they were vassals, and if they did not submit to his orders, his men would attack and enslave them. Just imagine what the Indians would understand, even if it had been shouted in their ears, since they did not have a command of the language. After observing these formalities, he made them slaves and took them to be sold on the island of Cubagua, Hispaniola, or Cuba. I have seen them arrive naked at the beaches of these islands, hunting snails or little shoots of grass so they would not starve to death, and I was ashamed to call myself a Christian.

These traffickers tried to move among the islands near the coast under the pretext that the Indians there were cannibals and seizing them was authorized; in any case, they took care to stay away from Chichiribichi out of the great respect that the Dominicans deserved. I am not saying that the former respected the latter but, rather, that they were aware of the influence that the Order had in Castile.

But to our great shame, one of the worst sinners of all arrived there, named Alonso de Hojeda, who did not fear even the devil, with whom I believe he ended his days. He was one of the few who was already rich when he came to the Indies, because he had been an agent of the guildhall of Seville, and so needed absolutely nothing, but he never tired of being rich, and he was one of the biggest investors in the fleets that enslaved the Indians. He wanted them for his fisheries in Cubagua, and he had no compunction, despite his age, about taking command of them.

In September 1520, accompanied by twenty young men, he arrived in one of those ships at the monastery of Santa Fe de Chichiribichi, at a moment when there was just one elderly friar and a lay brother there; the rest of the friars (as many as ten, I think) had gone with the superior, Friar Tomás Ortiz, to preach to the people on Cubagua. That was an unfortunate coincidence, and a major one; for if Friar Tomás had been there, he would have been more on the alert about these heartless men. But the old priest received them with his natural good will and even with happiness at being able to be with his countrymen, because he had no company but the Indians. Hojeda told the friar that they wanted to barter with the local lord, who was called Maraguay, and the old friar sent an Indian servant to fetch him.

Maraguay, who was by nature a fierce, wise, and cautious man, agreed to come because of the great confidence the friars had earned; but he himself did not trust other Spaniards because he had heard all about what they had done in the islands.

Hojeda very boldly ordered that a table and chair be placed in a clearing in the forest and asked the old friar for a sheet of paper and an inkstand, quill, and blotter that the lay brother, in his remarkable naïveté, brought him. The Indians looked on suspiciously at what Hojeda was doing, especially when he poised himself to start writing, because they knew that written papers brought them misfortune; they did not succeed in understanding that thoughts could be set down on paper, and they saw them as the white man's witchcraft.

Once the Indians were lined up in the clearing, with Maraguay at their head, Hojeda began asking if they knew of anyone in those parts who ate human flesh.

Informed as he was, Maraguay said in Spanish as soon

as he heard that: "No, no carne humana, no carne humana" ("No, not human flesh, not human flesh"), because he knew that that practice was a pretext for enslaving them. He immediately ordered them to break camp,
and the Spaniards, seeing how numerous and ready the
Indians were, with great regret had to let them leave.

The two friars, the old one and the lay brother, did
not have an inkling and were not at all suspicious of the
Spaniards' intentions. The latter left the monastery and
headed for Maracapana, north of the monastery, the master of which was a great friend of the friars because they
were among the first to be baptized, and he felt very
honored that they called him Gil González, which was
his first name.

Gil González received the Spaniards with caution but
hospitably, which is customary among those people. Hojeda, on his guard because of what had happened with
Maraguay, said he went there to collect some corn with
which to make bread; the corn he wanted was of very
high quality and had been grown by the Indians of the
mountains, the Tagares, who lived nine miles from there;
he showed them glass beads and other trinkets, of which
the Indians are fond, and also casks of wine, which is
another vile thing with which they had been shown how
to get drunk. Gil González sent word to the Tagares and
agreed with them that the next day fifty men would take
fifty loads of corn to the beach, where the ship was anchored.

The Tagares did as they had agreed, so the loads of corn
were on the beach at the appointed hour, and the men
who had brought them were lying on them to rest up

from the fatigue of their journey, which in the sierra was over a very rough road. Thus, taking advantage of their being off guard, Hojeda's men came out of the ship all at once, shooting with their arquebuses and culverins, and they fell upon the Indians, taking thirty-five prisoners and killing the rest, except for one who was able to escape and spread the alarm.

It goes without saying that Gil González was not very pleased and highly aggrieved, for the Tagares were his guests, and what had happened was an offense that the Cumanagotos could not forgive.

Via the Indians' means of communication, by smoke signals, the beating of drums, and relays of men who run through the forest like deer, the outrage that had been committed was known to those within sixty miles in four hours. The sun had not set when the lord of Maraguay and that of Maracapana, Gil González, met on a hill above the monastery and agreed to punish the Spaniards with death. Gil González said that the ones who had to be killed were those in Hojeda's ships, in order to rescue the Tagares who had been taken prisoner. But the Maraguayan answered that the friars who had given them shelter when they arrived also had to be killed. As a good Christian, Gil González defended the friars—but to no avail, for the Maraguayan explained to him how he had seen, with his own eyes, that they had been given paper and writing materials with which to make a list of the names of those who were to be enslaved.

Having made their plan, they reached agreement to wait until the following Sunday, the day on which the Christians were most off guard, to exact justice. Because

Gil González did not want to touch the friars, he reserved for himself the most dangerous part, which was to attack Hojeda. They did all this with great caution, so that the Spaniards would not have any warning. I mean Hojeda and not the friars, who knew nothing of what had happened and could not have had any inkling of what awaited them.

Gil González, who was very familiar with the activities the Spaniards enjoyed, ordered canoes to surround the ship that, under the protection of its cannons and culverins, rode at anchor near the same beach. They offered up fruit from the canoes, as though they were indifferent to the fact that they taken some Tagares prisoner, and the canoes also carried Indian women, who were wearing nothing but short skirts, and I believe that out of lust the Spaniards fell into the trap. Presented with these signs of friendship, Hojeda, with his lack of shame and great temerity, and without waiting until Sunday, landed on the beach on Saturday, together with ten or twelve of his men. Gil González received them with a big smile, as though nothing had happened, and took them to where they had set their trap. Some warriors who were waiting there set upon them, and Hojeda was among the first to fall dead; some managed to escape and swim out to the ship. Gil González' men surrounded them with their war canoes, shooting poisoned arrows at them, but the Spaniards, despite their small number and lacking their captain, defended themselves very well and managed to hoist sail, which was the main remedy.

The Maraguayan took his time in killing the friars. Through a servant of theirs, who escaped with his life, it was known how they died; the Father was already dressed to celebrate the Mass, it being Sunday, and the lay brother had just made confession in preparation for taking Communion. Maraguay rang the small bell at the door, and the lay brother went to open it, with a natural joy, thinking that it would be one of the baptized Indians who was coming to participate in the Holy Sacrifice, which they did on occasion, traveling several miles along a network of roads in the forest.

They killed him right there at the door with the blow of an axe to the head, and they stealthily went on to the sacristy; the Father had no warning, entrusting himself as he was to God in preparation for celebrating Mass at the altar, and with the same axe they gave him a blow from behind, to the head. Thus were both of them sent to receive Holy Communion, not sacramentally, but from the hands of our Lord God, and one can imagine with what joy he would receive them, for they had given their lives for him.

They then burned down the monastery, destroyed the surrounding fields, and killed with their arrows all the friars' domestic animals, including a horse that they used to pull a wagon.

The whole Pearl Coast rose up to give battle, with a great roar, urging each other on to prevent the Spaniards from getting near, and the innocents paid the same price as the rest. I say innocents because they were not to blame for the killings at Chichiribichi, but they were not totally free of guilt because all the Spaniards there had come for the same reason; Rodrigo de Bastidas, Andrés de Villacorta, and Juan Logroño, slave traffickers, unaware of the agreement that Maraguay and Maracapana had made, disembarked on the coast and paid for it with their lives.

The mayor of Cubagua, Antonio Flores, under the pretext that the island was in danger, ordered its evacuation; later it was learned that the Cumanagotos had never considered going to the island, because it was so well garrisoned that little could be done against it with arrows, however poisoned they might have been. But with this excuse, Antonio Flores, the greatest thief in the kingdom, confiscated four caravels and seized pearls that belonged to the Crown, worth twenty thousand pesos of gold, which he made off with and hid in a safe place. An investigation was conducted into all this after a time, but the pearls did not come to light; for the time being, this ruse allowed him to make an appearance in Hispaniola as if the world had come to an end.

The members of the Audience must have rubbed their hands together thinking about the benefit they would get from all this, and the first measure they took was to name Gonzalo de Ocampo, the late Alonso de Hojeda's son-in-law, as the captain general of the fleet that would have the task of pacifying the coast. In my opinion, if what they wanted to do was to exact justice, the most logical candidate would not be someone who, by his parentage, was more suited to being an avenger than a dispenser of justice. That is how things were done in Hispaniola, in the hands of Miguel de Pasamonte, the royal treasurer and the bishop of Burgos' principal agent in the Indies.

This Gonzalo de Ocampo was not one of the worst people, and I had a good friendship with him when the Hieronymite friars sent by Cardinal Jiménez de Cisneros believed what some said about the Indians lacking rationality and being unable to look after themselves, thus having been marked by nature to be slaves. Gonzalo de Ocampo, with a good deal of sense, spoke up and said that, after having been in the Indies for sixteen years, he knew they were not capable of living as the Spaniards did unless they were taught how to do so, but they were more than capable of living the life they led.

When I arrived in San Juan de Puerto Rico, Ocampo was finishing up the outfitting of his fleet, which would be setting sail for the Pearl Coast; I wasted no time in presenting myself to him and showing him the royal decrees that made it clear he could not cross over to the mainland without my authorization, since I was its administrator. Gonzalo de Ocampo could not get over his shock when he saw those papers, and he examined them, front and back, unable to believe his eyes. He called for one Juan Camacho, who was a lawyer participating in the expedition as such. He had no choice but to say that those titles were legal and that it was up to me to pacify the Indians who had risen up.

Gonzalo de Ocampo respected me, but it would be delusional to think that a captain in the Indies who was in command of a powerful fleet was going to let pass such an opportunity to make an impression. Very politely, but with the deceptiveness that is usual there, he said to me: "You can be certain that I will respect the measures you take, and I am willing to obey them . . . to the extent I am ordered to do so by the Audience of Santo Domingo. In the meantime, I have to continue my work and bring peace to those lands, so when you arrive there, you will find them in a very calm state."

This was one time I did not succumb to fury, for that would have got me nothing with someone who had the support of the Audience, and he even had a reasonable point; it was not for him to interpret my measures, for the lawyers of Hispaniola were there to do that, he told me. What Ocampo did wrong is that he did not wait until I went to Santo Domingo to talk to the members of the Audience; his pretext for going forward was that his assignment could not wait, which was not true. Quite on the contrary, there is no better way to pacify Indians than to let them sleep in peace, and if time cures many ills, in such cases it works miracles.

My idea was to let a few months go by and then present myself with the farmworkers, who would by then be dressed in their habits as Knights of the Golden Spurs, which is in effect dressed as friars, and I would patiently win them over to my side. An indication that it could have been done that way is that there was another mission of Franciscan Fathers on that same Pearl Coast, in the gulf of Cariaco, in a place that was later named New Toledo, and the Indians did no harm to them at all, and their mission and its beautiful orchard prospered and even had orange trees.

I explained all this in great detail to Gonzalo de Ocampo, and he nodded his assent at what I was saying, but behind my back he rushed the work of getting the ships ready to sail as soon as possible. Because I had no time to lose, I sent a message via a notary in which I ordered Gonzalo de Ocampo not to make war on the Indians in my district, and I prepared to go to Hispaniola, which is where the crux of the matter was.

Another big task was to reassure the farmworkers, for as soon as they found out that there was an uprising at the place that had been assigned to us, they could not get over their distress, and some might have even thought that they had been deceived about the Indians being peaceful by nature. I reasoned with them for a very long time, and they ended up understanding. It also helped for them to see the respect with which the people of San Juan treated me, especially the Indians who knew how I had fought for them; I am ashamed to say that when I walked through the streets, they knelt to me as I passed, wanting to kiss my hands, and even though I scolded them, that had no effect. There were only a few Spaniards, but they were not as arrogant as those of Hispaniola, because the island had neither gold nor pearls, but ranches and farms, and even though there were encomenderos, they were not as iniquitous as those who only pursued the mining of gold; they wanted to be at peace with the Indians and listened with pleasure to my speeches and with respect to my sermons about the equality of all men.

The proof of that is that they welcomed the farmworkers with fine spirit, distributing them among their houses and haciendas, and promising to take care of them, feed them, and teach them the customs of the land, while I would be in Santo Domingo arguing insistently for our rights. It helped me a great deal to have this development in the midst of so many bitter experiences.

Meanwhile, the ship *San Juan*, which had brought us from Spain, was making its way to its destination, Santo

Domingo, and I was left in San Juan with no means of transportation to Hispaniola. Since weeks could go by before another ship would dock there, and my task could not wait that long, I decided to go from one island to another (which were separated by nothing more than a channel called La Mona, which by my estimate was about 180 miles) in a canoe with Indian oarsmen, as they were used to doing. When the secretary of the council found out, he hit the roof, joined by others, saying that it was a blot on a man with the title of administrator of the Crown to navigate as the most wretched Indians do, quite apart from the danger of navigating in an open vessel during the hurricane season. I did not care much about the blot, but the latter point seemed to me to be more well-founded, because it was not reasonable to expose such an important matter to the vicissitudes of the elements.

I could not find a solution, but the secretary of the council told me that the royal documents, which authorized no one but me to enter a land rich in gold and pearls, were worth a lot of money and could be used to secure a loan, as it turned out. Under the loan, I was entrusted with a ship that cost five hundred pesos of gold; in Sanlúcar it would have cost me half that, but that is how things were in the Indies. It was a very seaworthy caravel, as was evidenced by the fact that we crossed the channel very easily and with few crosscurrents, despite the fact that we were caught in a hurricane that was not at all weak when we passed by the point of Aguadilla.

With me on that trip was Francisco de Soto (who had been working for me at the time of my attempt at peaceful colonization, which Luis Berrio had stymied) and another whom I trusted, but I did not want any of the farm-workers to come because it was better that they not know any of the customs of Hispaniola. We arrived in Santo Domingo in the middle of February 1521, and the members of the Audience received me with such signs of deference that for a moment I could dream that they were finally surrendering to the force of my papers. The president of the Audience was still the lawyer Lucas Vázquez de Ayllón, more famous for his licentious behavior than for his status as a lawyer, because he was the one I described as having to be publicly scolded from the pulpit by the Dominican Fathers: I have already described the fondness of the treasurer, Miguel de Pasamonte, for other people's belongings. They joined in governing Hispaniola, and from there all the Indies, for although the admiral's son Don Diego Colón continued to act as the viceroy, little attention was paid to him. Although they were corrupt, they were not stupid, and they knew that my royal decrees, issued by the emperor himself, had to be obeyed.

I was not stupid, either, and I knew very well that they would not yield willingly, but would be motivated to do so by strength and my tenacious determination. As soon as they accepted my rights on the Pearl Coast, which was the least they could do, I began to insist that they order Gonzalo de Ocampo to end his pacification of my territories, which they promised to do but did not, or when they did do it Ocampo had had time to do what he wished, as I will describe.

It is fitting at this point to introduce this consideration: there were some in Castile who mocked my effort

to pacify the Indians by using good Castilian farmworkers as well as how they were dressed, as a combination
of knights and friars. But in Santo Domingo, when they
saw me arrive in my own ship and learned that seventy of
those farmworkers were in San Juan, awaiting my return
there, they did not make fun of that, but instead really
trembled, for they knew that the project could succeed,
in which case forays against the Indians would come to
an end, their pearl fishing would come to an end, and
the gold mines would come to an end. How would they
be able to exploit the Indians to the point of death if the
emperor earned the same income or more from the haciendas and mineral deposits worked in harmony with
the indigenous people? How could the emperor not pre-
fer to have the population of his dominions as vassals,
good Christians, instead of enemies? What king wants
his territories to be barren, without any vassals to work
them, and the Crown to be without its share?

They could ignore this in Europe, where they were
used to a cycle of repeated smash-and-dash wars. But
Pasamonte and his ilk knew very well that the Indians
could be colonized peacefully, although they could no
longer do it, for all of their interests lay in branding Indians and mining gold—their interests and those of the
men who gave them orders from Castile as well as those
of the encomenderos of Hispaniola, Cuba, and Jamaica,
who had established their haciendas counting on being
able to enslave Indians. I have a mountain of documents
that say very clearly how they auctioned off the Indians
they seized in every foray; and how every member of the
Audience received a commission from the proceeds of

the auction; and how their closest friends were able to take Indians without paying for them, and their debt remained outstanding forever; and how the officials of the council, in Castile, retained their encomiendas without ever setting foot in the Indies.

This web of interests could choke anyone who wanted to disrupt it, and for that reason my dear Dominican Fathers, with Friar Pedro de Córdoba at their head, who welcomed me with open arms, insisted to me that I take shelter in the monastery, for my life in Hispaniola was in danger. This time I did not want to acquiesce, and I preferred to continue staying at the inn, although Francisco de Soto and others I trusted always accompanied me.

I found Friar Pedro de Córdoba as devoted as ever, although not as handsome, because tuberculosis had invaded his chest, I think because of so many penances, and although he was only thirty-eight years old, he walked like an old man. I am saying this about his physical condition, for his spirit carried on with the same fervor for making the Indians good Christians by setting an example, as Christ himself had done, and not with our swords. He enjoyed reading the royal decrees that I had brought and listening to my stories about the farmworkers who were waiting for me in San Juan de Puerto Rico. He was one of the most insistent in telling me to take great care, for the project I had been authorized to carry out could be the ruin of many encomenderos, who thought of nothing but buying Indians to set them to work in the mines. There were some who cost twenty pesos each, and in less than a month the encomenderos could gain twice as much from the gold that each Indian extracted. For that reason, the bidding at the auctions was very combative, and there were Indians who fetched ninety pesos, almost as much as the price of a black. But because there were very few Indians left in the islands, and those few had owners, the encomenderos had no choice but to take them from the continent; so one can imagine how they must have felt knowing that this cleric was the only administrator of those souls, and it would be no surprise that more than one of them would try to take my life, as they had already tried to do the last time I was there, when I held fewer titles that justified killing me.

Friar Pedro was not wrong, but there were other ploys that the villains in Hispaniola used to do me more harm than if they had been making an attempt on my life.

Not long after my arrival, on a very stormy night that made it frightening to walk through the streets because, since it was hurricane season, the waters washed away everything in their path, they called at the door of the inn. The innkeeper did not want to open it, for he said that it was not a night or the hour to give shelter; I was awake writing notes for the members of the Audience, and I persuaded him that it was not Christian, especially on such a night, to refuse shelter to a pilgrim. The innkeeper complied, and we found ourselves with a bearded man whom I did not recognize at first as the Basque Zamacoa, the pilot who had brought me to Hispaniola the first time and thanks to whose decisiveness and skill the lives of all of us on the ship *San Nicolás* had been saved when the *austral* came up in the latitude of Madeira. I have known many good pilots in my life, but none like Zamacoa. He

was the one who advised me later, when I was a boy
less than twenty years old, that I should not become a
miner and who wanted to take me with him, with the
best of intentions but in the worst of all businesses: the
slave trade. Twenty years had passed since then, and I
therefore did not recognize him until he told me who he
was. I then took him in my arms with great affection,
which was fitting treatment of a man to whom one owes
one's life, although I had heard that he continued to be
engaged in the contemptible occupation of slave trader.

"Step back, Father, because I am here to give you bad
tidings", he said.

This did not surprise me, for from the moment I became involved in the affairs of the Indians, for every good
piece of news, I got ten bad ones. Zamacoa must have
been around fifty years old, but he was a wreck, not from
his penances, like Friar Pedro, but rather from the contrary. He was an appalling man when it came to drink,
and he was not much better about food, for he even enjoyed betting about whether he could eat a roasted kid
goat all by himself. I say that he looked very old and di-
sheveled, with bloodshot eyes and a tongue thickened by
drink. Between that and the fact that he was not very
given to talking, as happens often with Basques, I barely
understood the bad forebodings he brought me. All he
said was that the next day, at the crack of dawn, I should
take my ship and my men and leave the island. I told him
that was not possible, in the wind and the downpour, and
I asked him to explain. But he shook his head no, all the
while drinking from a bottle that he had with him, and
the only thing he told me was that he was sure it would

be calm at dawn, and in this he was right, for even when he was drunk he knew the sea better than those who were sober.

I understood very well that he had come to do me a favor, and in order to reciprocate and at the same time show him the confidence I had in him, I said, "If you come with me, Señor Zamacoa, I'll order the ship to be rigged right now, and the sails to be set, but if the helm of the ship is in hands other than yours, I would be taking my men to their death."

I think he appreciated that, but again he shook his head no, and he answered, "I can't. I am with Chomin de Quitalia, and he should know nothing about this visit that I've made to you."

This Chomin was called Domingo de Guetaria, although it sounded as though he said Chomin de Quitalia; he was a Basque, like Zamacoa, but morally he was much worse. He had secured an appointment by the Audience as the head shipwright of Hispaniola, and his work consisted of examining the ships that came from Castile and repairing them as necessary; he had the only dry dock on the island, and shipowners trembled when they patronized it because he was so dishonest in his work.

But the great amount he robbed in his dry dock did not compare with the evil he wrought in chartering ships for the slave trade; two of them that Ocampo used in his exploits on the Pearl Coast, the *Concepción* and the *Sancti Spiritus*, were in his squadron. And when he could not charter them, he himself organized fleets to make forays among the Indians, and that is where Zamacoa acted as his pilot, with whom he partnered. Chomin was one of the evil men in the Indies.

Zamacoa was deficient in his inability, or more properly his reticence, in expressing himself, and I was deficient in my inability to understand him. I was preoccupied by the thought that the danger he was talking about was to my life, and I did not understand how they could make an attempt against it when I was surrounded by half a dozen well-armed men, in an inn next to the governor's palace and a stone's throw from the Dominicans' monastery. I was deficient in that, but not in relieving his conscience, which was sunk in the depravity of his many crimes. This did not happen that night because Zamacoa drank so much that he lost consciousness, and we had to put him to bed in the inn.

I understood at dawn why the Basque pilot was urging me to hurry. It was about seven in the morning when an official of the Audience presented himself at the inn to inform me that my ship was not seaworthy, and since its very bad condition was beyond repair, it had to be disposed of by being taken downriver to the sea and run up against the coast, to protect the lives of the people who would otherwise be sailing in it. At the beginning, I understood that the ship had been damaged by the strength of the hurricane during the night, and I could not understand how that could have been, because it was sheltered in the Ozama River. Even less could I understand how the official could have come with papers signed and sealed ordering the destruction of the ship if the damage was that recent.

We managed to wake up Zamacoa, who when he came to said only, "I warned you, Father." I replied, "But you warned me late and badly, Señor Zamacoa."

The maladroit idea had come from Chomin de Quitalia, who saw a great deal of danger if I took office as administrator of the Pearl Coast, which was where he, with his ships, enriched himself with his misdeeds. Because he was working with the members of the Audience, he proposed destroying my ship on the pretext that it was not seaworthy. Imagine the joy with which Pasamonte and his friends received that proposal, and they wasted no time in putting it in practice without paying any attention to my protests; these were among the most heated that I had ever made in my life, because for me to be without a ship to take me to the continent was the same as cutting off my legs.

I quickly looked for people who would attest to the grace with which the ship had made the crossing from San Juan and how well she had acquitted herself in the hurricane in Aguadilla, but the head shipwright sought out other experts who said what he wanted them to say, and the ship was broken up and pierced with holes so that it would sink to the bottom of the sea.

President Ayllón pretended he did not know about it when I went to see him, and he told me that he would order a file to be opened to investigate what had happened, which is how things are dealt with in the Indies. I say they are dealt with for people who do not want them to be dealt with, for they open hundreds of files but complete none of them.

All that I got from this whole muddle was a penitent,

Zamacoa, who told me that he could not live amid so much deceit and showed himself to be fearful of the accounts he would have to render to God quite soon. He lived about two years longer in considerable suffering, for he never gave up the evil vice of drink, and when he was delirious he saw the devil in the form of a horned iguana. To top it off, after so many acts of piracy, he was left without an *ochavo* and at the end had to rely on the charity of the Franciscan Fathers for food; but at least he stopped piloting ships that pursued Indians, and that was a great deal. It also consoled me to hear him say, when he was sober, that if he had money he would give it to me so that I could carry out my project of colonizing the Pearl Coast with peaceful farmers, which was the only remedy for the Indies.

In that region, we friars always had a lot of work to do with sinners who repented when they were approaching death's door; it is the great mercy of our Lord to grant that grace to such rabble, whose confessions would frighten anyone who was not used to hearing them. We listened to them with a will and even exercised restraint in the penances we gave them, supplementing them with our own sacrifice, for if we had imposed the ones they deserved, some of them would have perished in the attempt. What was most difficult for them was to return what they had sinfully gained at the expense of another, and on that score we could not yield an inch.

CHAPTER XIII

END OF THE
CHRONICLE OF A DREAM

Being without a ship was one of the most bitter pills I had to swallow in those days, although not the worst, as will be seen later.

Without a ship, I was left a prisoner on the island, because it was beyond imagination that anyone would dare to lend me another, mostly because all of them depended on the chief shipwright, who had so artfully deprived me of what was rightfully mine. I did not even know to whom to turn for advice, other than Friar Pedro de Córdoba, who could not have been, poor man, in worse condition. Tuberculosis had invaded him deeply, and he always carried a large red handkerchief to conceal the blood that tinged his coughs, which recurred repeatedly. Because he would drown, in effect, if he lay in bed, the brothers had him in a hard, high-backed chair, always in the shade of a silk-cotton tree that Friar Pedro highly admired.

I consoled myself with him and he with me, listening to my tales of woe and seeing that I was not of a mind to yield my rights, which were those of the Indians, although the emperor was in Germany, my workers were in Puerto Rico, Ocampo was on the continent, wreaking havoc on our dreams, and the encomenderos were ready to cut my throat to make it impossible for me to carry on with my efforts.

A ship arrived from Spain at about that time with the news that Cardinal Adriano, and all the governors of Castile, had put an end to the rebellion of the *comuneros* in the battle of Villalar and that the power of the cardinal, my patron, had greatly strengthened. This news was not at all welcome to everyone on the island, because there were some in the Audience who had expressed their support for the *comuneros*; seeing that I was in a difficult predicament, I began to boast about the only thing I had left, my friendship with the great chancellor Adriano, which was well-known in Santo Domingo, because he had signed some of the royal decrees that I brought, I let it be known that I was thinking about going back to Castile and returning from there with a fleet equipped with everything that was needed to take possession of the territories of the Pearl Coast.

I said it very fervently because at the time I was an impassioned cleric, very much in the grip of pride, and my desire would have been to arrive with that fleet well supplied with cannons so that no one would dare to get within thirty miles of my jurisdiction. In this I had taken leave of my senses because I wanted to pacify the Indians by making war on the Spaniards, and there I was imagining myself firing cannons at a caravel bearing Pasamonte, Ayllón, and the other members of the Audience.

Friar Pedro scolded me at length for these wicked thoughts, although he praised my decision to go back to Spain to continue insisting for the rights of the Indi-

ans before the high chancellor. And several things happened simultaneously in that connection. The first was
that Miguel de Pasamonte summoned me and told me
that all of us were servants of the same king and lord,
to whom we owed our loyalty, and so the proper thing
to do would be for us to carry out my project with the
farmers on the Pearl Coast.

To make a long story short, we ended up signing a
Capitulation in July 1521 in which each one sought to
protect and promote his own interests; mine was that,
instead of the fifty gentlemen who had to contribute two
hundred ducats each, so as to bring the total up to ten
thousand, that money would be supplied by the gentlemen of the Audience. The financing was divided into
twenty-four parts, of which six were allotted to the king,
six to this cleric and his workers, and three to Admiral
Diego Colón, the rest being shared among the four judges
of the Audience, the treasurer Miguel de Pasamonte, and
his subordinates.

During these negotiations, it sometimes seemed to me
that I was dreaming, and at other times that I was pawn-
ing my soul to the devil, because I was negotiating with
men who were so opposed to my views. They (especially
Miguel de Pasamonte) insisted more than I did that we
come to an agreement, out of fear of the protection that
the great chancellor Adriano might extend to me, and they
gave way on matters that I would never have imagined,
such as diving for the pearls in the waters of the island of
Cubagua in the way I wanted and more humanely; at bottom, I felt that they were seeking to continue capturing
slaves on the coast of Cumaná, on the pretext that they

were Caribs, or cannibals, and on that point they were prepared to break off the negotiations several times.

During those negotiations, Gonzalo de Ocampo returned from the Pearl Coast with his ships full of enslaved Indians captured in the wars of pacification; that is, he pacified them by putting a rope around their necks, so that there would no longer be any reason for concern that they would rebel again.

Ocampo came back very proud of his achievement because there were many Cumanagotos from Maracapana, and they were very battle-hardened, and he was able to defeat them all, applying the following stratagem: he ordered the ships to sail in convoy, and only the flagship sailed to the beach of Maracapana. He ordered all the men to hide in a lower deck, and he appeared on the bowsprit with just four sailors accompanying him. It did not take long for the lord of Maracapana, Gil González, to appear, mistrustful like all the others ever since the wretched arrival of Alonso de Hojeda. Ocampo cleverly pretended they were sailing along the coast to barter and that he was not even sure of where he found himself. Gil González approached the ship in his canoe, but with no intention of boarding it; the captain offered him Castilian bread and wine, which he knew the Indians found most tempting, but Gil González, with the few words of Spanish he knew, told them to throw them casks of wine and that they would reciprocate.

Ocampo had meanwhile arranged for a sailor who was very agile and a good swimmer and who jumped into the water, ostensibly to bring them one of the casks, but as soon as he arrived at the canoe, he took out a dagger that he carried behind him and embraced Gil González. They both fell into the water, and there the sailor repeatedly stabbed Gil González. This was followed by all the men who had been hidden away coming out to attack the other canoes with shots from arquebuses and crossbows. As the shots rang out, the ships in convoy spread out along the beach, and a great battle ensued; with their leader dead, the Indians thought of nothing but taking flight, and the Spaniards thought of nothing but taking them prisoner.

When I heard this account, I raged with all my strength, condemning this feat before the Audience with the utmost severity, and all I achieved was that the Audience reprimanded Gonzalo de Ocampo for having recounted these events exactly as they had happened. The rumor that spread afterward was that Ocampo had taken Gil González prisoner, along with other major caciques who had been his accomplices, judged them in accordance with Castilian law, and, having found them guilty, ordered them to be hanged from the lateen yard of the flagship. And this is the version that some who have called themselves chroniclers of the Indies tell in their books; but I heard the account I have given here from the lips of Ocampo himself, who openly repeated it, because it was very highly thought of there for captains to use stratagems to bring rebellions to an end more quickly, thus safeguarding the lives of their soldiers. Such captains were held in very high esteem by those who depended on them.

While I was deep in sorrow, they started to auction off the Indian prisoners, and Ocampo set out for the mainland to make the lesson complete. This matter of teaching a lesson is where I reacted most heatedly when President

Ayllón very pompously said that the Indians could not be allowed to kill two innocent friars (thereby admitting that Alonso de Hojeda was not so innocent) who just wanted to preach the gospel. As though he and his ilk cared about the Dominicans who were killed; rather, they were all a nuisance to them, because they belonged to the Order that denounced their abuses and protected this cleric.

It was such an infamy to enslave Indians under the pretext of serving justice for what had happened at Chichiribichi that the prelate Friar Pedro had himself brought into the presence of the judges of the Audience in a sedan chair because he could no longer walk. There, speaking with great effort but also very tenderly, he explained to them that friars were there to serve Christ and that part of that service was to die for him. If Christ, on the Cross, pardoned those who so wrongly inflicted such a cruel death upon him, how could it be that the Dominicans should not pardon those who killed out of ignorance, with the blameworthy intercession of bad Spaniards who provoked them to do it? As I listened, tears came to my eyes, seeing how he devoted the little life he had left to defending the Indians. I defended them, too, but Friar Pedro de Córdoba, in addition, loved them tenderly.

Anyone who did not have a heart of stone would have been moved by that speech, but Miguel de Pasamonte, who because he was the biggest troublemaker was the spokesman for all of them, answered him that it was not up to the prelate to extend a pardon that solely belonged to the Crown, under whose protection were all the Spaniards in the Indies. And on top of everything else, he allowed himself to quote the phrase in Scripture that requires us to render to Caesar the things that are Caesar's and to God the things that are God's. I held myself back out of respect for the presence of Friar Pedro, although that did not stop me from saying some very severe things to them.

But words were of little use in the Indies if they were not backed up by weapons, and because I had none of those other than the royal decrees, I clung to them. Seeing that I was not going to be able to prevent Ocampo from going to the Pearl Coast, this time to teach the lord of Maraguay a lesson and at the same time bring back twice the number of slaves, I signed the Capitulation in the form I have described. God knows whether I did the right or wrong thing.

I was unable to find out what Friar Pedro's judgment was because that very night he gave his soul up to God and I was left fatherless, although it consoled me very much that he died as a martyr in defense of the Indians. Another great consolation was the arrival of Friar Antón Montesino, who was in the north of the island and came for the burial, and I found consolation in his arms. He preached at the funeral and began with the verse that says: "Ecce quam bonum et quam iucundum habitare fratres in unum." (Behold, how good and pleasant it is when brothers dwell in unity.) He chose it because the funeral was held on the feast day of Catherine of Siena, a saint of the Dominican Order, and all of us were certain that that very day Friar Pedro would have joined with the Virgin of Siena, to whom he was very devoted, in heaven. But I applied it to myself in this earthly world and thought how good it was for brothers to be united, as the Do-

minicans were, whether they were Fathers or laity, and
no matter what their race. (At that time they had two
Indian novices, who later became laity.)

Miguel de Pasamonte's character as a thief was matched
by his diligence, and because I matched him in the latter,
the fleet that was to take us to the Pearl Coast was already
fitted out before the end of July. In charge of it all was one
Diego Caballero el Mozo (the Handsome; so named to
distinguish him from his father), who knew his work well
and had two fully manned and equipped ships ready, lacking nothing that was necessary for sailing and colonizing;
I never had been so well supplied with wine, oil, vinegar,
cheeses from the Canaries, equipment, munitions, and
trinkets to be used as presents, plus a license to take from
the island of La Mona 1,100 loads of cassava bread. The
ships were the *Concepción* and the *Sancti Spiritus*, which, as
befitted the situation, belonged to the chief shipwright,
Chomin de Quitalia. I was assailed endlessly by scruples
about having associated myself with such hostile people,
but I consoled myself with the thought that those ships,
which had been used to transport so many slaves, would
in the future serve to transport farmers and, with them,
a new manner of treating the Indians and teaching them
the gospel.

The master of the *Sancti Spiritus*, which had the deeper
draft but was older than the *Concepción*, was Pedro Hernández de Moguer, and he had a complement of seventeen
sailors, three cabin boys, and a shipwright; the master of
the *Concepción* was Juan Batista de Zumaya, with a crew
of nine sailors and three cabin boys. Thus, Miguel de

Pasamonte did not stint us, and at the last minute, at my request, two skiffs were added, with five oars each, which are very seaworthy and suitable for coastal navigation in well-intentioned search of Indians; they are not suitable for use by those with ill intentions, for they cannot be loaded with artillery.

We left Santo Domingo on July 27, 1521, and had a good crossing, with a calm wind and no hurricanes. Born as I was on the banks of the Guadalquivir, accustomed since childhood to seeing sails swelling in the wind and boats gliding like swans and cutting through the water, I think that if I had not become a friar I would have ended up as a pilot on the sea, I love it so much. When I traveled around Castile, from chancellery to chancellery, what pained me the most was not seeing the sea and being able to move on it. For that reason, I have never been afraid to cross the ocean, and there are few sounds that are more pleasing to me than that of the wind passing through the rigging to the sails.

We made a stop at the island of La Mona, and as soon as we loaded some cassava bread, I ordered the continuation of the voyage because I was burning with desire to arrive in San Juan de Puerto Rico, to take on the farmers, and continue heading for Cumaná. I dreamed of the joy that those who had been made Knights of the Golden Spurs were going to feel when they saw how richly supplied I was when I returned to San Juan, having left it six months before, loaded with debt, in a borrowed ship. At night, which sometimes brought out the full moon for us, I enjoyed going through the lower deck of the ship, counting the seeds and farming implements and thinking

of how they would be distributed among the families; I
even imagined the seeds as full-grown plants, the orchards
in bloom, the plowed fields, and the Indians working elbow to elbow with the Sorians, and with others who
would be coming behind them, to cultivate the only true
riches that are given to man in this vale of tears: soil. I
dreamed of it and delighted in it, for if I treasure the sea
and ships, I do the same with the beauty of fields that
have been well cultivated by men, which is when we are
the image of the Creator and most resemble him.

We first sighted the island of San Juan de Puerto Rico
on August 4, 1521, and that is when I had to drink the
chalice of bitterness down to the dregs. The arrival of
such a well-equipped fleet would have deserved a grand
reception, with salvos from the cannons, like the ones
that are given to ships that enter the port with pennants
flying along with the flag of Castile. The time of arrival
of such ships is known well in advance, when their sails
are spied from the capes and points of the island, and it
is customary for them to be met by the skiffs and canoes
of the local merchants themselves, who want to be the
first to know what goods they are bringing to be sold.

There was little of this, and when we anchored at the
beach, I feared that some pestilence might have broken
out, because hardly any Spaniards could be seen, and I
could not distinguish among them any farmworkers who
had stayed in the city and who, if they had been there,
would have been the first to come out to meet us.

Miguel Carriazo, the sailor who was a farmer in his
youth and had joined us on the journey from Spain to

Puerto Rico, finally appeared, and he was accompanied by no one besides Blas Hernández and his sons, Ignacio and Isidoro. I soon learned from them that the pestilence that had arrived on the island had been the same as always: greed for gold.

Before going on, I should describe the state of affairs in Puerto Rico at the time. The governor of the island was Juan Ponce de León, who was among those who went to the Indies in the second voyage of Cristóbal Colón; he had fought in the war for Granada and continued to fight in the Indies, thereby earning a great deal of renown for his feats against Indians in Hispaniola. Authorized by Governor Nicolás de Ovando to conquer the island of Puerto Rico, he had money with which to do so, and as he did, he founded important settlements, like the city of San Juan, which before that had been called Caparra. After that conquest, it seems that he became calmer, and instead of making war, he established a farm and a garden with all manner of fruits, plants, and animals native to the Indies that drew the admiration of everyone who saw it; it was one of the good things that was done there, and it was very instructive for those who came later. Seeing it encouraged me very much, for I understood that this farm was an example of how generous and fertile Mother Nature could be in those latitudes, and it showed that if Ponce de León could do it in San Juan, others could do it in the vast lands that surrounded us.

But, unfortunately for him, he heard about a mysterious island that they called Bimini and that later turned out to be a peninsula. He went there; he was so captivated by its beauty that he gave it the name Florida. As happened with every new conquest, they said things about it that did not turn out to be true, which was especially so about this one because they said it had a fountain and that anyone who drank its water would never lose his youth. Those who first went to the Indies were that ignorant, and they gave us friars a lot of work to do in arguing against such superstitions. They said the same thing about gold, and it seemed that one had only to bend down to pick it up off the ground. But I say that there must not have been as much in Florida as they said, when the first thing Ponce de León did was to join with Ayllón and Pasamonte in taking Indians out of Florida and transporting them to the mines of Hispaniola; for these members of the government, the surest gold continued to lie in capturing and selling slaves.

In that year of 1521, Ponce de León launched a second expedition to Florida, which would be his last, and because he already knew that the Indian inhabitants, who were called Seminoles, were very fierce, he wanted to fit out a very powerful fleet. There was no issue about the ships, for besides being rich, he bore the title of governor of Florida. But he could not find the men because they were scarce in all the islands. He soon cast his eyes on my farmers, but they were so committed to awaiting my return that he had to leave them alone and delay his expedition until he found the crews he needed.

Because bad news always travels faster than good news, even in remote places like those, the feat of the chief shipwright, Chomin de Quitalia, in destroying my ship was soon known in San Juan. From what Blas Hernández and

Miguel Carriazo said, the news was brought by an official from Hispaniola, one of Pasamonte's henchmen, who laughed long and hard when he recounted it; later, making it up, he added that I had headed back to Spain right away, never to return. I do not know whether he did it intentionally or not, following instructions from his master, but I do know how much harm he caused because I suffered greatly from it.

It is easy to imagine how much this news must have pleased the farmers, who were so many miles away from their homeland, living on charity in someone else's house. Blas and Andrea, who had known me for so long, insisted that it would not be characteristic of me to abandon people to their fate, and Miguel Carriazo, who hardly knew me, also came to my defense, saying that if I had gone to Spain I would surely return. Ponce de León's men wasted no time before descending again on the farmers and telling them that, if I had been left without a ship, there was little I could do for them. Others told them that, if I had abandoned them, they were free to undertake new adventures, and they would find no better one than the one in Florida.

The worst of all these men, according to Miguel Carriazo, turned out to be a servant of Ponce de León, a black *ladino* from Seville named Juan Garrido, who had been in the first expedition to Florida with his master, to whom he was very devoted; Garrido gave the Sorians to believe that Florida was a land of milk and honey, where wheat grew without having to be planted, as did the gold for anyone who preferred that. Miguel Carriazo challenged the black, and they had a fight from which neither one emerged unscathed. It could even have earned Carriazo a stint in prison if the black had not been a slave.

It does not surprise me that the farmers ended up leaving me, nor do I blame them for it, if they had been led to believe that I had abandoned them. What surprises me more is the loyalty of Blas Hernández and his sons, who preferred to stay in San Juan and be left to their fate. Not to mention Miguel Carriazo, although because he was more familiar with the Indies, he knew that a lot of expeditions like Ponce de León's ended in failure. He was the one who insisted the most that they should wait for news from me and that three months in the Indies were not the same as in Castile, where everything is a stone's throw away.

One regrettable fact is that some of the wives of the farmers contributed to the disaster that lay ahead, urging their husbands not to waste such a great opportunity to enrich themselves, the chance they were being given to pursue such a chimera.

For it was a chimera, and it ended in disaster for all of them. A chimera because Ponce de León, who was already of an advanced age (more than sixty), was in a hurry to colonize the peninsula, perhaps to leave a greater inheritance to his children, and he went there with just two ships and no more than 120 men, which was not much for a land inhabited by Indians who were very aware of the continuous invasions made by the slave traffickers.

By my estimate, the fleet left San Juan de Puerto Rico in May 1521, carrying all the farmers for whom I had gone through so much, but none was taken as a farmer, each one having been assigned a task that would serve a fleet bent on conquest and building small forts. That was absurd: How could men who knew only how to handle a hoe and a plow serve as soldiers or sailors? For that is how things were done in the Indies, and sometimes things turned out well and at other times disastrously.

All of them left except those I have mentioned, for in the end Ponce de León convinced those who were undecided by advancing them a month's pay, which in Puerto Rico was very high; many of them had never seen such a large sum before. That is what our Saint Thomas cites as *concausae*, for in human affairs there ordinarily is no one cause but, rather, several concurrent causes. And this concurrent cause, this blasted sum of money, was what convinced the most reluctant ones.

That expedition caused great joy in Hispaniola when it became known that it included all the farmers who would have come with me to the continent. The Spaniards there mocked me, and they regarded me as insane, considering, on the contrary, that it was very sane for those poor Castilians from Soria to have chosen to go after the gold instead of being Knights of the Golden Spurs, but with a mattock in their hand. "We did not come to the Indies to dig", said those who in their homeland had done nothing else. There was rejoicing, and a good deal of it, in Hispaniola, in Cuba, and in the other islands, because without farmers there would be no peaceful colonization of the Pearl Coast, and they all could happily and contentedly carry on their business of encomiendas. All of them rejoiced except the Indians, who suffered from them.

I say that it was a chimera and disaster for all because

that expedition of Ponce de León's was one of the most ill-fated in memory in the Indies, from which few emerged with their lives. At Christmas time in 1521, when they were pursuing their attempts to settle there, they were attacked by the Timucua Indians, who are the Seminoles' enemies, but they were greater enemies of the Spaniards, and they dispatched all of them. Ponce de León himself was so badly injured that he died soon thereafter; the survivors, as far as I know, could be counted on the fingers of one hand, and one of them was Juan Garrido, the black *ladino*, with whom I crossed paths in Mexico years later when he was in his old age. He did not even remember the farmers from Soria or how he insisted that they join the fleet; he thus could have a clear conscience.

These are the ways of the Lord our God; those men who were to have served to show how the Indies could be peaceably colonized went to their frightful deaths on the cape of a remote peninsula. God alone knows why.

I went on with my ships to the Pearl Coast to try to complete my mission, but I knew that the endeavor had been ruined when I lost the farmers, for although I continued to be the administrator of the Indians on that coast, the title was worth little because it lacked substance. I describe all of this more extensively in the *History of the Indies* that I have written, and it need not be repeated here. I will add only that sometimes the Lord is pleased to give a hundredfold in a way that is evident here on earth, and he did so with those who stayed with me.

Blas Hernández, Andrea, and their two sons made the crossing to Cumaná and stayed in a mission of the Franciscan Fathers there, the ones who had an orchard that even included orange trees, north of Chichiribichi. They began working under the Fathers' protection, but later they were among the first to have their own lands on the coast of Cumaná, which they worked profitably with mares that became the main part of their business. They were also among the first to bring over Castilian sheep and all kinds of seeds, but what gave them the highest return was corn, which they ultimately grew on plantations that were more than two days' ride in extent. As the best evidence of the favor that the Lord showed for this family, Andrea gave birth to a little boy, despite the fact that she seemed to have passed the age at which she could conceive; I do not say it was a miracle but that it was a great mark of heaven's favor. Their married daughter in Soria also came with her husband and newborn son, for on her father's lands there was work for many. The sons married well; the elder with a woman from Castile and the younger with a Cumanagoto. They were all known as the Blases, and I think their number grew to more than fifty, and they were very powerful in the region. In their dealings with the Indians, they always behaved like good Christians, and the slaves they had were blacks, but treated with great respect, with an eye to not separating parents from their children.

As for Miguel Carriazo, he married a Cumanagoto cacique, and he himself became one of the most esteemed caciques, for to defend his people he did not hesitate to take arms against the bad Spaniards, especially those from the island of Cubagua, who continued to be determined to plunder along the coast. For defending himself from one of those raids they branded him a traitor to the Crown, and the governor of the mainland, who was at the time Pedro de los Ríos, put him on trial. His defense was successful, for he was able to prove that those who lived on his lands were good vassals of King Charles, to whom they paid tribute, while those who had attacked were Spanish ruffians, who cared only about their interests and robbing their neighbor, contributing little to the Crown. I was the bishop of Chiapas in Mexico when this happened and was able to testify on his behalf; but if Pedrarias Dávila had continued to be the governor of the continent, I would not have been able to do much for him, just as very little could be done for Núñez de Balboa, whom Dávila had beheaded on lower charges.

And here I end the story of my youth and my time as a cleric and of the endeavor that I pursued with the greatest effort of my long life, that of peacefully colonizing the Pearl Coast, which would have served as an example to many, for the good of mankind and charity for the Indians. God, in his inscrutable designs, allowed it to fail because of the greed of those who governed the Indies and of the encomenderos who supported them. With this imprecation, and with glory and honor to God, we have come to the end of this book.

CHAPTER XIV

EPILOGUE

Bartolomé de Las Casas arrived on the Pearl Coast in the autumn of 1521 to take possession of his post as administrator of the Indians in the region. He explained to the natives that there was a new Spanish king who intended to hold them as vassals, peacefully, and he described to them the powers and projects that he was bringing with him. To do so, he relied on an Indian lady called Doña María, who spoke Spanish, and on the help of the Franciscan missionaries, who gave him a very good reception.

But while he was preaching peace, the encomenderos of the island of Cubagua continued to harass the natives, sometimes pestering them to sell boys and girls in exchange for jugs of wine, for which they had acquired a taste, and at other times robbing them in the usual way. Invoking his authority as royal administrator, Bartolomé de Las Casas presented claims to the mayor of the island of Cubagua, Francisco de Vallejo, and all he got was death threats, because his determination to change the system of exploitation of the pearl fisheries was a threat to the interests of the encomenderos and the ruling class.

Furthermore, the soldiers and sailors who came with him in the two ships that he fitted out as authorized by the Audience in Santo Domingo abandoned him once they realized that he was not going to give them permission to take their booty, in accordance with the customs of the time.

The only thing Las Casas could do was to build a storehouse next to the mission of the Franciscans, on the bank of the Cumaná River, which is today called Manzanares, in Venezuela, and store all the provisions from the ships in it. Francisco de Soto remained at the head of his diminished expedition, along with Blas Hernández, his sons, and Miguel Carriazo, whom I have already mentioned. Because the threat to Las Casas' life was growing, thanks to the machinations of the people of Cubagua, the Franciscans begged him to return to Hispaniola and, from there, to write to the emperor to tell him what was happening and to seek confirmation of his powers and reinforcements that would enable him to use them.

Though he felt great heartache and his conscience suffered, too, he decided to follow the advice of the Franciscan Fathers, and he left the mainland in the month of December 1521. After a very hazardous passage to Santo Domingo, from which he sent several messages to the emperor, he stayed there to wait for his reply.

While he was waiting, he experienced what has been called the *second conversion*. As had happened in his *first conversion*, he maintained very close relations with the Dominicans of Santo Domingo, and one of them, his confessor Friar Domingo de Betanzos, showed him that perhaps his vocation lay on a path of greater abnegation. The cleric let himself be persuaded and took the Dominican habit in the city of Santo Domingo in September 1522. As he himself recounted in his *History of the Indies*, his decision occasioned great happiness, but for different reasons. The friars and the good people of the island rejoiced over the path of sanctity that he was choosing; the lay encomenderos and the governing class also rejoiced, but because they saw him as being buried by his decision, which would rid them of such an insistent and nagging enemy in the argument over the encomiendas and abuses that were committed in the Indies.

He was thirty-eight years old at the time, and he had forty-four more years to live. Despite his age, which was very advanced for the times, he completed his novitiate with the Dominicans in the normal way, refraining from any public activity for four years.

In 1526 he was named prior of a newly established monastery in Puerto Plata, on the north coast of Hispaniola. There he began preaching to Indians and Christians, and he began writing his *History of the Indies*.

From that moment on, he again devoted himself indefatigably to his activity on behalf of the Indians, and his unceasing travels were perceived with true surprise and awe. He traveled to Mexico, Panama, Nicaragua, and Guatemala, and he crossed the Atlantic several times to defend the rights of the Indians in the emperor's court. He suffered various persecutions and imprisonments, but nothing daunted him.

In 1534 he succeeded in subduing the rebellious cacique Enriquillo. He was an illustrious cacique, educated in a school that the Franciscans had on Hispaniola, who had rebelled in the sierras of Barouco against the atrocity committed by his encomendero, Francisco de Valenzuela, of raping the cacique's wife, the noble native Doña Lucía.

He managed to build up an army of four thousand rebellious Indians, to extend the rebellion into the mountains in the north of the island, and to keep the authorities in check for more than fifteen years. Friar Bartolomé secured the permission of his superiors and went to the sierra in search of Enriquillo, whom he found and with whom he stayed for more than a month, during which he celebrated Mass daily and secured confessions from the cacique and all his captains, who also turned over their arms. This would not be the only occasion on which he would have the opportunity to intervene in order to pacify rebellious Indians.

Some believe that his most important act in favor of the Indians was his participation in the drafting of what are called the New Laws of the Indies, which Emperor Charles V signed in Barcelona on November 20, 1542. Las Casas was the main driving force behind the New Laws, which greatly improved the condition of the Indians; thanks to those laws, there was no extinction of the indigenous race in later conquests on the American continent, as had occurred on the islands that were discovered first.

Charles V held him in high esteem and wanted to name him, in Barcelona, the bishop of Cuzco, but Las Casas, who did not want either to be appointed to a post or to be granted a privilege, fled to Valencia. The emperor later succeeded in naming him, via a clever maneuver, the bishop of Chiapas, in Mexico, a diocese over which he presided from 1544 to 1551.

In his fight against encomiendas and abuses, he did not hesitate to confront the highest authorities, both ecclesiastical and civil. In 1555, the encomenderos of Peru, taking advantage of the painful situation in which the royal treasury found itself as a result of the interminable wars in Europe, proposed to Philip II, the young monarch who had just inherited the throne, the concession in perpetuity of the encomiendas, for which they would pay nine million ducats. The king accepted, seeing it as a solution of his fiscal problems; when Friar Bartolomé found out about it, he protested against the injustice that this sale of vassals entailed, and he sent Philip II a very harsh memorandum, in which he warned him that, unless he changed his decision, the king would be complicit in the hardships suffered by the Indians. The result was that the pretensions of the Peruvian encomenderos did not prosper.

Friar Bartolomé's very hectic life did not prevent him from writing what can be described as a vast body of work, numbering some four hundred works on the Indies, some as long as his *History of the Indies*. Altogether, his writings are estimated to consist of no less than three thousand pages in Latin and Castilian, because he wrote in both languages equally well. The most polemical of all his writings was his *Very Short Account of the Destruction of the Indies*, in which he denounced the excesses of the conquest and which was seized upon by Spain's enemies to concoct the Black Legend.

When in 1561 Philip II established the court in Madrid, Friar Bartolomé moved into the common house of study that the Order of Saint Dominic had in the sanctuary of Our Lady of Atocha, on the outskirts of the capital. From there he followed the events in America, with the purpose of influencing the policy of the king, at the same time that he petitioned the Holy See regarding the new churches in those lands.

He died in the aforementioned monastery on July 18, 1566, and, in accordance with his instructions, he was buried with great simplicity, with a wooden crozier. But his funeral *de corpore insepulto* was very solemn, and it was attended by all the prominent figures of the court, but the simple people were also present.

BIBLIOGRAPHICAL SOURCES

For the writing of this novel about Bartolomé de las Casas, which covers the period of his life in which he was a prospector for gold, rancher, and cleric, until he took the vows of a Dominican friar, I have consulted the following texts:

El Plan Cisneros-Las Casas para la reformación de las Indias, by Manuel Giménez Fernández, 1984 edition of the Consejo Superior de Investigaciones Cientificas, Escuela de Estudios Hispano-Americanos.

Bartolomé de Las Casas, capellán de Carlos I, poblador de Cumaná, by the same author and also published by the aforementioned Consejo Superior.

Manuel Giménez Fernández was a professor of the University of Seville and reconstructed the life of Friar Bartolomé between 1516 and 1523 on the basis of original documentation in the Archives of the Indies with a faithfulness and attention to detail that are difficult to surpass. His work may be characterized as monumental, and the two volumes that are cited amount to more than two thousand pages.

Quien era Bartolomé de Las Casas, by Pedro Borges, Ediciones Rialp, 1990 edition. It is a book of great interest on account of the excellent systematization with which it treats the different periods in the life of the subject of the biography.

Historia de las Indias, by Bartolomé de Las Casas, edition of Agustín Millares Carlo and a preliminary study by Lewis Hanke, for the Fondo de Cultura Económica de México. It comprises three volumes with more than 1,500 pages altogether, and it is of foremost importance to the understanding of the subject and of the conquest of the Indies; it has the value of being narrated by a direct witness of the events described.

Brevísima relacion de la destrucción de las Indias, by Bartolomé de Las Casas. It is his best-known and most polemical work. Published by André Saint-Lu, for Cátedra, Letras Hispanicas.

Fray Bartolomé de Las Casas, by Isacio Pérez Fernández, published by OPE, Caleruega, Burgos, Spain, 1984. The author, a Dominican friar, is a specialist in Bartolomé de Las Casas.

Juan Latino: gloria de España y de su raza, by Doctor Calixto C. Masó, published by Northeastern Illinois University. It is an interesting short work on the problem of slavery in the sixteenth century.